The Repulse Chronicles
Book Six

Operation Repulse

by
Chris James

www.chrisjamesauthor.net

Also by Chris James

Repulse: Europe at War 2062–2064
Time Is the Only God
Dystopia Descending
The Repulse Chronicles, Book One: Onslaught
The Repulse Chronicles, Book Two: Invasion
The Repulse Chronicles, Book Three: The Battle for Europe
The Repulse Chronicles, Book Four: The Endgame
The Repulse Chronicles, Book Five: The Race against Time

Available as Kindle e-books and paperbacks from Amazon

Copyright © Chris James, 2023. All rights reserved.
Chris James asserts his moral right to be identified as the author of this work. All characters and events portrayed in this novel are a figment of the author's imagination.

ISBN: 9798854165945

*Dedicated to the memory of Jo-Anne
A dear friend and steadfast supporter*

Chapter 1

05.15 Wednesday 1 August 2063

Captain Pip Clarke felt the restraining straps dig into her body when the autonomous air transport dived. Her Squitch announced: "Prepare to disembark under fire."

The AAT decelerated and Pip's stomach fell. She and her troops had trained for this, but it was the last thing any of them wanted.

Pip blinked and zoomed the tactical view in her lens but saw little to reassure her. The AAT was coming down close to an urban area that the Scythes had not fully cleared. Digital markers denoting friendly and hostile elements flashed and moved around the terrain in a kind of super-AI-choreographed dance.

Their wing was part of the force designated to take control of the *Deltawerken*, the series of barriers built to keep the rising North Sea out of Europe that the enemy had destroyed earlier in the war, flooding huge areas of the low-lying Netherlands.

She opened comms to her troops and yelled her deduction, "Something on the line has gone to rat-shit—"

A shuddering thump shook the whole craft as it touched down and bounced, throwing everyone against their restraints like rag dolls. The AAT crunched down to earth once more and remained still. Through the small windows opposite Pip, smoke swirled and obscured the early morning sky.

"Remain seated," Pip's Squitch instructed.

Her glance flitted over the troops sitting on the opposite side of the fuselage. Faces creased in shocked surprise. The urgency of the approach and descent hit an abrupt pause.

Her Squitch repeated, "Prepare to disembark under fire."

Air hissed through Pip's clenched teeth and she stared at the door through which she'd lead her troops into battle.

Then the instruction came: "Exit the AAT now with your weapon raised."

Everyone unclipped their restraints, turned and pulled their Pickups from the brackets on the fuselage next to them, and stood.

Pip said, "Follow me and keep your eyes open. Remember your training and don't fumble." She strode towards the doorway. It slid up in front of her to reveal grey terrain outside. She leapt from the aircraft and landed with a crunch on loose gravel. She rolled hard to her right. The tang of muddy sea air on a persistent breeze invaded her senses and took the edge off the bitterness in her throat.

Incoming fire split the air, fast and destructive. Yelps and shouts followed, along with metallic thumps as shots hit the AAT.

"Aim and fire at the buildings in front of you," her Squitch said.

Lying prone, Pip aimed her Pickup and fired until her magazine emptied. The shells did not even make a mark on the bland warehouse on the other side of the field. She ejected the empty magazine and leaned up slightly on one elbow to reach into her webbing for another. The movement allowed her to glance back at the aircraft and see her troops leaping out and throwing themselves to the ground. Another fusillade of enemy fire suddenly punctured the soldiers as they emerged. Three of them slumped one after the other onto the bodies of their comrades.

Her Squitch announced: "Cease fire and prepare to advance."

"Why are you getting my troops killed?" she hissed, not expecting a response.

As Pip rose to her knees, a young man rolled in at her side. His name and rank resolved in the air as she glanced at him. Sergeant MacManus's dark skin shone with sweat and glistened on the stubble around his chin. He spoke in a voice that quivered: "Bugger this, ma'am. There's at least three dead. How come did the super AI dae this?"

Pip shared his frustration, but this was not the time to question the super AI. "It's different now," she said. "We're not defending; we're attacking, Mac. And however well organised the invasion is, we're going to take casualties."

Despite ensuring she spoke with authority, confusion made the bone above her eyes ache. Why had they disembarked under fire? NATO should have been in control, and her troops should not—

"Standby to advance in ten, nine, eight…" her Squitch broke in.

MacManus muttered, "Here we go."

A wing of Scythe ACAs swept into the battlespace from nowhere. Another wing followed, and another. Pip enlarged the tactical view in her display and caught her breath at the speed and dexterity of the new NATO aircraft. The sound of rushing air above her did nothing to drown out the

Squitch's countdown, "...three, two, one. Advance towards the designated target now."

Pip leapt to her feet, sensing the troops around her do the same. Ahead of them, indistinct flames flashed over the buildings. Corrugated metal sheets on the roofs melted like ice in the sun. The concrete pillars shattered and windows exploded. In the sky, the ACAs banked and peeled off, climbing high.

Cradling her Pickup, she ran towards the pall of smoke and dust that now obscured the building. The activity caused a familiar exaltation: out in the open, gasping in breaths of warm air.

Her Squitch cautioned, "Approach the target and stand by to engage remaining enemy warriors."

MacManus called out, "No way did any of them survive that."

Pip slowed to a trot. Glancing left and right, she saw the other troops follow suit, certainly having been told to do the same by their battlefield management systems.

She veered nearer to MacManus and replied, "Don't bet on—"

"Danger. Drop and fire where indicated," her Squitch said.

Pip fell to the ground in an instant and stifled a curse when she landed awkwardly, scraping her elbows but keeping her Pickup clear.

Her Squitch added, "Surviving enemy warriors are in the debris ahead of you."

A few metres to her left, a similarly prone MacManus offered: "So, now we wait for the Scythes to make another pass. Aye?"

Concern burned Pip's chest like indigestion. The yellow terrain of dead grass spread out in front of her, flat and even. The canal on her left ran straight towards the smoking ruins, but the open field offered no cover whatsoever. She fired at the damaged buildings. She could not make out definite targets and wondered if they were all simply putting down supressing fire. Her magazine emptied and she reloaded.

Her Squitch said, "Cease fire. Standby to advance."

"Casualties?" she asked as a droplet of sweat broke free from her eyebrow and stung her eye.

"Low," her Squitch answered evasively.

"Why are we having to clear this—?" Pip broke off when another wing of Scythes fell out of the sky, pivoted in a gracious parabolic arc directly above them, and then swept a few metres over the ground towards the ruined buildings. There came more distant cracking and hissing when their Pulsars came to bear.

Her Squitch said, "Advance where indicated."

Pip pulled herself up and ran, again cradling her Pickup while trying to keep her body low. Pounding feet either side of her lifted her spirits. Warmer breezes alternated with the residual cooler air of the previous night.

Pip slowed with the line of advancing NATO troops as they neared the target. She asked in a quiet voice, "Have we got backup?"

"Affirmative," her Squitch replied.

"What's the probability of any enemy surviving those ACA passes?"

"Less than ten percent."

She opened comms to her teams and barked, "Look sharp, everyone. And remember the residual heat from our lasers. Keep moving and don't touch anything you don't have to." Then she said, "Mac?"

"Aye?"

"Get your squad in close."

"Mine and a few others."

An indicator in Pip's lens flashed red to warn her that any remaining enemy might attack before her Squitch could caution her.

The shattered buildings loomed in front of her, a mass of twisted iron rods jutting from broken concrete and steaming debris. On Pip's left, a human figure encased in metal stood in a sculpture of frozen agony, hands raised to the sky. The enemy combatant looked like the ash-covered victims of Pompeii, only this warrior had been covered by molten metal when the roof came down.

The local tactical situation that Pip's Squitch overlaid in her view abruptly zoomed out to show a digital representation of her section of the front. Several plus and minus time indicators flashed yellow, telling her that the need to secure the area had become urgent. She deduced that the reason they'd been obliged to disembark under fire must've been to keep the line of advance on track.

She blinked to refocus her view on the debris ahead, noting that the ruined warehouse in front of them was only the first building at the edge of a business park. Murmurs of instructions and confirmations came through in her comms. On both sides of her, troops padded with caution over broken concrete and glass, while masonry dust hung in the warm morning air. The heat from the cooling metal dried her throat.

A sudden, guttural shriek broke the tension. The familiar sound of rapid gunshots followed. Pip crouched. Her view flashed red as NATO troops yelled to take cover. Chunks of rubble crunched under unseen boots. There came a pop and an unlucky squaddie collapsed without fuss or further movement.

"You might want to hang back, Mac," Pip said, aware of her sergeant's inexperience in battle.

Pip's Squitch overlaid indicators of the enemy's likely locations while her mind demanded to know how anyone could've survived the ACAs' assault on the buildings. She climbed the rubble ahead of MacManus, hearing his footing slip as the debris shifted under his weight.

More shouts and exclamations carried on the still, morning air. Her sense of unease grew. She scrambled as loose debris pulled at her boots like grasping hands beneath her. She crested the rise holding her Pickup and fired without aiming. She leapt onwards. The dust cleared and the bright, hot sky bore down on her. A flicker of movement caught her eye.

Her Squitch said, "Fire now where indica—"

A second sense demanded that she take cover. She spun around, dropping her Pickup, and threw herself at Mac. The sergeant grunted in shock as they fell into a depression in the rubble, tumbling down a slight incline.

Above them, volleys of gunfire rang out. A wing of Scythes finally hissed overhead, leaving another cacophony of dull crashes and splitting masonry in their wake.

Silence followed.

Her Squitch announced, "The battlespace is secure. Prepare to continue to advance."

Freshly disturbed concrete dust irritated her eyes and mouth. She blinked moisture under her eyelids and worked up some saliva around her gums. She spat the dust out of her mouth and a headache began.

She pushed herself up and asked, "You okay, Mac?"

"Aye," Mac answered, also clambering to his feet.

"Sorry about shoving you like that."

He dabbed at fresh blood matting his hair and said, "Could've been a wee bit worse. Looks like I owe you one, cap."

She brushed the dust from her smock while checking the tactical situation in her lens. She ignored his observation and asked, "How bad is that injury, sergeant?"

Mac shook his head and replied, "A scratch."

She turned around to survey the rubble. Ahead of the line of attack, distant ACAs swept down to leave new palls of smoke rising behind them. Small arms fire crackled among the other damaged warehouses, but in the absence of a warning from their Squitches, no one moved.

Her Squitch said, "Advance where indicated."

Pip looked at Mac's blood-stained face and said, "Right, let's crack on."

"I did nay expect it to be like this," Mac said.

Pip replied, "And it's only just the start—"

A new voice suddenly yelled, "Got one. I got me a scimitar."

A lumpen, awkward young man slipped and stumbled as he crested the rubble in front of Pip. Digital text resolved in the air next to him. Pip read, 'Private John "Barny" Hines, 33 Armoured Engineer Squadron.'

The moment Hines caught sight of his commanders, his face fell. The squaddie coughed and the warrior's blade vanished behind his back. Pip thought to issue a reprimand, but Mac cleared his throat pointedly.

Hines turned and scuttled away. Pip glanced at Mac.

"He led the assault on the position," Mac said. "Ran ahead of the rest of the line. He does nay ken what fear is."

"Understood," she replied with a nod, realising she might need to keep an eye on Hines for both good and bad reasons.

Chapter 2

06.17 Wednesday 1 August 2063

Maria Phillips pressed the battlefield GenoFluid pack against the bloodied stump of the soldier's upper arm.

"Christ, it hurts a bit," the young man uttered through clenched teeth.

"I know," Maria said. "Just concentrate on breathing. The bots will relieve your pain very soon." The display in Maria's lens gave the soldier's name as Zander and detailed over fifty pieces of shrapnel that had penetrated his body, mostly around his right shoulder and in his legs. Maria urged the bots inside the pack to hurry and dull the agony the young man had to be enduring.

Zander caught his breath and then relaxed back into the dried, yellow grass lining the narrow country road. The bots were working. Relief surged through Maria.

His eyes glistened and he said, "You medics always look so sexy when you're work—". Zander emitted a sudden, truncated gulp. His head lolled and he died.

Maria recognised the life fade from Zander's eyes as the soldier's body became fully limp. The indicative colour of Zander's details and list of injuries in Maria's vision changed from red to white, confirming death.

Maria's Squitch spoke: "This casualty has expired. You should proceed to the individual highlighted in your lens, who requires attention."

"What happened?" Maria mumbled, still holding the GenoFluid pack on the bloodied stump of Zander's missing arm, unwilling to accept his death. "I reached him in time, the pack was in position and the bots doing their job. He should have stabilised."

Her Squitch repeated, "This casualty has expired. You need to proceed to the individual highlighted in your lens—"

"Cause of death?" she demanded.

"Severance of the spinal cord at the third verteb—"

"How?"

"The casualty attempted to lift his head, causing a piece of shrapnel to move approximately two-point-one-six millimetres and sever—"

"So tell the bots to keep his brain oxygenated until we can get him to—"

"Insufficient time is available," her Squitch said with finality.

Nabou suddenly yelled in her ears, "Maz, can you help me?"

Her friend's urgent plea forced Maria to tear her eyes away from the young face beneath her. She let the GenoFluid pack fall onto the dirt. She stood, shook her head in silent apology to Zander, and ran along the road towards where Nabou had gone on ahead of her. The crump of an explosion shuddered through the ground. Indicators flashed in her vision describing casualties all around her.

She yelled through truncated breaths: "Where do you need me?"

Nabou replied, "Come to my location. I am... overwhelmed."

"My Squitch isn't—"

"Because I need you here," Nabou cried, an urgency in her voice that Maria had never heard before. She hurried on.

"Danger," her Squitch said. "Enemy counterattack imminent in your immediate vicinity. Seek cover immediately."

She cast her gaze skywards as her breaths became more laboured. "No, not now," she muttered.

"Maz, hurry," Nabou pleaded in her ear.

Maria ran faster as the lane dipped and turned to the right. Too many warning lights flashed in her vision. Dread welled inside her. Memories of previous injuries and the pain they caused chilled the sweat on her exposed neck.

A pall of grey smoke drifted over the road in front of Maria and new screeching filled the sky. The fear of what it hid did little to reassure her.

"Seek cover immediately," her Squitch repeated.

She stopped and crouched at the side of the road close to a large, dead oak. A break in the smoke allowed her to glimpse the sky peppered with distant black dots. Experience had taught her that such a view was more than enough to be a prelude to the most extreme—

The atmosphere around her evaporated suddenly, as though sucked up into a giant, unseen vacuum. Maria's throat constricted in response. She fell forwards, her face scraping against dry, crumbly bark. Heat rolled over her head and the hairs on her head shrivelled. A new wave of cooler air rushed in and Maria gasped, staggered at how the pain increased.

The bark on the oak broke off in her hands as she pulled herself upright. She brushed the flakes from between her fingers, gasping as her throat stung. Blinking her eyes to get some moisture into them, Maria staggered on.

Her Squitch said, "Proceed along the road."

She put a hand to the top of her head and patted the brittle mass there. The air around her was thick with heat and the sound of flames crackling nearby.

"At a junction fifty metres in front of you, turn right. You must leave the battlespace and seek medical attention."

"Shit," Maria muttered, pain and confusion swirling like the smoke around her. "Nabou?" she called.

Her Squitch cautioned, "Increase your pace."

"Why?"

"Enemy warriors have survived the initial attack in preprepared positions to the southeast. Continue to proceed where indicated."

The thinning brocade on her right gave way to a dry, red field with a copse of spindly trees. She asked through gasps, "Why don't you kill them, then?"

Her Squitch answered, "You will be able to advance in less than four minutes. Assist the casualties ahead of you if you feel able to."

Maria fought growing disorientation. Her chest ached. She entered the expansive field and stumbled on uneven clumps of dried mud. A collection of tangled and charred bodies of NATO troops greeted her. In her vision, only white indicators hung over the victims, denoting that all were dead.

She slowed to a walk and asked, "I can't help dead casualties."

"There are wounded two hundred metres ahead of your position."

As if confirmation, new indicators flashed denoting casualties beyond her own field of vision.

"Nabou? Where are you?"

There came only silence.

"Where is Field Surgeon Faye?"

The voice of her Squitch didn't waver as it informed her, "The location of the body of Field Surgeon Faye is indicated now."

Maria heard a sound escape her mouth like a moan. Her eyes welled, causing the indicator in her view to shimmer and warp over the scattered scene in front of her. She stopped. She judged from the crater in the field that a Spider had detonated in the midst of a deployment of supporting troops. Questions flooded her shocked mind: Why had the super AI failed to defend them? What had gone wrong, to leave a crater of dirt littered with the body parts of NATO troops who'd been told that they had the edge—finally—against the unstoppable Caliphate?

Maria blinked back the tears, her jaw locked in a rictus of denial. "Please, no," she muttered in vain. She stumbled, her right hand automatically reaching into a pouch on the thigh of her combat trousers to grasp the burnt foot of Billy the Rabbit, her good luck charm and crutch in moments of stress.

Her Squitch said without fanfare, "Enemy warriors have begun counterattacking. Obtain a discarded weapon and follow the directions in your lens."

"What?" Maria asked, confusion threatening to overwhelm her. She needed time to absorb the loss of her friend. The constant changing situation and priorities left her untethered.

"Arm yourself now," her Squitch instructed.

A frightened sob escaped her lips. She stumbled among the broken, dried clumps of earth, bending over to scoop up a discarded weapon that lay close to a lump of bloodied flesh wrapped in a torn NATO uniform. Her Squitch immediately linked to the Pickup and authorised Maria to use it.

"The magazine in your weapon has insufficient rounds remaining. You must obtain—"

Maria threw herself to the ground as dozens of black dots swept out of the azure sky and down to tree level. The air hissed with their passage. The clumps of brown, dry earth were as hard as concrete, but Maria gripped them in anticipation of another explosion—

The ground trembled and shook when more detonations erupted among the barren countryside. A sudden gust of wind blew hot and hard over her, carrying metallic whines. Maria scrunched her eyes closed and buried her head in the dry dirt, unable to face the same fate that had befallen her friend. Alone, her courage deserted her.

Silence followed.

"What's happened?" she squeaked, still confused by the chaos and that her Squitch had stopped instructing her so abruptly.

"Move into position where indicated and prepare to engage the enemy."

Maria's blood froze. She'd been close to combat before, but then she'd had support like other troops and the Falarete defences at Dover Port. Now, she knew only that she did not want to die.

Her Squitch repeated its instruction and then added: "A failure to comply will be reported to your senior officer."

With a sudden shout of frustration at that threat, Maria pushed herself up and began running. Her lens guided her towards a depression where the field ended in high brocade. She tripped and stumbled over the dried mud, but remained upright, hurling her body forwards, determined not to be punished for any perceived cowardice if she happened to survive the day. Her fear gave way to acceptance of what the tall growth in front of her might hide. Above her, black dots whizzed and hissed and pirouetted, moving almost faster than her eyes could follow.

Her Squitch said, "Enemy warriors are advancing on your left. NATO troops are in front of you, moving to engage them."

"Why?" she gasped, confusion adding to her discomfort. Her mind shrieked that Operation Repulse wasn't supposed to be like this. It should be the machines doing the fighting, not flesh-and-blood—

"Seek cover immediately," her Squitch said.

Beyond the digital data overlaid in her view, Maria made out a very real black shape spinning out of the blue sky towards her, trailing the smoke of its partial destruction. In an instant, it filled her vision, looming large like some dark, evil vulture swooping in to kill her. She had just enough time to realise she should move out of its way, but then it smashed into the earth no more than twenty metres in front of her. She caught her breath as the machine skidded past her, a jagged piece of bent bodywork slicing her right arm above her elbow as it did so.

Chapter 3

08.19 Wednesday 1 August 2063

Journalist Geoffrey Kenneth Morrow winced under the furious gaze of the belligerent Royal Marine. The man, appropriately named Savage, had been assigned responsibility for Geoff's safety as he 'tagged along' on their section of the front.

"I will tell you this again," Savage hissed, the black bristles of his ample moustache adding to the menace of his expression. "And for the last fucking time, Journo."

Geoff nodded and kept his eyes downcast, certain that Savage could beat him to a pulp without breaking a sweat.

"Do not—ever—delay when disembarking an AAT. Don't trip. Don't fucking glance around to admire the fucking scenery, and do not ask anyone if they need a fucking hand—"

"But that private snagged the strap of his Bergan on the flange—"

"Which he's been fucking trained to deal with," Savage almost shouted. "It is not your problem, Journo."

"Right, okay. Got it," Geoff muttered, his own masculinity withering under Savage's narrow-eyed gaze. He scratched his wiry hair where it poked out from under his ill-fitting helmet. The reality of his objective redundancy came home to him: he was useless to Savage. Geoff had body armour but no weapons. They'd trained him to apply a battlefield GenoFluid pack, but otherwise he was just a tourist.

He glanced up at Savage to see the man's square jaw move in terse, quiet utterances as he communicated with his Squitch. Geoff's lens was linked to the British Army's super AI, but the latter would block anything spoken by the other soldiers that it deemed Geoff did not need to know. The one fact of which his chaperone had made him fully aware was how angry the unit all were to be in the second wave of the invasion, not the first.

"Come on," Savage yelled back at Geoff, standing and following the rest of the squad as it moved towards the ruined buildings at the edge of the small Dutch town.

Geoff followed, hurrying to keep up. Savage had explained about keeping the right distance in case the enemy had left behind mines and other traps. An image comforted Geoff of the brute of a soldier striding ten paces in front of him suddenly getting blown to bits. Such realisation—that getting blown to bits was now a distinct possibility—combined with the morning heat to prickle his skin. His sense of safety had evaporated like a puddle in the sun, the conviction growing that he should've stayed in England.

But, then, Alan at *The Guardian* would hardly have put him on the payroll unless Geoff were prepared to risk his neck. Besides, Geoff's massive scoop the previous May, when the Medway Towns had been decimated in a rare, successful enemy attack, meant that Geoff enjoyed a little more respect from editors like Alan, even if the government had stuck an R-notice on it and spiked the story.

Fine dust kicked up by the soldiers' boots clawed at the back of Geoff's throat. In reaction, he unclipped his canteen from his belt and took a swig of water. Ahead of him, members of the squad waved their arms in what Geoff took to be caution. He stopped walking when the line came to a halt. There followed a silence and Geoff's lens told him that the soldiers were discussing potential dangers ahead of them.

The sky burned hot and blue. Red roof-tile dust mingled with old cement to make the dry air taste like burnt chalk. Geoff noted the randomness of the damage—some houses sat unscathed next to smashed and charred ruins on the next plot.

The squad resumed its advance. Foreboding grew inside Geoff without apparent reason. The street along which they walked expanded: the houses became larger and more refined, the damage more extreme. Memories from earlier in the war, of helping to dig bodies out from under the rubble in Spain, of being paralysed when the monorail was hit in southern France, reasserted themselves. The intimation came to him that those awful experiences—singularly overwhelmed by losing Lisa and their child when he'd finally got back to England—might not be the worst he would be obliged to face before the end of this war.

Geoff ducked as a sudden roar of displaced air overhead announced the passage of a wing of large autonomous air transports. The bulbous, ungainly craft defied gravity with all the grace of a thrown shotput, until they changed direction or altitude, which they seemed to do effortlessly.

Derisive laughter came to Geoff's ears. A smile creased Savage's mean face. The Royal Marine said, "They're transports delivering construction replicators for the Delta Works. No need to be such a scaredy-cat."

Geoff threw him a wan smile, not caring if any of the soldiers thought he was a coward. The AATs slowed and descended beyond the shattered rooftops.

An indicator flashed in Geoff's vision. He twitched an eye muscle to open the communication, the system set to audio only lest a thumbnail in the corner of his view caused him to miss something dangerous.

"Update?" Alan asked.

"We're entering a town now. I said I'd be in touch," Geoff replied, irritated.

"Wires are saying your wave is moving inland quickly. The construction replicators are in—"

"Yeah, right. Nice of you to point that shit out from the safety of your London office—"

"Whoa there, Geoff, my boy. The other embeds with your attack group—"

Geoff terminated the connection when he noticed the look on a squaddie's face. The young man stood guard at a doorway to a damaged suburban house on a street of many such typically Dutch, wood-frame buildings. He looked downcast and exhausted, but Geoff sensed something more.

As if in confirmation, Savage turned back and said, with a nod to the same building, "Our super AI says there's a load of stiffs in there."

Geoff broke out of the line and strode to the guard. The young man stiffened as if preparing to salute, until he must've realised that only a civilian hack approached him. His eyes narrowed when Geoff reached him.

Geoff nodded at the house beyond the squaddie and asked, "What's in there?"

The man's white, blotchy complexion creased into a frown and he said, "You don't wanna know, mate."

Geoff heaved in a breath and said, "You can see I'm a journo, so you must know that not only do I want to see what's in there, I've got to. It's my job."

The squaddie shook his head. "Nope. It's sealed off. Crime scene."

"Ask your CO, would you? Tell him I'm an embed with the Royal Marines, and my report will make your regiment look good to the rest of the world. Show them what you're doing; what you're up against, you know?"

The squaddie's left eyelid twitched. He said, "Yes, sir... He's with *The Guar*—yes, sir. Will do." The young man looked at Geoff and said, "All right. You can go in. But don't touch anything and no puking. Got that?"

Geoff nodded.

The squaddie stepped aside and said, "If you need to chunder, use your helmet, right?"

"Roger that."

"My CO said to make sure you're back out of there in less than two minutes, or I'll come and get you."

Geoff began to protest, but the squaddie cut him off and said, "Mate, you won't wanna stay in there for a second longer than you have to, trust me."

"Where's the interesting stuff?"

"At the back. The middle of the abattoir is the living room."

Geoff passed the guard and entered the anonymous single-storey dwelling. Plunged into the relative darkness of the interior, he stopped to let his eyes adjust from the bright daylight. The odour in the dimness triggered a recollection deep in his memory; a smell that represented a common thread through all of his most brutal experiences in this war.

He paced along a short corridor, noting a series of small watercolours of bucolic windmills hanging askew on the grey wall. Light increased with the stench of watery rust as he reached the threshold into what had been a spacious living room. The furniture had been pushed back against three of the walls, while the furthest led out onto a terrace. In the middle of the room lay the partially naked bodies of at least a dozen women.

Geoff's mouth dried. He tried to whisper a curse but only strangled air escaped his throat. His mind divided: one half into shock; the other maintaining journalistic dispassion. All of the bodies were female. From the little flesh that was not covered in blood or blood-soaked clothes, he judged them all to be in their teens or twenties. There appeared to be no obvious causes of death other than by blade. They must've been killed within the last couple of hours because of the smell.

All of the victims had another thing in common: they'd been undernourished. Slender legs were entwined with thin arms and draped over bony ribcages. Most of their throats had been cut.

A shout of "Oi!" came to Geoff's ears. "Time's up. They've found another one a few streets away. Twice as many down there."

As in Spain the previous year and when Lisa and their child were killed in the London attack on 2 June 2062, the searing determination that no victim of this war should be forgotten reasserted itself like a forgotten rage of anger. Geoff nodded in grim acceptance of the scene around him. It wasn't his job to identify these victims now. Soon, army support elements containing medics and forensic experts would arrive and find out who these women were and where they came from. And he'd contact those experts and obtain access to that data. He'd record their names and anything else he could find out about them. Other questions would also have to be answered: why did the enemy kill them now, when they had to withdraw? He shuddered to think of the lives these women must have led in the last eighteen months, to have survived that long only to be murdered just before the moment of rescue.

Geoff turned and retreated into the narrow corridor with its small watercolour pictures hanging on the wall, his nose already used to the smell of fresh blood. In the bright doorway ahead, the back of the squaddie stood in silhouette.

While the desire to record every victim of this vile war burned anew, the rational part of his mind noted the unreasonableness of such an objective. Then again, if not him—who? Millions had been killed or displaced; mainland Europe had been raped in the foulest manner imaginable. Someone had to try—

Re-emergence into the bright, hot morning sunlight stung his eyes. "Thanks," he muttered to the guard, squinting to see how far Savage and rest of the troops had gone.

"Not so pretty when they've been sliced up like that, are they?" the guard said in black humour.

"Fuck off," Geoff replied.

Chapter 4

08.58 Wednesday 1 August 2063

Maria Phillips stared at the harassed doctor as he said, "Field surgeon, I need you to get to your assigned sector and assist the wounded there. We're going to have a lot more coming in."

Maria nodded absent-mindedly, still fighting to cope with the morning's events. She muttered, "Yes, sir. Of course."

He turned and lumbered off to where an autonomous troop transport had just rolled to a stop. Maria took in the scene of chaos around her, as other medics and surgeons moved among the injured soldiers.

Her Squitch instructed, "Proceed southeast for three hundred metres, as indicated. At the temporary stores there, collect ten battlefield GenoFluid packs and then follow directions to sector zero-seven-one and administer the packs."

"Right," she answered. A familiar pain that had dogged her since she'd discovered Nabou had been killed returned under the bone above her eyes. The sorrow aggravated her own injuries. She hurried between the rows of injured troops sitting or lying on the warm ground, the bright morning sun increasing in heat with every passing moment. She took the longest strides she could and asked her Squitch, "Please state the current location of Field Surgeon Nabou Faye."

"Field Surgeon Faye's body is in a temporary mortuary awaiting repatriation."

Maria said nothing, fighting a loneliness she'd not felt since a Spider had blown up her parents' house. She followed the indicators in her lens that led her to more casualties further on in the barren field. From the west, autonomous troop transports rocked slightly as they drove over the ground. Low in the sky, aircraft also gathered.

Her sense of professionalism forced itself out from under the weight of her grief. She reached a pallet of stores over which a cargo net was draped. "Okay, tell me again, what do I need?" she asked.

Her Squitch repeated, "Collect ten battlefield GenoFluid packs and proceed where indicated in your lens."

As she did so, she asked, "We're going to need a theatre for the more seriously wounded. Where is it?"

"An AAT is inbound with the required equipment for you to oper—"

A sudden and vast volley of hisses overhead drowned out the rest of her Squitch's answer as a wing of Scythes raced above them. Maria gave an involuntary shiver at the noise. She looped the lanyards on the corners of the GenoFluid packs over her shoulder. Her training told there could be no danger, else her Squitch would've said something, but this first morning of a new phase in the war had already placed a heavy toll on her.

Once she had five packs slung over each shoulder, the load on her right arm aggravating her own minor injury, she turned from the pallet and her view lit up with digital indicators over casualties lying or sitting on the dry dirt in front of her. Most were yellow, meaning the injuries were not life-threatening; some were orange. She could not see any reds. Advancing into the rows of injured, her motivation clarified. Memories of Nabou faded, yielding precedence to those who needed her help now.

"Please?" a man's strained voice called out when she reached the head of the nearest row.

She shrugged a GenoFluid pack from her shoulder as the casualty's personal details resolved digitally in the air next to him. He already had a pack over a stomach wound. "Hang on," she answered. Her lens linked to the soldier's Squitch and relayed that the current pack was performing at less than seventy percent capacity due to stress damage incurred during the casualty's evac. "You can manage, yes, private?" she asked.

The soldier nodded his confirmation.

Maria handed him a new pack. "Replace the one there with this one," she instructed.

To her right sat a young woman who appeared uninjured, but whose head rested on her knees. Maria glanced at her straight brown hair and the digital details informed her that this soldier's internal organs had suffered a level of blunt-force trauma that meant they'd begun to shut down.

Maria crouched beside her and said, "Okay, I need you to lay on the stretcher now."

Seconds passed. Maria put her arm out to ease the casualty downwards when the young woman murmured, "It hurts."

"Sergeant Bay, please lay down on your front."

With a whimper the young woman did so. Her pained expression contorted further and Maria saw they must have been about the same age. Maria rolled up the woman's smock laid a pack on her lower back.

A moment later, her Squitch announced, "This casualty is now stable."

"Good," Maria said, standing.

A comms icon flashed in the bottom-right of her view. Concern gripped her when she saw that it was her older brother. "Martin? What's happened?"

"Nothing's happened to me, Maz," he replied, a familiar note of defiance in his voice.

Maria said, "Thank god." She moved to the next casualty and lifted another pack from her shoulder. Further along the row, the indicator above an injured soldier turned red.

Her Squitch ordered: "Prioritise Second Lieutenant Lavigne, as indicated."

Martin continued, "Three of my guys who got hit half an hour ago. Their transport's coming in at your location. Can you take care of them?"

"What?" Maria asked in confusion. "I don't get to decide who I treat. You know that."

"Yeah, yeah. They'll contact you. Two are still mobile but the other one really took a hiding. They're my guys, Maz. Please."

"Right, I'll do what I can," she replied, hurrying towards the critically injured soldier.

"Thanks."

"Just make sure you don't end up on one of those transports."

The connection ended.

Maria reached Second Lieutenant Lavigne. The young woman lay in a foetal position, grasping her stomach as spasms wracked her small body. Blood soaked her uniform and congealed in the dirt underneath her.

Maria knelt and shrugged all of the GenoFluid packs from her shoulders. As she did so, in her vision more of

Lavigne's fading vital signs resolved in the air around her. With care, Maria slid her index finger under the chinstrap of the soldier's helmet, and then prised the clasp open with her thumb. The scent of sweat mixed with the rust of fresh blood invaded her nose again. The patient continued trembling and a gave moan of exhausted agony when Maria lifted the helmet and wiped the moisture from the back of the soldier's neck.

The countdown to Lavigne's death dipped below thirty seconds. Maria laid one of the small packs across the top of the victim's exposed neck, and breathed out. She'd done what she could. She watched the pack, trying to visualise the billions of nanobots traversing the membrane and entering the soldier's body at the top of her spine. The woman's trembling faded and stopped. Her breathing slowed and blood-soaked hands fell away from her stomach to reveal white flesh oozing more blood.

"Data, now," Maria requested.

Streams of new digital information from the pack splayed out in her view in front of the casualty. Maria muttered, "Oh, no. Please," as it became plain all of the nanobots in the pack could not repair the injuries nor stem the loss of blood.

Maria said, "This casualty needs an operating theatre. She needs fluids."

Her Squitch answered, "A casualty clearing station will not be established before this individual expires."

An unfamiliar emotion burst like a bomb inside Maria. She hated—for the first time in her life she *hated*—the euphemism 'expire' to describe the young woman's approaching death.

"Stop it happening," she said, her voice sounding plaintive, a deeper instinct telling her that to hate was futile, even now.

Her Squitch said, "Proceed to the next casualty, as indicated."

"No. Why can't you induce a coma until we can get a theatre set up?"

"Fluid loss is too great. The bots in her system now are easing her pain prior to expiration."

On her knees, Maria cradled the young woman's head in her hands. She pleaded, "But if it will only be a few moments, can't the bots keep the blood in her brain oxygenated enough?"

But the Squitch replied, "Second Lieutenant Lavigne has lost too much blood."

The countdown reached zero. Lavigne became limp. The red indicator turned to white. Maria asked in bitterness, "So what was the point of my even trying to save her?"

"The casualty's Squitch estimated her internal injuries to be survivable. This estimate transpired to be incorrect. You should proceed to assisting the next casualty, as indicated."

Maria laid Lavigne's lifeless head on the dirt, sat back, and made to collect the discarded packs. The next casualty lay nearby, a yellow indicator flashing over him despite injuries that included shrapnel embedded in much of his torso. Maria stepped over to the stretcher and saw that the GenoFluid pack tucked into his tunic had lost much of its contents, probably due to leakage since he'd been evacuated.

She knelt down to repeat the process that hadn't helped Lavigne, safe in the knowledge that this casualty's injuries were not life-threatening. A coarse dryness irritated her throat. She asked: "When will we have a water replicator? And a proper casualty clearing station, with surgical GenoFluid packs? And some more fucking help?"

"Medics and a doctor from First Army Medical Corps are inbound."

"ETA?" She undid the soldier's tunic, pulled it open, and placed a new pack over the man's throat. Streams of digital data resolved, one of which told her that out of two-hundred-and-twenty-seven pieces of shrapnel that had penetrated his body armour and uniform, sixty-three percent could be dissolved by dedicated nanobots to leave his body in urination and excretion. Of the larger pieces, only one would have to be removed by invasive surgery, while the rest could be plucked out. The new pack reconfigured the required dissolution bots while confirming sufficient bots remained to dull the soldier's pain until the casualty clearing station could be established.

Her Squitch said, "Information: an injured member of Sierra squad from the Royal Observer Corps is requesting con—"

"Approved," Maria broke in.

A strained male voice said without fanfare, "We're coming down close to your position. Can you help?"

"Yes," Maria answered. She stood and squinted at the approaching autonomous air transports in the sky. She said, "Squitch, reassign as required so I can deal with that request."

"Confirmed."

"Well?" she asked impatiently. "Have you got someone?"

"Affirmative."

The first small Airbus AAT bumped down on the ground just a few metres beyond the furthest row of injured. A few larger Boeings followed. The hatch on the Airbus slid up and three figures emerged, one after the other. At once, digital information resolved in Maria's vision stating the names and ranks of the new arrivals.

A medic hurried up to her. She passed him the GenoFluid packs with a "Thanks, Reggie," but the man just nodded in confirmation, doubtless being told what to do and where to go by his own Squitch.

She strode towards the AATs, asking, "Which one has Sierra squad in it?"

Her Squitch replied, "Collect a surgical GenoFluid pack from the medical transport, as indicated. Then proceed to the casualty."

She arrived at the medical transport and stood aside as two medics carried out one-metre square panels. She entered and collected a full-size pack, relieved to get her hands on better-quality kit. Outside again, she glanced at the four panels standing on edge and arranged in a square. "How long till we can operate on the more badly injured ones?" she asked.

"Approximately seven minutes and thirty-one seconds," came the answer.

She hurried to Sierra squad's transport, noting burns and scarring on its bodywork. A familiar click-clack came from behind her when the panels on the dirt snapped open and began to arrange themselves into what would shortly become a rudimentary operating theatre.

Maria reached her destination as two men emerged from the dark, narrow slit in the body of the AAT, both faces creased in pain. Their names and ranks appeared in the air next to them. The taller one, called Ed, grasped his upper-left arm, which was broken and bleeding. The shorter one, Mason, limped into the hot sunlight with his right hand on his bloody right thigh. The data next to him described multiple pieces of shrapnel that threatened to require a knee replacement.

The taller one acknowledged with a nod, "Ma'am. Your brother sends his regards. Jamie's in there. He's not good."

Maria shook her head at the absurdity that Martin would ask his injured subordinates to give her his regards. She looked at them and said, "Why haven't you got battlefield packs on those injuries?"

Ed shrugged and looked at his boots, mumbling, "Dunno. It happened pretty quick, ma'am. One minute we're advancing, expecting to find only dead ragheads; the next, a poxy Spider's loose and causing all kinds of shi—er, trouble."

"Go and try and make yourselves comfortable over there," she said, indicating the nearest row of casualties. "Someone will take care of you."

She didn't wait for their reply, and blinked at the relative darkness as she entered the cool interior of the AAT. Blood dripped from a gurney that had been hurriedly strapped to the fuselage, spatting on the metal floor. The corporal lay on his front, the back of his smock shredded and soaked in blood. A red indicator began counting down ominously. She took a small knife from a trouser pocket and slit the soldier's uniform with care. Blood obscured the extent of the damage to his back. She peeled the material away. With his injured flesh clear, she laid the pack down onto his back.

"Okay," she said to herself. The unconscious man's face looked familiar. Then she remembered the casualty she'd lost earlier in the morning. What was his name? Zander. Young and handsome. Then suddenly dead. And here, now, lay another one, a young face smeared with dirt and dried sweat, eyes closed and—

A sudden dizziness swept over her. She gripped the gurney and tried to regulate her shallow breaths.

Her Squitch announced: "Information: your blood-glucose level has fallen to an unsafe level. You require water and electrolyte."

Maria murmured, "In a minute." She stroked Jamie's soft blond hair. The red countdown stopped and the indicator changed to orange. He was out of immediate danger, and the realisation dispelled the sick feeling and allowed her to stand steady again.

But Zander, Nabou, all those other NATO troops in the field were dead, and the day had barely begun.

Chapter 5

10.21 Wednesday 1 August 2063

Geoff Morrow's throat stung when he swallowed in reaction to the view in front of him. Even the confrontational Savage reined in his pugnacity when the super-AI confirmed that they did in fact stand on the precipice of a vast execution pit.

Savage muttered, "There must be thousands in there. The super AI says that mess could be two metres deep."

Geoff didn't answer. He cast his eyes around the perimeter of the sports stadium. However, instead of rows of seats in the stands surrounding the pitch, there stood burnt and blasted mobile laser units, vaster than any western lasers Geoff had seen. These metal boxes angled down to point into what had been the pitch. Each metal box had, on the side facing the pitch, an emitter. Although Geoff strained to see from outside, he shuddered to think of the heat that size of lens would be able to emit.

As if reading the journalist's mind, Savage said, "That's a max of two shots and anything line-of-sight for four klicks is reduced to a puddle of burnt, steaming sludge with bones sticking out."

"When do you think those people were killed?"

Savage shrugged. "Difficult to say." Air hissed through his teeth and he speculated, "A while, though." He pointed a finger and added, "The patches of skin that didn't burn look pretty leathery."

Geoff reflected that the soldier had a point. There rested the congealed remains of thousands of people whom the Caliphate had executed via incineration. But their lasers did not vaporise the victims entirely; they merely reduced the mass of humanity to a sea of cooked meat and fat that, after months or years, resembled a sea of brown and grey with points of white bone sticking up at jagged angles.

Savage asked, "Want to take a closer look?"

Geoff's face dropped but his morbid curiosity peaked. "Yeah, all right," came out of his mouth before he realised he'd said it.

Savage's head dipped forwards and he muttered, "Roger that. Going to take a look… The stadium's called Wilhelmus Veteranen… Nah, I'll take the Journo with me. Max ten on this and then we push on… Roger."

As Geoff followed the soldier to the chain-link perimeter fence, he cursed again his lack of access to the military's super AI. He blurted out, "It's pissing me off only getting half the conversation."

Savage stopped in mid-step. He turned back to Geoff, his thick eyebrows coming together in considered thoughtfulness. He shook his head and said in a concluding tone, "Nope, I absolutely do not give the slightest fuck about anything that may or may not be pissing you off, Journo."

The Royal Marine turned back to face the rusted chain-link fence that enclosed the sports ground. He extracted a small, gun-like device from his smock. He aimed it a few centimetres from the rudimentary lock holding the single-person gate.

A series of bright blue flashes came from it and stung Geoff's eyes. He squinted and complained, "Jesus, couldn't you have warned me?"

Savage glanced back and replied in the mocking tone of an affected young girl's voice, "Oh, sorry. Bright lights, bright lights."

Geoff smothered another curse lest Savage thump him for expressing it out loud.

The gate in the fence swung open with a dull metallic rustle, and Savage returned the device to his smock. He strode into the sports stadium as though he owned it. Geoff followed. The deep grey concrete led to pre-cast steps of the kind found in thousands of small, local sports stadia all over Europe. Geoff's journalist's eye alit on the bland traces of those whose lives had ended here: a shrivelled and twisted man's jacket; a woman's broken blusher compact, the faded russet of the makeup smeared in the dirt; a child's running shoe, blackened and frayed.

Savage touched the metal casing of the closest laser, stroking it in uncharacteristic admiration. "This is gorgeous," he said.

"Gorgeous?"

"Look at the size of it," Savage said, gesturing to the lens. "We haven't got anything that comes close."

"Oh yeah?" Geoff questioned. "The Yanks' surface ships have the Pulsar Mark—"

"No, no," the soldier broke in without rancour, "NATO's most powerful laser has a lens with a diameter of just under a metre. How big does that lens look to you?"

Geoff conceded, "Bigger than that."

"Yup," Savage said, slinging his Pickup over his shoulder and hopping down three of the concrete rows. He stood in front of the huge machine. "See? That beast is nearly two metres." Savage stuck his fists on his hips and sighed. He turned to look at the other lasers sited around the stadium and said, "They must've lifted them into position with a crane. Look at the brackets holding each of the things at the right angle to cook everyone on the pitch."

Geoff couldn't help but concede Savage's observation. Now standing next to one, Geoff saw that each laser consisted of a metal box the size of a shipping container, only narrower, with the vast lens on one of the longer oblong sides. He asked, "So what actually powers these things? I've read about our gear—"

"In the British Army, we call it 'kit'," Savage interjected.

"Er, yeah, okay," Geoff stammered. "Anyway, NATO lasers are reckoned to be the biggest and most powerful they can be because there are limits on the frequency—"

"And now we've got them, that's what we're going to find out, isn't it? How could these bastard, backwards ragheads come up with kit so much better than ours?"

Geoff turned to the pitch a few metres below them and its impossibly grotesque harvest. "Those poor bastards were probably wondering the same thing," he said, images of the terrified people they must've once been assaulting his mind's eye: scared children, panicked men and women, confused senior citizens. A sudden thought occurred to him. He said, "How the hell is anyone going to identify those remains? There must be thousands of people in that mass."

Savage shrugged in apparent indifference. "Don't know. Is it important? They're dead. Probably some forensics types will come by sooner or later, but right now we're on day one of the operation to take Europe back and seriously kick the raghead's arse, you know?"

"But they need to be remembered, acknowledged. There will be relatives, other survivors…" his words trailed off as Savage began mumbling.

"Uh-huh," he said. "Good… Right…"

Geoff moved down the rows of precast concrete steps, drawn by morbid curiosity. Specks of white that he thought might be other debris he realised had to be bone. He put a hand out to steady himself. His spirit reeled in revulsion at the enemy's cynicism. He stared up at the lasers, deliberately placed to kill as many people as effectively as possible. He could picture the fear, hear the screams, smell the burning flesh—

"Hey, Journo? You coming?"

Geoff spun round. "What? Where?"

Savage's face broke into a satisfied smile and he said, "We've been reassigned to the first wave, at fucking last. We've got an AAT inbound back at junction 7-A."

"But," Geoff stammered, unable to process this sudden change, "I'm an embed, reporting—"

"Yeah, the lads all think you're way too much of a coward to come along. You best stay here until the next wave lands." Savage waved a hand at the pitch behind them and added, "You can be all morose over what's left of Europe's biggest barbeque."

Geoff leapt up the steps, anger giving his legs more power. He said, "I'm coming with you."

Savage smiled in belligerent satisfaction. He shook his finger as he said, "You do exactly what I tell you. And if we come under fire and you shit yourself, I'll double-tap you myself, got that?"

Geoff smothered a curse. Memories of running away from Lisa and their child in London during the attack fourteen months earlier made him hate himself a fraction more for his cowardice that day. He clenched his eyes shut and, as he'd expected, Lisa's voice resonated in his head again: "You're a bastard, Geoff Morrow." When he opened them again, Savage had exited the sports ground. Geoff hurried after him. His own lens recorded every single thing he said and did, and, if he were lucky, he would survive this war and write the book that had already begun to form in his mind's eye.

As he also exited the ground, he muttered under his breath, "And cowardice is not going to play a part of it, so you can also fuck off, Sergeant Savage."

Savage turned and demanded: "What did you say?"

"Only that I'm coming with you."

"Congrats on finding some balls, then, Journo."

Chapter 6

11.57 Wednesday 1 August 2063

For the first time he could recall, Field Marshall Sir Terry Tidbury wished there were a NATO soldier equal or superior to him with whom he could discuss his concerns. He wanted to contact Suds but knew that his brother-in-arms in America had his own hands full. Besides, Suds wouldn't likely appreciate being woken in the middle of the night as it was over there. On the other hand, a half-smile formed on Terry's face at the mischievous consideration of spoiling Suds' beauty sleep.

He glanced out of his private office in the War Rooms to the main area beyond. In silence, the array of screens above the stations flashed and blinked and displayed thousands of pieces of data. Operatives tapped lights on the consoles at which they sat, often muttering soundlessly, now and then glancing up at the screens.

His adjutant, Simms, stood at the central display directing and advising or deferring in Terry's temporary absence. He would soon go out there and do his best to exude the calm confidence he knew was expected of him. Terry gulped down the hot, sweet tea and tried to ignore the aches in his joints that, despite his wishes to the contrary, spread out into his limbs. He silently questioned again if the lack of sleep might cloud his judgement in a manner similar to the aggravation it caused his fifty-seven-year-old bones. But at once he reflexively chided himself for being so self-involved at this time of greatest urgency.

The fact remained that his most significant concern lingered unarticulated—as it should for the head of any army on the execution of its most important operation. Terry smiled ruefully at the thought of those times of high drama for NATO leaders since the alliance's formation in 1949, some one hundred and fourteen years ago.

Still grasping the mug of tea, he left the office and approached Simms at the central holographic display. "How close are we?" he asked.

His adjutant's eyebrows came together in consideration and he answered: "Quite." He indicated one of the figures in the display, "According to Squonk, we are on schedule to achieve all day one objectives—"

"Day one, already?" Terry broke in. "It's not even midday."

"And at the lower end of forecast casualty numbers. Ground is being gained continuously, sir. Indeed, both attack groups should achieve all of their objectives within the next four hours."

"Any material irregularities so far?"

"No, sir," Simms replied with his usual tight smile.

"How about support? Are the advance units getting everything in a timely manner?"

"Some of Pakla's elements of Attack Group East north of Amersfoort were delayed by seven minutes awaiting air deployments of Abrahams tanks."

Terry murmured his acknowledgement and then said, "Squonk, show casualty numbers and locations, Attack Group East."

The super AI answered, "Confirmed."

Terry watched in silence as the map zoomed towards the Netherlands and detailed locations where NATO troops had suffered setbacks.

"The Wessex units have taken a bit of a beating. Make a note for me to speak to their CO when the day is over."

Simms replied, "Very good, sir."

Terry said, "Squonk, overlay group progress with R-plus-one objectives."

The three-dimensional image tilted and withdrew to show real-time locations of the advance units; a lighter shade indicating where they should be at certain times. Terry then told the super AI to do the same for Attack Group South, in the area between Caen and Rouen.

"Over five thousand casualties," he observed.

"From an operation involving nearly two million troops and supporting elements, field marshal?" Simms said.

Terry nodded in consideration of his adjutant's point. He said, "I suppose it is a far better situation than any of our forebears enjoyed."

A silence settled between the men. Terry concentrated on the display, watching in real time each incremental gain by NATO forces. His eyes flitted over to the screens on the periphery of the room, above the operators' heads, and back again. The sense of his own redundancy became exacerbated, producing a chill sweat on the back of his neck. He had control and the power to approve or reject any adjustment in this most meticulously planned invasion. But, ultimately, no one really needed him.

As if reading Terry's thoughts, Simms asked, "Would you like to take some rest, sir?"

"No, I would not," Terry responded more testily than he'd intended. On reflection, he added, "Ever since this war began, I believe we've relied too much on our computers. They missed all of it, Simms. Can you remember, eighteen months ago, when this chaos began, how likely did our so-called super artificial intelligence claim such a war as this was?"

"Just eight percent, if memory serves," Simms replied.

"And now look," he said, waving his arm at the central display. "Again, we rely on them. Yes, I know," Terry said in anticipation of his adjutant's counterargument, "we have no choice; that such an operation could not possibly be managed without them."

"If we consider that our enemy also depends to a great extent—"

"Yes, a battle between computers, with millions of very real human casualties. But when I look at these screens, there is one question I cannot stop asking myself; a question that I don't want to ask the computers."

"Sir Terry," Simms began, "we are committed, and you have an important role to—"

"No," Terry said, cutting him off with a raised hand. "We are again relying on percentages and probabilities in the same way as before this war started, and, if the computers are wrong again, I believe we will be just as impotent as we were then."

"I understand, sir," Simms said with a note of diplomacy. "But the decision to bring the start date forward from October should still transpire to be the correct one, especially given the advantage in our weapons' capabilities."

Terry didn't answer. He kept scanning the displays all around him, noting the names of his generals and their designated sectors. NATO forces spread inland like a dry paper towel soaking up spilt liquid. His subordinates included many commanders at all levels who brought some human intelligence and intuition to the battle, but Terry secretly worried that some might also rely too much on the computers.

He said, "The decision to bring the start date forward hardly matters now, Simms. Nevertheless, I cannot help but ask myself: when? When will it happen?"

Simms nodded. "It might still be too early, sir."

Terry grunted his agreement. "But it has to come, and it can't be long. The enemy's computers must be urging him that he cannot allow us to gain a foothold. Although," Terry added, "it does seem we already have."

Simms said, "Operation Repulse is proceeding according to plan."

Terry gave his adjutant a withering look and said, "You sound like Squonk."

"Ah, sorry, sir. I merely wanted to—"

"Never mind. The fact remains that all the time Tazirbu can keep producing weapons, the enemy's counterattack will come. And when it does, it will be costly to repel."

"Sir," Simms replied, "the Americans' insistence on bringing the start date forward necessitated certain compromises, but these have been factored into the plan. Provided that Hastings can keep to the schedule, our casualties should not be materially higher than under the scenario with the original start date."

Terry added, "And until we can confirm if he succeeds or fails, we have no way of knowing his or his team's status."

Chapter 7

18.00 Wednesday 1 August 2063

Two hundred metres under the Mediterranean Sea, Colour Sergeant Rory Moore stomped along *HMS Spiteful*'s narrow passageway with a toxic mixture of frustration, apprehension and regret burning his throat like rising stomach acid. He stopped and pressed his back into the cold metal bulkhead as one of the sub's ratings, a small woman the same height as Pip, passed with a curious nod. Rory stared after her for a moment.

A modern submarine was not an ideal place for a man who stood nearly two metres tall. Rory resumed towards the galley, head dipped constantly forward, wondering how he could've allowed himself to be talked into undertaking another mission on this vessel. The previous year, the discomfort hadn't felt so bad. He and Pip had escaped the enemy's sudden, unstoppable assault on Europe, and the *Spiteful* had returned both of them back to England.

But now, with the prospect of Operation Thunderclap and its risks looming ever closer, Rory found himself battling a negativity he'd never anticipated. Too many things on the submarine drove him to distraction: the hideous 'hot-bunking' that obliged him to sleep in the same tiny bunk—unamusingly called 'coffins' by the regular crew—as ratings about whose personal hygiene he could not be sure; the toilet that seemed even narrower than it had been the previous year; the shower inside which he could hardly clean himself—

"There you are. Come on," Nick Bird, the team's navigator, said from the doorway to the wardroom. "You know his nibs don't like no tardiness, you great lump."

Rory followed Nick through the doorway.

"And there we go," Harry Dixon pronounced with a flourishing wave towards Rory. "Good of you to join us, sergeant."

Rory threw him a sardonic smile and replied, "The pleasure's all mine, Captain Dixon. Although I must reiterate my complaint about the shoddy board and lodging on our little cruise."

The other team member, Declan Gardner, snorted a laugh and said, "You'll be liking the sightseeing he's got planned for us in a couple of days, so you will."

Rory sat at the small table. His knee hit the support, as it always did, when he forced his thigh under the low, thin wood. "Christ," he muttered, "bloody pygmies. Bloody world's built for them."

Harry ran his fingers through his thick blond hair and said, "Sorry to break it you, old chap, but I rather think you're the abnormality, not the rest of the world. Still, if you want—"

"It's not like the guvnor to be late," Nick broke in, curiosity in his Estuary English accent.

"The XO's probably fluttering her eyelashes at him again," Declan said.

"Don't be a sap," Rory said. "I was on this boat last year when she was chief petty officer, and she was a tough nut. I wouldn't give her any shi—"

"What makes you think she doesn't have a soft side, then?" Declan asked, eyebrow raised.

"I'm not saying—"

"I do think our giant might be feeling a little jealous, chaps," Harry said to jeers from the other two.

"Piss off, captain," Rory responded, smiling.

"Careful, mate," Nick cautioned, "or Harry will have you up on a charge."

Declan nodded towards Harry and said, "Might be an idea to plug Captain Dixon in to the boat's batteries and give him a proper charge."

"Seconded," Rory said, chuckling.

Harry sighed and shook his head in disdain. "Honestly, look what passes for humour among you lower-class types. You really are such a shower. Deary me."

Rory sensed all of them catch their breaths when the door clicked open. General Maximillian Hastings stepped nimbly into the wardroom and shut the door. Rory had taken to observing his CO's pencil-thin moustache to see if he let it grow or not. So far, Rory thought the general allowed the sad black worm to get a little longer before reminding it of its place with a trim.

Hastings began: "Apologies for my lateness. I think each of us has his issues with our current environment. Despite everyone on *Spiteful* being as accommodating as we might reasonably expect, I understand this is probably the most trying part of the operation for us. As I mentioned to you during training, we need to regard this period as a time to focus on our ultimate objective and review and recall all the work we carried out so diligently before embarking. These few days of relative peace have given us a chance to recharge our batteries, as it were, before we arrive off the coast of North Africa. Well, there is not long to wait now."

Hastings stepped back and forth in the limited space, emanating a familiar awkwardness as the wardroom was too small to allow him to pace around as he usually would when addressing the team.

Nick Bird stuck his hand up as though he were a student in class. "Er, general," he began, "is there any news on the progress of Operation Repulse?"

Rory smiled when Hastings gave the Londoner a withering look. The general replied, "Of course not. What part of 'we are running silent to avoid any risk of enemy detection' did you not understand?"

"Right," Nick said, "only I overheard a couple of the crew talking earlier today—"

"That's enough of the tittle-tattle," Hastings said with a wave of his hand.

Harry leaned into Nick and muttered, "I think they might've been teasing you, old chap."

"But they didn't know I was there," Nick protested.

Declan said, "Have you not twigged it yet that everyone on this boat knows everyone else's business, so they do?"

Rory added, "And they do enjoy a good wind-up, mate."

Nick looked crestfallen.

Hastings clapped his hands together and said, "Now, depending on local conditions, we're approaching the fully active phase of Operation Thunderclap." He glanced behind him at the picture hanging on the wall and ordered, "Computer? Show map three and follow my directions."

Rory watched the apparent oil-on-canvas painting of a nineteenth century ship-of-the-line dissolve into a map of a section of coastline.

"Right. *Spiteful* has sent forward several shoals of proximetres to swim above and below us. If they bump into anything and send their short-burst pulse back to the boat, the captain will know the enemy has placed defensive traps along his coastline, and we may end up having a slightly longer swim than we'd planned."

The map zoomed into a vast bay in the middle of the North African coast that Rory knew to be due north of the target at Tazirbu.

The general went on, "Despite all of our hard data on the enemy being years out of date due to his relentless jamming, we can still be fairly confident of many of our calculations, especially the locations of towns on this part of the coastline, mainly thanks to some autonomous observations where newer data was obtained before the devices were neutralised."

The map zoomed in further and a more detailed area resolved, sea to the northwest, sand-coloured land to the southeast.

Hastings said, "The captain has acknowledged my desire to get us in as close as possible to minimise the distance we have to swim. On the other hand, he does seem to be awfully fond of his boat and does not wish it to be damaged by, for example, running aground."

"That's a rather selfish attitude, if I may say so, sir," Harry chipped in, in his best Old-Etonian accent.

The general nodded and replied, "Quite so. In any case, the proximetres will be the ultimate arbiters of just how close we can get. We will also need moonlight and a relatively calm swell. So, while we shall arrive in the vicinity in the next six-to-eight hours, we may not be able to commence immediately. Any questions so far?"

Declan stuck his hand up and said, "Have you made a decision regarding my request to reconsider using the boosters on the cylinders we talked about before we left?"

Rory's ears picked up at the Irishman's question. The idea of the boosters had been one of the main topics of conversation among Declan, Nick and Rory. A day before they left England, Declan had had the idea to replicate and fit a small propeller on the back of each of the eight cylinders. Each booster would be able to run for a few minutes from compressed air and promised to assist the swimmers with their loads. Each of them was convinced there would be no risk of detection.

Hastings stroked his moustache with the knuckle of his index finger and replied, "Yes, I have. And the answer has to be 'no', I'm afraid."

Rory saw other shoulders slump in disappointment in addition to his own.

The general went on, "It's a sound idea, no mistake about it. But it's come too late. While planning this mission, I have attempted to avoid or minimise any potential risk of discovery by the enemy. And these 'boosters' are in my opinion not worth the increased potential for discovery."

Nick said, "But they might really save us some exertion, sir."

"And that is the reason we shan't use them, bombardier. We have planned on having to cover fifteen hundred to two thousand metres. Yes, pulling our kit through the water will require effort, but this is hardly the most onerous fitness challenge the British Army has ever demanded of its soldiers. The boosters increase the detection risk at the questionable benefit of us not being quite so out of breath when we reach the shore. And that, gentlemen, is simply not worth it."

"Fair enough," Nick mumbled.

Hastings said, "I do understand the physical demands this first part of the operation will place on each of us—and I should like to add that I am by far the most senior in years—

but there are other complications. For example, what if a cylinder ran off course? How would we recover it? What if one of the boosters otherwise malfunctioned or failed to perform? We would've taken the risk only to be back at square one."

Rory watched the others around the small table and sensed their acceptance of the general's explanation.

"Next," Hastings continued, "is the importance of assembly and traversing the distance to the target. Again, we trained thoroughly on these aspects and we know the potential for problems."

The blue on the map disappeared. A uniform sandy yellow covered the screen and an indicative dotted line resolved, heading south.

"We have all familiarised ourselves with the Triumphs, their handling and their performance. Do any of you feel the need to revisit any aspect of that part of the mission?"

Rory shook his head while the others mumbled in the negative.

"Very good," Hastings said. "Success in this second part of the operation will, to a large degree, rely on us being able to cover the six hundred kilometres to the target as swiftly as possible. To do this, we will utilise traditional night-vision goggles—"

Rory tutted in obvious disapproval.

"Yes, sergeant?" Hastings said in invitation.

"Sir, I remain unconvinced they're worth the risk."

The general stepped back, shrugged, and said, "The risk is minimal while the gain is substantial."

Nick tipped his head forward and said, "It's not as big a risk as the bikes themselves. We can't hardly cover the whole bike and rider with a giant BHC sleeve, can we? If you accept that risk, those old-fashioned goggles should not cause you any trouble at all."

Rory argued, "They're still going to be emitting an electromagnetic sig—"

"Not so much as you might think," Hastings broke in. "And only in a very limited area."

Nick added, "Look, I've got to get us an effing long way in the least time in enemy territory, with only paper maps and a compass to lead the way, right?"

Rory said, "Yeah, I do know th—"

"Those goggles will let us see the terrain in front of us for far enough that we can really crack on through the night. We're going to have to deal with everything the desert's got to offer on the way, Rory: shale and stone; sand dunes, dried riverbeds. You don't want to go plummeting into a bloody wadi at eighty Ks an hour, do you? Without those goggles, it'd take three times as long to get there."

Hastings addressed Rory, "Bombardier Bird is our navigator, and I agree with him that the pros outweigh the cons by quite some margin. In any case, we are hardly going to be silent or invisible. The motorbikes will be emitting noise and heat, as will our own bodies. Ultimately, we are relying on the fact that the North African desert is a very large, very hot, and therefore very hostile, environment which the enemy does not in fact trouble himself to patrol or otherwise monitor outside populated areas and established transport routes. The very nature of this mission has to rely on enemy complacency to the smallest degree."

"Yes, sir," Rory replied quietly, wishing he felt more mollified than he did.

"Now," the general went on, "we come to the third part of the operation: arrival at and disabling of the target."

The map enlarged again. The dotted line swerved to the west to run parallel with a key highway that led into the centre of the city. To the north appeared an arrangement of small rectangles.

Hastings said, "Now, this is where things get interesting, particularly our military advantages over the enemy, about which he does not, or at least should not, know." The general pointed his finger at the highway to the east of Tazirbu. "Here we have a major, six-lane highway for autonomous vehicles that links the city with the rest of the enemy's population centres. Here, to the north, is the ACA production plant. As we can expect, it is made up of several buildings. And we will only have one night to confirm which are the most important and to lay the sonic mines."

Nick's forehead creased and he asked, "Excuse me, sir, but how can we be sure about any of this? No one has been inside and escaped from the Caliphate in, like, forever."

Rory wondered too, although he'd heard plenty of rumours over the last year, ever since he, Smith and Heaton had supported the Poles in a contact to capture the first enemy warrior alive. And Smith had paid for that contact with his life.

"Chaps," Hastings began, "what I'm going to tell you is classified as secret, so I trust you all to be discreet, post-operation. For some time now, any of the enemy we capture in battle alive or who surrender, are shipped across the Atlantic to a medical facility that scans their brains. All of their lifetime's memories are extracted and analysed by the computers for any useful intel. In this case," he said, thumbing back at the overhead plan of the target city, "one casualty who was scanned a few months ago transpired to have actually grown up in Tazirbu—the brute had memories of the whole area."

Declan asked, a note of confusion in his voice, "What do you mean, like, all of their memories? Are you saying everything they can remember or everything they ever saw in their whole lives?"

Hastings replied, "The latter."

"Would you believe that?" Declan asked rhetorically, looking at the others.

Hastings went on, "Our computers extrapolated these details from one wounded enemy and were able to cross-reference them with others' memories, snippets of conversations, glimpses of battle plans, and so on and so forth."

Harry glanced around at the rest of the team and said, "Not sure why something like that should be classified secret."

Rory said, "If the rumours I've heard are true, there's every reason to keep something like that secret."

The atmosphere thickened. Rory caught the general's glance and sensed his acquiescence.

Harry looked from the general to Rory and asked, "Well? What do you two seem to know that the rest of us don't, eh?"

Rory said, "The act of scanning their brains kills them."

"Honestly?" Harry said.

"Yeah," Rory said, "basically means NATO is killing prisoners of war. Or even 'murdering' them, if you get my drift?"

Nick chirruped, "Can't say I've got a problem with that, to be frank."

"I'll second that, so I will," Declan added.

Hastings said, "We're not going to debate the rights and wrongs of current NATO policy. But when this mission is over, do keep your mouths shut. And that, gentleman, is an order. Now, the fourth and final part of the plan: extraction. Assuming the sonic mines work as intended, I think we can expect the enemy to start looking for the culprits."

Ironic chuckles floated around the small wardroom. The map withdrew more slowly until the North African coastline again edged into view. Rory shifted his position, leaning forward, and the fading walnut veneer on the table smelt like dried, decayed flowers.

Hastings said, "However, our computers insist we will enjoy a minimum window of two hours during which each of us needs to disperse. Firstly, the enemy will or should be in shock and will not understand what has happened. Remember, one of his primary weapons' production facilities will have been destroyed without an apparent agent—there will have been no ACAs, missiles or explosions, nor any indications of the cause of the violence. Most importantly for us, there will be no evidence of enemy presence, let alone activity. Indeed, the computers give a good chance of the enemy believing that the cause might actually have been a natural earthquake.

"During this period, it will be vital for each of us to get as far away as possible. Remember, with appropriate navigation, our bikes are capable of returning to the infiltration point on the coast in less than ten hours. We can be a long way from the facility even before the enemy begins to comprehend that some external, unnatural force was at play."

Rory sensed the tension in the room. With each facet of the mission laid out so plainly, he realised that if they succeeded, the enemy would be seriously hindered and at the same time absolutely confounded.

Nick nodded in thoughtful consideration. He sniffed and opined, "Yup, it's a good plan, that. I like it, general. I reckon it stands a chance."

The others laughed and the tension broke. Hastings threw the Londoner a withering glance.

Chapter 8

20.22 Wednesday 1 August 2063

Pip's body ached from the day's exertions. She sat with her back resting against the slats of a damaged wooden fence. In front of her, across half a dozen fields, lay the outskirts of the Dutch town of Breda. The sun set behind her, the horizon ahead already black with the darkness of night.

Sergeant MacManus approached and held out his hand. He said, "Need something to eat that's nay replicated, cap?"

Pip offered a wan smile and replied, "Thanks, I've still got my bar. I'd forgotten about that. Take the weight off?" she added with a nod at the ground next to her.

"Aye, I will. Thanks," the slim young man answered. He almost fell down next to her.

Pip pulled the Velcro strap open on a small pouch on the thigh of her combat trousers. She took out a nutrition bar wrapped in paper. She tore the top off, pushed the bar up with her thumb and index finger, and bit hard on the nut-and-nougat combination. While chewing, she said, "Tastes like it's out of date."

"Nay," Mac replied, "that's just the heat. Makes the nutrients a mite manky."

Pip smiled. She asked, "Where are you from, Mac? And I don't only mean Scotland."

The young man scoffed and replied, "A wee town on the Clyde called Glasgow."

Pip chuckled as Mac accentuated his accent so the name of his home town came out as 'Glaz-geh'. She said, "My map's showing the nearest useable billet is at least two klicks behind us."

"Aye, but the nights are drawing out now. We're getting cooler air so it's easier to sleep outdoors."

Pip opened her mouth in reply, but then her Squitch spoke the one word that could galvanise the most exhausted limbs: "Danger."

"Shite," Mac hissed, pushing himself off the ground.

Pip's Squitch reported, "Enemy activity five hundred metres northeast of your position. Prepare to advance and engage."

"Have you some ammo, cap?"

Pip spoke as she rose, stuffing the half-eaten bar back in the pouch. "Still a couple of mags, yeah. You?"

"Aye, at least—"

The boom of a vast explosion nearby cut Mac off. For a second, the area lit up like daylight. A forest of burning debris cascaded down and vanished, the darkness returning like an evil magician hiding the light.

"Right," Pip said, hurrying to the nearest tracked pathway. "Check in, please."

A new voice spoke in her ear: "Roger, Sierra three-five. We're on our way in. Thirty seconds."

"Thanks, Toby," Pip answered.

Her Squitch updated her, "Enemy warriors are defending a hemp processing plant."

"So destroy them," Pip said in exasperation.

"They have civilian hostages," her Squitch replied.

Pip followed the directions her Squitch displayed in her view and jogged inexorably closer to the site of the explosion.

Her Squitch announced, "Information: an autonomous air transport is enroute to provide support."

"Negative," Pip said, "it will be a target."

"The aircraft has no human occupants."

The sounds of flames crackling and popping grew. A whine carried on the air above them and a bright, white spotlight abruptly shone at an angle onto what, Pip assumed, was the centre of the drama. Large, irregular gouts of thick black smoke billowed upwards.

"Status?" Pip asked, her mouth tasting cinders in each breath.

"Enemy warriors are attempting to retreat with hostages."

Mac asked, "How did they nay know what's going on?"

"Don't know; don't care, Mac," Pip replied. In a corner of her view, a tactical overview showed that four members of Sierra three-five had arrived fifty metres on her left, behind a brittle hedge.

Mac said, "We've got Hines to the north."

"Good," Pip replied. She slowed her pace, weapon ready. The hemp processing plant consisted of two warehouses. The larger one, on Pip's left, had been destroyed by the explosion. The small remaining warehouse had corrugated metal sides and roof, the narrow waves of metal glinting grey and black under the AAT's spotlight. She analysed the side of the building in front of her, now well within small arms' range, and noted a pair of double doors and four narrow, rectangular windows. Smoke seeped through the tops of the windows as though a giant inside were blowing it.

"Should we nay be taking cover?" Mac asked, any trepidation in his voice lost against the background noise of the growing flames and creaking metal.

"If your Squitch hasn't told you to, then the answer's no," Pip replied, wishing the inexperienced sergeant would stop asking stupid questions. "Looks like the back of the building was damaged when the bigger warehouse went up. Don't reckon they can stay in there much longer."

Her Squitch said, "Information: the airspace is secure."

Thirty metres of tarmac road separated Pip and the building. The fire brightened her surroundings with demonic clarity. She asked, "Nearest medics?"

Her Squitch answered, "Approaching from the south. Aim where indicated and prepare to engage the enemy."

She heard MacManus utter a foul curse at the same time as the door in the plant swung open. She aimed her Pickup, but her view alerted her that the individual in the doorway was a non-combatant. She spoke clearly, more for the sergeant's benefit than her own, "No biggie. We've trained for this. Keep tight on the hostiles." Determination surged inside Pip and she paced towards the doorway.

"Cap?" Mac said.

"Back me up," Pip said. At the end of her barrel, the eyes of a young woman in a dishevelled dress glared back. A thick, brown forearm was clamped around her neck. The hand grasped the shaft of a dagger, its straight-edge blade suggestive of a Persian *kard*.

Mac said, "You've got a load of firepower behind you, cap."

Her Squitch spoke, "You should not engage the enemy until the hostage is out of immediate danger."

Pip swore under her breath. The last thing she needed was the super AI stating the blindingly obvious.

Other chatter from a few disparate voices came to her ears from the members of Sierra three-five: "It's too hot round the back. No one's coming out that way."

"Smudge? How's it burning on the east side?"

"Lots of smoke. I count seven ragheads wanting to move out. Each has got a hostage, either by the throat, hair, or round the waist."

"Look sharp."

"Pity we don't have pacification ammo."

"This is a war, corporal, not fucking crowd control."

"Roger that."

"Shitheads are clearing the building, heading east."

"They don't seriously think they're gonna get back to their lines, do they?"

"Reckon so, Smudge."

"They must be out of their tiny m—"

Another explosion lit up the building and road in front of Pip. She lurched when the ground trembled and a sharp, deep pain stabbed at her eardrums.

"Shit, shit, shit," Mac cursed behind her. She sensed and shared his frustration that their Rules of Engagement insisted they could not risk harming the hostage, even if the hostage had already been harmed.

When her view cleared, Pip watched the enemy warrior stagger along the front of the building, dragging his hostage. The warrior appeared determined to reach his—

A series of gunshots rang out from the other side of the building. Pip's fear for the hostages increased.

"Ragheads down—"

"They did their hostages—"

"Smudge, call in emergency evac—"

The warrior in front of Pip stopped, righted himself, and dragged the *kard* across the hostage's throat. She collapsed. An instant later, Pip felt more than heard Mac fire his weapon. The top of the warrior's head flipped off and the body fell straight down less than a second after the woman.

Pip broke into a sprint. She reached the hostage to see the young woman had lost consciousness. Blood leaked out of the neck wound but did not spurt. Pip put her weapon down and pulled at the straps holding her webbing. Crouching next to the victim, she struggled to see the extent of the injury.

"Give me your pack, now," she ordered MacManus when he arrived.

Pip strained to see the extent of the pooling blood because the light from the fire did not penetrate fully to ground level. Then, the AAT descended on the other side of the plant and its spotlight vanished. Flaming shadows danced so that she couldn't even tell if the victim still breathed.

"Here you go," Mac said, offering the small battlefield GenoFluid pack.

"Wait." Pip discarded her webbing. She rolled her top up her torso and over her head, grateful that she'd decided to wear a bra. She leaned in, slid her left arm under the young woman's head and shoulders as gently as she could, and pressed her sweat-stained top onto the wound. She glanced back at Mac and said, "Tear the arm of her dress and get the pack on her skin, now."

Without speaking, the sergeant did as he was told.

Pip shifted her weight onto her hip to ease the effort of holding the makeshift bandage over the girl's wound. She said, "Squonk, tell the bots in the pack to do whatever they have to keep her alive."

"Confirmed."

Pip knew the bots would do that anyway, but saying it out loud made her feel somehow that the girl's fate was not entirely dependent on the nanobots in the pack.

More chatter, which her Squitch deemed relevant to her situation, came to her ears: "The AAT is down right here, guys. Kudos to Hines for showing some real grit."

"Let's move these girls. We need to get them to the nearest CCS."

"The whole place is gonna collapse soon. Step on it, Smudge. Captain Clarke? My Squitch says you have another injured civilian on your side of the building. Can the casualty wait for assistance?"

Pip answered, "Negative. This one could bleed out before then."

"So, you need to get here and board the AAT."

Pip spoke her concern out loud, "I'm not a medic. I'm not sure we can move her."

"Then you stay and wait."

MacManus tapped her knee and urged, "Cap, let's carry her."

Pip nodded. They lifted the casualty and, struggling in the heat, carried her around to the east side of the building.

"Dead raghead behind you," Mac cautioned.

"Come on, please," a voice urged above the noise of crackling flames.

Pip stepped over the body of an enemy and reached the narrow doorway of the small Airbus C440. She backed in and followed someone's instruction to put the casualty down by the forward bulkhead. She sat on the floor and cradled the woman's bloodied head, hoping the human contact might somehow help.

"Okay," Mac said laying the girl's legs on the floor. "I'll be off—"

The hatchway slid closed and the engine whine increased in pitch. Pip threw Mac a tired smile. The AAT lifted off and accelerated.

"Status?" Pip asked, staring at the unconscious girl she held.

Her Squitch replied: "The casualty is stable and will survive depending on a successful blood transfusion and minor surgery within the next hour."

"How long till we reach the nearest casualty clearing station?"

"Approximately eight minutes and sixteen seconds."

Pip glanced at the other young women in the cramped fuselage, also obliged to lay on the floor of the aircraft. She realised her equipment and weapon remained on the ground where she'd left them. With a twitch of her eye, she filed the appropriate notification so they'd be retrieved.

She shifted her position to ease the ache in her back. With adrenalin deserting her, exhaustion suffused her limbs. She closed her eyes and slowed her breathing. She suddenly noticed a tiny icon blinking in a corner of her vision. She raised it. The information panel included a link to the casualty's lens. Pip activated it. The young woman she held was called Esmée and was twenty-two years old. She came from Delft and had been studying interplanetary propulsion engineering at the recently established University of Europe before the war. Pip then rotated through a gallery of images: Esmée celebrating a sports success with her parents; Esmée taking a selfie on vacation with her siblings; Esmée partying with her university friends. Pip settled on a picture of Esmée smiling flirtatiously at the camera, with white, even teeth shining out and eyes that glittered with happiness. The girl in the picture looked nothing like the near-dead, bloodied mess whose damaged head rested on Pip's lap.

"What is it?" Mac asked.

"What?"

"You just said, 'Oh my god'."

"Did I? I don't know. I just saw images of her before the war."

"Aye."

The AAT descended and she said to Mac, "At least she's going to live."

But his response surprised her: "And you think that's a grand thing, do you?"

"What?"

Mac nodded towards Esmée, "I saw the look in her eyes too, when her captor held that knife at her throat. And she did nay look like she wanted rescuing, not by a long way."

"But that was then," Pip protested. "She'll recover, get better—"

"Recover?" Mac broke in. "Poor bairn's been suffering the worst abuse for the better part of eighteen months, maybe thinking it would nay end till they killed her, and you think she can just 'recover'?"

Pip didn't know how to respond to the sergeant's observation.

"Aye," MacManus concluded, "if you say so, cap."

Chapter 9

05.59 Thursday 2 August 2063

Frustration burned inside Colonel Trudy Pearce. She'd never thought her military career might lead her to the situation where a vast clash of arms in Europe was in progress, yet she had been so 'successful' that she was almost completely removed from the battle. Determination surged to find some resolution to this dilemma, driven by needs she still fought to dominate.

Today marked three hundred and twenty-three days since she'd last enjoyed a vodka and tonic. As the time passed, the addiction did become easier—well, less-worse—to manage, but it never went away. If she closed her eyes and concentrated, she could feel the liquid slide down her throat, its warmth so utterly comforting, reassuring, calming; its flavour so mellow, delicate, enticing. She missed the lightness in her head and restfulness in her limbs. And she could always talk to Dan more easily.

And now, this incredible, ridiculous situation that kept her from fighting with her troops threatened to undo all her hard work. The memories of the lightheaded pleasure alcohol gave her strengthened, gaining clarity, instead of fading, which she knew they would if she remained away from combat.

She looked at the wall screen. Pinprick lights and basic geometric shapes shone on the topographical map of northern France. These denoted the locations of tens of battalions around which orbited hundreds of teams of varying strengths. Units dispatched from Crowhurst, part of Attack Group South, had reached their R-plus-one objectives the previous evening with fewer than a thousand casualties.

"Add in current movements," she ordered.

Numerous thin, coloured lines appeared, zipping across the map as though weaving a web. They stretched from southern England to northern France and denoted the progress of air and ground transports. Trudy marvelled at the level of organisation required to coordinate the movement of over two million troops and their equipment in two spearheads, and then ensure that support arrived in a timely manner and sufficient quantities, while wounded combatants and civilian victims were either evac'd or taken to local facilities. But, staring at the image, a new feeling began, driven by her depthless hatred of the enemy.

She instructed the super AI, "Add in current totals of all NATO and enemy ACA losses, combatant losses, and known civilian victims."

"Confirmed."

Half a dozen rows of numbers splayed out across the top of the screen in blocks in the foreground and background. Trudy took them in, nodding to herself, impressed but unsurprised.

"Display concentrations of enemy ACA destruction on the map."

Blobs of light differing in size resolved with digits next to them. Trudy studied the numbers and considered what the enemy had in fact launched into the battle. She reasoned that

NATO's attack had enjoyed the element of surprise, and the enemy had, at first glance, thrown what defences were available into the battle. But the total of a little under a quarter of a million Blackswans and Lapwings destroyed by NATO's seventy thousand Scythes struck her as more than favourable to NATO.

She said, "Speculate: could the enemy have defended its positions any more effectively with the resources it had to hand?"

The super AI answered, "Affirmative, although not to a degree that would have changed the outcome and prevented NATO from gaining all of its R-plus-one objectives."

Curiosity piqued inside Trudy. "Expand?"

"With more effective deployments, the enemy could have inflicted between ten and thirty-five percent greater casualties."

"Really? So why didn't it?"

"Extrapolations are based on detailed post-factum operational decisions and their potential alternatives in the time period in question."

Trudy smiled. "You mean to say 'based on hindsight'? Fair enough." Her gaze centred on the locations of units she thought of as her own: those deployed from Crowhurst barracks. Her original concern returned, tempered with another abrupt realisation. She had to act.

She said, "Squonk, I want to leave a message for Field Marshal Terry Tidbury."

"Your immediate superior is General Abrio," the super AI replied with a hint, Trudy thought, of tartness.

"Yes, thank you," she replied with heavy sarcasm. "Just let me leave a recorded message for him, okay?"

"Confirmed. Speak when ready."

"Good morning, field marshal," Trudy began, her thoughts crystallising as she spoke. "Firstly, please accept my congratulations on the operation's success on its first day. Secondly, my apologies for contacting you directly. However, on analysing the enemy's apparent retreat—"

A thumbnail appeared in the bottom-right corner of the screen. Terry Tidbury's face squinted out of it. "Colonel Pearce? Good morning. How are things at Crowhurst?"

"Oh, good morning, field marshal. I didn't expect you to be at your post quite so ea—"

"It's not early, colonel. How can I help you?"

Trudy overcame her surprise and replied, "Sir, I've been looking the results of R-plus-one and I'm concerned."

"Oh?"

"Yes. I can't help feeling yesterday went a little too well."

"I disagree. We took thousands of casualties. The numbers are at the lower end of what the computers forecast, but there were some very hot battles, colonel. Plus, there were more than a few of the enemy who preferred death in battle to surrender or retreat."

A shiver of brutal excitement ran through Trudy. Enemy warriors who preferred death over retreat were exactly the ones she sought. She maintained her professional, soldierly composure and replied, "I see. Nevertheless, in the first twenty-seven hours of Operation Repulse, the enemy has made no serious, coordinated counterattack."

Terry shook his head and replied, "That is quite probably due to us enjoying the element of surprise."

Trudy knew what she wanted, and it was not a debate over whether and how much surprise they'd had. She decided to get to the point: "Sir, I do believe that a counterattack is imminent. It has to be. I worry that our forces are being lulled into a false sense of security—"

"And what do you propose we do about it?" Terry asked.

Trudy caught the faintest sardonic tone in his question. She answered with her most diplomatic voice, "Sir, there is little any of us as individuals can do. But I would like to request permission to move my headquarters across the Channel. Given my, shall we say, notoriety among the ranks, this might help... buttress? morale. When the inevitable counterattack does arrive, it could help in some small way to show how confident we are in the success of the operation that a senior commander is already in the field."

She held her breath as Terry considered her request.

He nodded, "Very well. Permission granted."

"Thank you, field marshal."

"And Colonel Pearce?"

"Yes, sir?"

"Keep a close eye on discipline. We are supposed to be more civilised than the enemy."

"Of course, sir," Trudy replied, holding her professional half-smile until the field marshal's face vanished. When it did, her expression changed to a grimace—as if he could understand the motivations of those who had actually lost loved ones in this war. Oh yes, she thought, discipline would be the very last thing she would keep a close eye on. Now she had only two objectives: to find the remains of her beloved Dan—missing in northern France since 5 June the previous year—and killing as many of the enemy as she could to extract the highest possible price for them murdering her family and taking Dan from her.

Her grimace transformed into a confident smile. She ran her fingers through her blonde hair, just the way Dan used to do, and said, "Squonk? Arrange the transport of a mobile command vehicle for me. One of the larger models. Get me as close to the front as regs allow."

"Confirmed."

"Also, assign Master Sergeant LaRue and Sergeant Lyon. And my adjutant, obviously."

She waited, watching the screen and analysing the map. Somewhere in there, Dan's mobile command vehicle had been overrun during the Battle for Europe. She would start at the last known loca—"

"Information," Squonk said, breaking into her thoughts. "A Boeing 828 autonomous air transport has been assigned to convey you, your personnel and equipment to the Netherlands. When do you wish to leave?"

"As soon as possible," she replied with suppressed irony.

"Confirmed. Your AAT will arrive at hangar W4 in approximately nineteen minutes and eleven seconds. You should collect your personal equipment and be ready to embark in due time."

"You can count on that," she muttered. Then she said, "Marta?"

After a moment's pause, a somnolent, "Yes, ma'am?" came to her ears.

"Are you awake?"

"Am now, ma'am," her adjutant, Marta Woodward, answered.

"Good. Pack your things. We're going to Europe."

Chapter 10

18.55 Thursday 2 August 2063

Senior Tech Janis Bagget dabbed the tears from her eyes. Now, she'd have to repair her makeup before she could go to the next meeting, in five minutes. But she needed a moment to contain the overwhelming guilt that, when the bad moments came, suffused every limb in her body. Her room in dormitory block B at NASA's Jet Propulsion Laboratory had become both a sanctuary and a prison since she'd found out the truth about her sister in New York.

She asked the empty bed, "Do the others know? Would they even care if they did? And why does knowing the truth never get any easier, no matter how much time passes?"

NASA's super AI, known as 'Muffy' in honour of Neil Armstrong's ill-fated daughter, spoke in a light, female voice, "Would you like to expand your thoughts on this to receive a speculative answer?"

"No," Janis mumbled. She passed into the cramped bathroom to retouch her eyeliner. The depth of her guilt had its roots in her 'charmed' youth. At first, her teachers thought she might've been a math prodigy. But it transpired she was only a genius. Still, she was easily smart enough to get into Stanford. Money, however, was the problem. She had no father and her mother had mental health problems that included drug addiction. She had one sibling, a sister called Janet. Their similar names were only one manifestation of their mother's problems, or more likely her deranged sense of humour.

Janet, five years older than Janis, went to work in New York while Janis was still at high school, amid the uncertain future of who could support her kid sister's genius. She always claimed she had a successful career in advertising, even running her own agency. Janet paid for her kid sister to go to Stanford, join NASA, and enjoy the career she now had. Janet always said that her kid sister should also do well. Janet told Janis that there'd come a time when the older sister would need the younger's help; there would come a time for payback.

Janis clicked the tube of eyeliner open and leaned close to the mirror. She stroked the small, black pencil along the bottom of her right eye.

The only problem was that Janet's life had been a lie. Janet had earned plenty of money, enough to pay for Janis to go through university and get the kind of results that NASA would not ignore. However, Janet's career had not been in advertising. Janet had been a high-class hooker.

Janis drew the eyeliner across the bottom of her left eye. In a higher part of her vision came the indication that she needed to leave and make her way to the meeting room in the admin section of the building, a two-minute elevator-ride-and-walk away.

But the most awful part was that Janet had to die for Janis to find out the truth. On 13 October the previous year, those mad bastards in the Arab or Persian desert or wherever they were, had attacked the United States. Openly. Brazenly. They'd blown up some island in the Atlantic to cause a massive wave, and then sent their bombs to destroy the damns—those miracles of American ingenuity—that kept the rising Atlantic away from the east coast.

Janet's apartment had been on the fourth floor of an apartment block in Newark, but it hadn't been high enough, and the second surge of water, a massive tidal wave hundreds of feet high, smashed into her block and killed her. It was only then, when Janis had been informed of her sister's sudden death, that the subsequent access to her business affairs revealed the hidden truth: Janet had become a high-class hooker to earn the money so her kid sister could fulfil the potential that Janis's teachers had found in her.

Janis clipped the eyeliner back in its little tube and put it back on the narrow glass shelf below the mirror.

The power of the memories threatened to make her cry again. She stopped, concentrated, and swallowed back the wave of regret that Janet had never spoken to her about her true 'career'; that she could never have trusted her kid sister enough to tell her the truth, even after their mother died all those years ago.

"And now, you've left me, Janet. I'm on my own," she said to her reflection. "And how the Goddamn am I ever supposed to pay you back now, huh?" She heaved in a truncated sob and sniffed. She grabbed the rouge brush and gave her cheekbones a couple of swift swipes.

She left her room in the dormitory block and hurried to catch the elevator. The doors opened and the faces of the two admin people already in it lit up in awe when they recognised her. They said, "Ma'am," in a breathless unison with which Janis had become familiar some time ago. She wanted to tell them that she hadn't done anything out of the ordinary, but the successes churned out by Reyer's team carried a wave of adulation ahead of the members that she neither understood, appreciated, nor cared for.

The doors opened at her floor. She threw her co-workers a tight smile and got off. Outside the row of windows on her left, the California forests fought to survive in an increasingly hostile environment. Years ago, scientists had tried to genetically engineer and nurture trees that needed less water, but there were too many glitches for the program to succeed. Janis noted the handful of green pines on the hillside, congruous among the scattered brown and yellow branches of others that were all-but-dead.

The clicking of heels drew her attention to the entrance to the conference room. "Hi, Janis," said Emily Hays, a fellow senior tech.

"Hi."

Emily's narrow face motioned towards the door to the conference room. "This promises to be one hell of a JTDC meeting."

Janis liked her colleague's English accent, but lately she'd been trying too hard to use Americanisms. Janis replied, "Sure, I can't wait to find out, either. Is Louis feeling any better?"

"I don't think he'll miss this no matter how he's feeling. Come on."

Janis followed her teammate into the modest, semi-circular auditorium. The tiered rows fell away steeply to a small stage. She nodded to the other members of the Joint Tech Development Committee. Many of the faces wore smiles in anticipation of the news they were about to receive.

None of their enthusiasm reached Janis.

She sat one row further down from Emily and poured a glass of water from the carafe in front of her. Their leader, Louis Reyer, sat in the row closest to the stage. On the surface in front of her sat a pair of glasses. She put them on and the scene around her transformed. Holographic representations of some of the many hundreds of people around the world who helped the JTDC resolved in the rows below her. As she glanced at an individual, their name, specialisation and other details appeared in the air next to them.

In the centre of the small stage, the image of a man in military fatigues materialised: small, with a typical crewcut on his flat head and his chest puffed out. The information in the air next to him told Janis that he was Colonel Long, CinC of the US Army's Logistics Corps. Janis narrowed her eye and twitched a muscle. The word 'CinC' expanded to become 'Commander in Chief'. With that curiosity settled, she let out a satisfied sigh.

Long's chest deflated a little and he stepped forward. "Ladies and gentlemen of the Joint Tech Development Committee, time is short so I will be brief. In the first thirty-six hours of Operation Repulse, NATO's new armaments have performed in the upper range of super-AI forecasts."

Janis nodded in satisfaction. Suddenly, the sleepless nights and the stress and the rows and the compromises had all been worth it.

Long stuck out his arm and a three-dimensional digital image of northwestern Europe resolved behind him. He said, "The more northerly of the two NATO spearheads, Attack Group East, had, as of zero-eight-hundred hours CET today, reached all of its objectives with near-as-damnit thirty percent fewer casualties than the median forecast."

Reams of data splayed down over the map above Belgium and the Netherlands.

Long dragged his hand over his crewcut and went on, "Okay, ah, this is the summary performance for the first twenty-four hours of the operation. On this front, we deployed around twenty thousand X–7s and five thousand X–9s. The full-depth data of every aspect of their flight performance is being transferred to your super AI now."

The image shifted to the south. Belgium and the Netherlands moved upwards and northern France became the dominant landmass, with Paris to the right.

"This front was a little bit broader and more spread out. While Attack Group East advanced into more built-up areas, where the Scythes could utilise support elements like tanks, Attack Group South was—and for sure still is—faced with more open countryside surrounding generally smaller urban centres. As a result, here we deployed around thirty-eight thousand X–7s and seven thousand X–9s."

Again, data resolved over the image and Long repeated, "Uh, the full-depth data of every aspect of their flight performance is also being transferred to your super AI now."

Janis twitched her eye, her senses tingling at the prospect of analysing the complete flight performance data of the Muon-Catalyst Power Unit, or MCPU, version 8C. She recalled the meeting when she herself had introduced it to NATO leaders and politicians. Finally, almost a year later, she would be able to see how that theory had actually performed in real-life battle conditions. Janis appreciated that the militaries had made the effort to present this information in person, as it were, rather than just sending a notification.

Long continued, "Although there are many variables, so we can't assign a real figure, I do wanna highlight the fact that the Scythes are outperforming the enemy's ACAs by such a hell of a margin it must translate into a lot of saved NATO lives. And before I handover to the next speaker, this is what I'd like to stress to you folks. All reports we're getting back from the front lines are full of praise for these machines. And a lot of that is down to you and your hard work."

Janis sensed a ripple of pride roll through the room.

"Now," Long said in a tone of conclusion, "I wanna hand you over to Supreme Allied Commander, Europe. Here to talk to you, ladies and gentlemen, is Field Marshal Sir Terry Tidbury."

Janis's mouth fell open in shock. From somewhere behind her came the strangled exclamation, "No freakin' way!", which vocalised her own reaction.

Colonel Long and his map of northern-western Europe vanished. In his place the image of a small, bald man sitting at a desk appeared. His eyes shone bright and piercing, but otherwise Janis reflected just how ordinary the great leader looked. In any crowded place, surely no one would give him a second glance.

The field marshal sat upright and said, "Members of the Joint Tech Development Committee, thank you for allowing me to address you directly."

"That's real smooth," Janis muttered under her breath.

"Firstly, I echo Colonel Long's words and would also like to convey my sincerest thanks—along with the gratitude of thousands of NATO troops from every country in Europe and beyond—to each of you for your role in creating the powerpack that gives the Scythe ACAs their incredible speed and dexterity."

"Whoosh," Janis whispered, vocalising the feeling the field marshal's words caused in her and, she suspected, everyone else in the JTDC.

"However," the soldier went on, "now is not the time to rest. The enemy will—he must—deploy new weapons long before we can declare Operation Repulse to be a success. Thanks in large part to your efforts, we have today regained a foothold on the European mainland. But there remains the very material risk of a counterattack; one that could, conceivably, yet lead to our defeat. The one certainty we can rely on today is that the enemy will counterattack with superior weapons.

"With that in mind, I would like to ask you all to continue your research. The enemy now knows what we are attacking him with. The element of surprise that worked so well in our favour has now expired. Even as I speak, his computers and his military experts are developing countermeasures to stop us taking back that which is rightfully ours. In the immediate future, we can expect that these will be minor developments to his existing munitions. However, we can also be sure he is already designing an ACA that will be able to defeat the X–7 and the X–9. And that is why I am asking you to consider and anticipate the enemy's next step, and design something superior to counteract that."

The field marshal paused, presumably, Janis thought, to let the gravity of the situation sink in. Janis wanted to tell him that he needn't have worried.

"I do understand," the soldier went on, "the effort and personal sacrifices you are all making. I assure you that these are appreciated immeasurably here in Europe. Thank you all and good luck." The field marshal vanished.

Janis glanced left and right to see a few heads shake in a disbelief she herself shared. From close to the stage, Louis Reyer stood up with care. He hobbled up the step onto the small stage using a metal cane. Janis hadn't seen him need a walking aid before and her concern increased: not yet thirty years old, their leader still should have much more life in front of him. At least he was safely outside Europe and here in California, where there was no question of him getting the very best medical care.

Reyer turned to face the auditorium. In heavily accented English, the Frenchman said, "So, my friends, all vacation leave is cancelled until further notice."

A ripple of laughter floated over the rows of seats.

Reyer's smile faded and a more familiar dour countenance returned. This was the Reyer that Janis recognised and respected. He said, "I rather prefer not to think we are simply back at square one. That is not really the case. But the field marshal, who was kind enough to accept my invitation to speak to us today, makes a most valid point. Until NATO wins, we cannot stop. We must now design and develop the next-gen ACAs for our comrades in the armies. For today, I think we will enjoy looking at the data—and there is much of it, I should add—from the performance of the 8C power unit. At tomorrow's meeting, we will set out a framework to proceed. No questions today, please. Thank you all for attending."

Janis watched Reyer shuffle from the stage. Emily leapt up from her seat to help him. Around her, remote attendees vanished. She removed her glasses to see that only a handful of the team had attended in person. She sipped some water and considered what she'd heard, idly watching Emily and Reyer leave the auditorium. She muttered, "If he's that bad, why'd he even bother turning up?"

She stood and left the auditorium. Janis Bagget derived satisfaction that her work as part of the JTDC had helped to save the lives of so many NATO troops. But, as she returned to her small room in the dorm several floors above, she regretted again that she could do nothing to save the one life she'd cared about so much.

Chapter 11

07.12 Friday 3 August 2063

Officer Mark Phillips, 3rd Airspace Defence, reclined in his usual monitoring pod and put the headset on. He waited while Squonk confirmed his identity and assigned him a sector of the front to monitor.

A familiar voice called in his ears, "Babyface Phillips? Do you know what day it is today?"

His view came alive with a three-dimensional topographical image of a section of NATO's forward units in the French countryside. He replied, "Good morning, Captain Shithead. To what do I owe this displeasure? Have you already run out of kittens to drown this morning?"

"STFU, you little idiot."

"I'll shut the fuck up just as soon as you do, Captain Shithead."

Since passing out and graduating to full Air Defence Officer, Mark had decided to fight fire with fire where Captain Joe Neely-also-known-as-Shithead was concerned. Oddly, however, Captain Shithead hadn't seemed to mind Mark's abuse, responding in kind and not otherwise caring. Mark spoke to his friend, Simon, who told Mark that sometimes it was better to just accept that other people must be okay with a certain situation, and not to question it or them too much.

Captain Shithead continued, "Listen, my feeble little helper. Today is R-plus-three. Can you remember what the objectives are for today?"

Mark shivered. Of course, he remembered. He'd had a sleepless night remembering, staggered at the contrast between this life and his old life of gaming in the Universes. That life had been a child's life. Now, his observations and reactions could mean the difference between life and death for real, living soldiers and civilians, not silly digital creations in a stupid game.

He replied with as much sarcastic nonchalance as he could muster after only two coffees, "Yeah, sure. The cleaning staff are going to have a collection to raise money to buy you a second brain cell. No, wait, my mistake. That's R-plus-four. Today the objective is for the lead elements to reach and enter Paris."

Shithead replied, "Okay, Babyface, before your wit begins to exceed the inherent genius of amoeba, just remember to keep your useless, blind eyes on any innovations the enemy might deploy. This is your reminder, Babyface: Squonk says today—R-plus-three—is the most likely day our brain-dead ragheads might actually come back at us with something innovative. Got that?"

"Goodness me, sir," Mark answered in feigned astonishment, "do you really think they really might do that?"

"Fuck off, Babyface."

Mark smiled when Captain Shithead ended the connection. His attention returned to the data in front of him. He considered that the geometry involved in coordinating NATO's combined forces as they advanced should qualify as some kind of work of art. With a wave of his hand or blink of his eye, he could travel from low-Earth orbit, observing NATO satellites guarded from thousands of metres below by the new SkyMasters, a piece of engineering that Mark had come to admire in the three days they had been in operation above the battlefield.

Beneath them, at altitudes ranging from ten thousand metres all the way almost down to ground level, flew the two variants of Scythe ACA, describing patterns in the sky that minimised any potential enemy attack while providing maximum cover for the ground troops. And even then, on the ground NATO troops enjoyed the protection of autonomous tanks—always ready to advance and clear any building or trench or obstruction the Scythes could not guarantee were free of enemy combatants.

And after those defences, NATO troops carried with them the famous Falarete, in all of its variations. Their Boeing and Airbus air transports had built-in Falaretes for defence; the ground transports also carried them. In addition, all brigades and other formations carried specialised Falarete fire teams, always close to or in the battlespace to defend against any stray Spider or Lapwing that might somehow manage to sneak through the impenetrable defences ranged against it. Finally, each unit and troop detailed at least one soldier who slung a portable Falarete tube over his or her shoulder to be ready to defend them in the worst-case scenario.

Mark conceded that despite all of this, soldiers still died. Gaps opened during the advance that required split-second decisions—even the super AI could not anticipate every potential vagary of chance. The super AI might need human approval of tactics the time required for which might often involve deciding which poor squaddies lived or died.

Nevertheless, a deep sense of satisfaction swelled inside Mark Phillips. Finally, he belonged. At last, his life made sense as his unique abilities found what Simon half-jokingly called 'gainful employment'. From here, Mark acted as the very human intersection with the cold, calculating skills of super artificial intelligence. For no matter how much human-generated data super AI processed, quantum computing could still not compensate for the very human instinct to survive. After so many months at 3rd Airspace Defence, Mark understood that the vastest machine intelligence could only mimic the uniqueness of humanity, never imitate it to any notable degree.

He watched and analysed as the contacts between NATO and enemy ACAs increased. Scythes probed enemy defences to make way for ground forces to advance on the outskirts of Paris. The enemy's Blackswans and Lapwings, now comprehensively outgunned and outmanoeuvred, did what any self-respecting artificial intelligence would do, and created a measured, cautious retreat to allow enough time for their human elements—Caliphate warriors—to pull back.

Squonk broke into his thoughts, "Information: SkyMaster Delta–7 is tracking increased enemy ACA activity at the indicated reference—"

Mark waved his hand and sent his view zooming into an area of France fifty kilometres to the west of Paris. Little spots of light shone as enemy ACAs emerged from the fog of jamming the enemy still deployed further behind the lines. Mark considered that the enemy would hardly announce its counterattack if it didn't have to.

"Caution: the enemy is deploying more ACAs than at any time since the commencement of Operation Repulse."

"Shit, shit, shit," Mark muttered as his view came alive with tens of new data streams. One stream notified him that multiple waves of Blackswans and Lapwings were emerging from jamming from the direction of Spain. He concentrated on his sector of the front, which centred on a town called

Conches-on-Ouche. He instructed, "Open comms now to all senior commanders."

"Confirmed."

"This is Airspace Defence. You have multiple enemy ACAs inbound. Scythes need to be reassigned from your sector but the gap will be filled by ground assets." Mark exhaled gently lest any physical movement somehow cause a ripple to the situation on the map in front of him. He withdrew his view to see thirty wings of X–7s and two of X–9s roll, peel out and surge in two directions: half to the northwest to support the defence of Attack Group East, and the other half to the southwest to help meet the emerging threat from the enemy machines flying up from Spain.

"Squonk, anticipate other, unexpected threats," Mark instructed, the gamer in him already convinced that the enemy had to have something else up its sleeve; that simply throwing several thousand more Blackswans and Lapwings at the new Scythes could not reverse NATO's advances.

"There are several hundred potential ways in which—"

"Most probable—now?"

"The battlespace is too dynamic to sust—"

"Jesus Christ," Mark hissed. "You're supposed to be super artificial intelligence and right now I wouldn't use you to organise a fucking party—"

"Information: autonomous main battle tanks advancing at sector six-three-tango are reporting ineffective Falarete contacts."

Mark's eyes widened in shock. "What?" he nearly shrieked. "That can't be right. Explain."

Squonk's voice didn't waver as it reported, "Tanks are under attack from enemy Spiders. Falaretes are engaging their targets without success." There came a brief pause, then, "Fifteen tanks have been destroyed. The remainder in sector six-three-tango are now retreating."

"No," Mark said, a deep sense of shock following on from his realisation. He stabbed an icon in his view to open an emergency comms link. "Attention, all commanders in sector six-three-tango. Falaretes can no longer neutralise enemy Spiders. Your super AI should react accordingly."

He puffed air in his cheeks, knowing that he'd done what he could, but also hearing the doubt in his voice on the word 'should'. The lack of humanity in super artificial intelligence systems was well known—Mark and everyone at Air Defence specifically dealt with this aspect in military situations. But, for the first time in his life, the practical implications of this chilled Mark in a way he'd never known before. The enemy had developed a countermeasure and, as demanded by military logic, had combined its novelty with a powerful counter-assault.

Mark Phillips realised that many NATO soldiers down below on those battlefields were about to die. He zoomed his view, driven by morbid curiosity, to see which formations would bear the brunt of the enemy's first serious counterattack. As the sectors affected, all to the west of the town of Conches-on-Ouche, rose up in his view, he noted their designations: the French 2nd Dragoons, commanded by General Abrio; US Marine Corps., 2nd Battalion, 12th Marine Expeditionary Unit; Royal Observer Corps—

"Oh, no," Mark muttered, when he realised that his older brother, Martin, was in the battalion that lay in the path of the counterattack. He paused, watching as pinprick flashes noted engagements between the combatants. "This is bullshit," he said aloud. He considered trying to contact Martin directly to warn him, but realised that not only might such an effort distract his brother at a critical moment, but also his brother's Squitch would do a better job of keeping Martin alive than a garbled warning from him.

Nevertheless, that didn't mean he just had to sit by and watch. "Squonk? Why have the Falaretes stopped destroying the Spiders?"

"The are four options avail—"

"Most probable?"

"The ability of the Falarete to overcome the Spider's shielding has been compromised."

"How?"

"Shielding frequency variation."

"Shit. How long before we can develop and deploy a countermeasure to restore Falarete effectiveness?"

"Approximately one hour and fifty-five minutes."

"Shit," Mark repeated. He stared at the digital representation of the battlespace. He said, "Hold on, brother. You've managed for over a year. Just get through the next two hours."

Chapter 12

07.18 Friday 3 August 2063

As she ran, Captain Sabine Oberst of the French 2nd Dragoon Regiment barely noticed the sweat prickling her cropped hair and itching her scalp. She avoided a horse track and, to save time, leaped through the dry vegetation on the forest floor towards the nearest mobile command post, her limbs light and her breathing urgent in the rush of an emergency.

"Where are my Scythes?" she hissed.

"Ma'am," her sergeant's voice replied in her ear, "it looks like a counterattack and the computer has had to redirect our supporting ACAs."

"So stop all advances."

The reply came to her ears laced with Gallic indifference, "Of course, the computer has already done this."

"Good," she said. "Now order all forward units to start withdrawing. Without air superiority, we dare not—"

A new voice overrode her present link. "Where are you?" demanded Major Boyer, her superior officer.

"On my way back to the command po—"

"But my display shows you in the forest to the south."

"Yes, sir."

"For the sake of the Lord, why?"

Sabine slowed enough to catch her breath. "I prefer to ensure that my mobile Falarete teams are in position and ready."

"Whatever for?" Boyer demanded. "Those teams have been trained quite thoroughly."

"Sir, I believe motivating one's own troops—"

"Get back to your mobile command vehicle."

"Yes, sir," she said, containing the bitterness at Boyer's indifference. The soldiers under her command needed the best support she could offer. She reached the edge of the trees and emerged into a large, flat field. In the distance, the brown roofs of the town shimmered under the growing heat of the day.

Her mobile command vehicle sat waiting for her a hundred or so metres to the north, on the track. She twitched her eye and turned left and right to confirm deployments. At the far southern edge of the field, the three-soldier Falarete team she'd been visiting in person now also jogged back towards the mobile command vehicle, Falarete tubes jolting up and down as they went, to prepare for a potential withdrawal. She listened to her troops' background chatter, satisfied that their morale remained good.

Her Squitch said, "Information: the two squadrons of Challenger and Leopard tanks have engaged the approaching enemy ACAs."

She resettled the strap of her Pickup on her shoulder and resumed running. While her body followed the treeline, her mind tried to process all of the data in her lens. The enemy's counterattack did not concern her as greatly as she thought it might. She and her troops—along with just about all of the NATO armies—had spent months training in

England, and with good military discipline had practised defensive drills in anticipation of a range of countermeasures the enemy might take once Operation Repulse kicked off. None of them, from the lowest squaddie to the generals, expected the enemy to roll over and allow NATO to reclaim Europe without—

Her thoughts were broken by the repeated crumps of explosions nearby. Sabine staggered as the ground under her boots fell away and then came back hard, as though trying to knock her off her feet. She looked to the east in fear and saw giant, ice-cream scoops of dirty black earth thrown into the sky. Her senses screamed that something, somewhere must have gone wrong.

Her Squitch reported, "Both tank squadrons have been destroyed. You should reach your mobile command vehicle and withdraw."

"What?" she exclaimed. "How?"

"Danger: enemy Spiders approaching from the east. You are among their targets. Distance eight hundred metres, closing in a straight line. Take defensive action immediately."

Sabine stopped running, unslung her Pickup and crouched on one knee without conscious thought. A moment later, the reassuring hisses of Falaretes launching came to her ears. The view in her lens lit up with warnings of multiple Spiders approaching. From her right, the Falaretes sped in like deadly flies to meet them. She waited for the resulting explosions—but nothing happened. The Falaretes vanished. The Spiders' eight articulated appendages snapped out from their bodies and they hit the ground at the far end of the field.

"Aim where indicated and fire now," her Squitch said.

She fired short bursts, not understanding how the Spiders could still be advancing. Her shells made the target Spider's shielding flash green. It continued racing towards her. The magazine emptied and she ejected and replaced it with another from her smock. Months of training simulations of just such an attack allowed her to fire long enough and accurately enough that the Spider detonated more than a hundred metres away. She grimaced when dust and dirt thrown up by the explosion returned to earth.

Her Squitch repeated the instruction, "Aim and fire where indicated now."

She turned her head in time to see the nearest mobile Falarete team—with whom she'd been chatting less than five minutes earlier—facing three Spiders hurtling at them with a terrifying click-clack sound. As she looked, the leading machine exploded under a hail of shells. She raised her Pickup, fired the few remaining shots in the magazine and replaced it. By then, the other Spiders had gained on the mobile fire team. There came another flash when the second Spider detonated under withering fire. But the force of this explosion pushed the three defending soldiers onto their backs.

Sabine kept firing until the last Spider reached the team and exploded in a deadening thump that made her hate the enemy a fraction more than she already did. Broken and twisted bodies fell back to earth with the dust and dirt.

"What about the other fire teams?"

"All squads to the south of your current position have been destroyed."

She turned back to seek out the mobile command vehicle but the track was empty. She twitched an eye muscle to bring up the relevant map showing its location. "How long before I get there if I run?"

"Four minutes. However, the battlespace is too dynamic to guarantee that the mobile command vehicle will remain in that location for that length of time."

She turned, shouldered her Pickup, and resumed running, adrenalin once more lending fleetness to her strides. As she went on, the sounds of other NATO troops also running for their lives came to her. She looked to her left to see three figures sprinting through the forest, heads lowered, arms powering up and down, without Pickups or other kit. She stole glances while making sure the track ahead was clear.

She accelerated, analysing the local tactical situation in her lens. The tanks that should have supported the Scythes in clearing the way into the town had been destroyed. She damned whatever the enemy was doing elsewhere to deny her and her troops aircover. Without the Scythes and without the tanks, all of them were hopelessly exposed.

She expanded the view in her lens to a wider level and realised that more drama was taking place further along the axis of NATO's advance. A sudden surge of relief that she was not personally the main target of the enemy's counterattack lent some additional strength to her tiring legs. She slowed her pace as she approached her mobile command vehicle.

She converged with the three other troops, her display telling her they belonged to the British Army, Royal Observer Corps.

The tallest man in the lead slowed to a fast walk and said through heaving breaths, "Nice to meet you, Captain Oberst."

Sabine read the text in the air next to his affable smile and replied, "Likewise, Captain Martin Phillips." She nodded ahead and added, "The vehicle is just on the track there. You need a ride, yes?"

"Thank you, yes," the Englishman replied.

Sabine had never found anything particularly attractive about the English. The way some of them still clung to an arrogance of entitlement annoyed her as it did most mainland Europeans. But this one had a warm smile even in this most demanding of situations. She decided that, if they survived the engagement, she would endeavour to get to know him better.

Phillips asked, "We passed through your defensive line back there when our ATT was damaged. Did any of your mobile teams get away?"

Sabine shook her head.

"Sorry," the Englishman offered.

Sabine nodded to his two comrades and asked, "And are the three of you all who are left in your team?"

Philips nodded.

"Such is this war, captain. Come on." She resumed a fast jog towards the vehicle.

Her Squitch advised, "Increase your pace. Further wings of Blackswans are approaching and are likely to target your location."

"*Merde*," Sabine cursed, accelerating. The three soldiers of the Royal Observer Corps followed her. She hissed, "Tanks?"

Her Squitch replied, "Six squadrons are moving into position to increase the time available for human assets to withdraw."

She led the others to the mobile command vehicle. The flat metal door of the MCV slid back to admit them. Sabine leapt up the step and entered the relative darkness.

Sergeant Roche said, "We need to move, now. The computer wanted to retreat sooner but I threatened to smash it to bits if we did not wait a little longer for you."

"Thanks, Roche," Sabine replied with a smile.

The three Englishmen entered and the door slid closed behind them.

"Strap in those seats," Sabine told them, indicating side-mounted, pulldown seats at the front of the vehicle. The men did so and it began to reverse westwards.

Sabine grabbed a seat at the rear and pulled it down. She stowed her Pickup in a bracket and strapped herself in. The instant she was secure, the vehicle accelerated.

Discomforting bumps knocked her spine and thighs when the vehicle turned off the track and entered the forest. Sudden immobility after the exhilaration of running and fighting real Spiders—instead of those dummies they'd trained on—engendered a creeping foreboding. Despite all that training, the real Spider's speed and dexterity had terrified her, and its explosive yield had dismayed her.

Sabine gripped the restraining straps on her shoulders and watched the screens above her. With a twitch of her eye, she linked her lens to the same data streams. "We are not going to make it," she said to herself.

Her Squitch replied, "All possible measures are being taken to protect human asse—"

"Shut up," she replied tersely. "Those tanks have less than one minute before they are destroyed. What is wrong with the Falaretes? Why do they not work?"

Any reply her Squitch might have made was lost in an abrupt, violent sequence of manoeuvres. The forest through which the super AI drove the mobile command vehicle dipped and then fell away in a steep incline. As Sabine tensed all of her muscles to limit the impacts of these juddering shocks, she realised how dependent on the Falarete NATO forces had become.

One feed in her lens described a digital representation of the squadrons of autonomous tanks as they fired their Falaretes and then resorted to their secondary armament: either missile batteries or Pulsar lasers. As it must have been the previous year during the enemy's relentless advance across Europe, the Blackswans kept coming on, releasing Spiders to drive NATO forces backwards.

With a growing dread inside her, Sabine watched the tanks go offline, either brewing up when a single Spider somehow got between the giant wheels, or being blown to pieces when swamped by multiple Spiders simultaneously.

A brief flash of hope flared when a new icon shimmered into life to announce that previously diverted Scythes had turned around and where racing back to provide aircover. But the numbers didn't add up: the Blackswans carrying their deadly cargoes were closing too quickly and would arrive seconds before the Scythes.

The mobile command vehicle slowed and levelled. The map in Sabine's lens showed a low gorge a few hundred metres away that would provide cover, until she recalled that there could be no cover against Spiders. From the opposite direction, the digital representation of an approaching Blackswan broke into fifty new lines as it released its Spiders. They spread out on their own trajectories, with a single Spider heading for her mobile command vehicle far faster than the super AI could reverse them away.

Captain Sabine Oberst scratched a final time at the sweat irritating her scalp. She peered towards the front of the vehicle to see the handsome Englishman and his comrades swapping nervous glances. So, she would not, after all, have the chance to get to know him better. In her display, the Spider that had targeted them rushed in with annoying rapidity. If it were just a little slower, then perhaps a Scythe might—

The breath left her body when the front of the vehicle lifted upwards and split open. She thought she heard howls of pain and shock, and then she lost consciousness.

Chapter 13

07.21 Friday 3 August 2063

Pip Clarke heard the panic in her young sergeant's words. He cried, "Cap, the Falaretes are nay working anymore. What's going on?"

She fixed him with a look she hoped would keep the whine from his voice. "Take it easy, Mac. We've trained for this. It's no big deal—"

"Maybe not for you—"

"And neither for you, sergeant," she snapped in irritation. "Just make sure you've got a full mag—"

"But we've lost aircover," Mac said. "The Scythes have—"

"Get a grip. We have to support each other if we're going to get out of this, right? So, remember your training, Sergeant MacManus."

The young man blinked, swallowed and croaked, "Yes, ma'am."

She turned away from him and placed her Pickup carefully in the sand. She and her squad had been advancing on the town of Tilburg. They'd had the Scythes and tanks clearing the way ahead, their advance delayed by enemy elements who hadn't retreated. Then, pandemonium had erupted. She and her team were now trapped on a golf course to the west of the town.

With care, she raised herself up to see over the lip of the bunker. A road bisected the golf course, along which the super AI had proposed sending an autonomous troop transport to collect them and take them to the rear. She spoke to Mac over her shoulder, "Listen, if you get a Spider coming straight at you, you just need to hold your nerve, right?"

"Aye."

"You'll get the time to fire two mags, and that should be enough if it's been hit with almost anything else beforehand." She felt some empathy for the sergeant, as she had far more battle experience than he did.

Her Squitch said, "Information: ACAs have been reassigned to your sector and six squadrons of tanks will be within range to provide defensive fire in ninety seconds."

"Where's the ATT?" she asked.

"Approaching your position."

She turned her head and saw the troop transport racing along the flat road. She muttered, "The taxi's arrived, team."

Across the expanse of the dull yellow grass, military figures darted between sandy bunkers, doubled over. The first to leap into her bunker was the redoubtable Barny Hines.

"Did ye find anything?" Mac asked him.

"Nah," Barny replied, a look of disgust on his face, "only bloody lost golf balls everywhere."

"Aye, there's a mystery."

Pip's Squitch said, "Advance towards the road."

"Come on," Pip said to the others. Further away, the other team members ran to catch up. She left the bunker and sprinted over the dry, brittle fairway. She reached a small copse of mature oaks, most of which were dead.

Her Squitch announced, "Danger: an enemy ACA has targeted this sector."

"Check your mags, guy," Pip told the others. She shivered, knowing from experience that the situation could deteriorate with little further warning. She pushed herself into the light brown, shredded dead bark. Behind her, the autonomous troop transport rolled to a stop. She looked at it and asked, "Is anyone on that th—?"

"Yes, ma'am," came an urgent voice in her ear. "Corporal Grayson. I've got a few injured here."

"Shit," Pip swore under her breath. If even a single Spider came out of the sky now—

There came a truncated gasp in her ears. Out on the road, the ATT reversed in a straight line.

At the same time, her Squitch said, "A Lapwing has targeted your location. Aim and fire where indicated."

"You must be fucking kidding me," Mac said, raising his Pickup and aiming into the sky, despite the fact that they were surround by mature trees.

Pip's spirit sank: she knew Spiders; there was a chance against a Spider. But she'd never heard of anyone surviving against a Lapwing.

The air above her hissed as the Lapwing swept out of the sky. It decelerated with a suddenness that Pip scarcely believed. She stepped forward in a mix of curiosity and trepidation to give herself a clear view of the road. The bulbous Lapwing hung about fifty metres above the trees, its fins offering a veneer of aerodynamic acceptability to an otherwise lumpen machine.

Shells from other troops firing from the ground pinged green off the ACA's shielding, making little difference beyond giving the Lapwing data on their precise location.

Trying to retreat almost directly underneath the Lapwing, the autonomous troop transport veered left and right in a vain attempt at evasion. Its wheels blew out. Steam and smoke shimmered and hissed from the vehicle's metal plates. Then, under repeated, invisible pulses from the Lapwing's laser, the sides wilted and buckled like molten plastic. The surfaces of the ATT bowed inwards before the vehicle burst into flames.

"Now the wee bastard will come for us," Mac said, unnecessarily.

Pip aimed and fired at the Lapwing, wondering how many shells from the Pickups would be required to defeat its shielding. Her magazine emptied, and as she had done so many times before, she dropped the empty, grabbed another from her smock, and snapped it into place. The Lapwing rose up from its handiwork on the ATT and accelerated into the sky. Pip hoped none of the troops would mistake the manoeuvre for any kind of withdrawal—this was simply the most expedient way for it to reorientate its line of attack to its next targets: them.

Her Squitch announced, "Blackswans have entered the battlespace and deployed Spiders. You should seek cover."

Pip glanced back at Mac to see no change in his expression, which suggested that only she had been informed of the fatal worsening of their odds. She swung her Pickup skywards again. The black dot representing the Lapwing was identified in her view. It completed its pirouette and began a sweeping descent on an axis that would ensure it could burn as many NATO troops as possible. Pip didn't want to burn. She had seen the victims.

Pip fired the last shot in her magazine—and the Lapwing exploded with a distant pop. It lost its grace in flight and twisted erratically before thudding into the ground on the other side of the burning ATT.

She heard Mac curse, "What the actual fu—?"

"We've got aircover back," Pip yelled. She spun around to the east, where, through the dead trees, half a dozen Spiders arrived on the golf course. Their appendages flicked gouts of sand and dirt into the air as they raced towards her and her team.

The lumpen form of Barny Hines led the charge out of the sand dunes with a yell of fury. MacManus and the other troops followed, but Pip knew the Spiders would be on them in seconds.

Her Squitch instructed, "Cease fire and take cover now."

"What?" Pip queried, confused at the advice.

Metallic hissing suddenly filled the air above her. In reflex, she crouched as a wing of Scythes came in from behind her. They raced overhead, from west to east, and the Spiders' shielding flashed green as the invisible laser pulses hit them. The Scythes rose high into the sky after making their pass. An instant later and from Pip's right, a second wing of Scythes streaked over the Spiders flying south to north. Pip looked on aghast as each Spider slumped or exploded, their appendages buckling and twisting from the heat.

Then, the air was still. The trees on the fairways burned, sending wafts of pale grey smoke up into the empty sky. Pip couldn't tear her eyes away from the Spiders, looking for any sign of danger, even though her senses told her that they had been destroyed.

She struggled for breath. She said, "Report."

Her Squitch replied, "The battlespace is now secure. A medivac unit is enroute to your location."

Her ears registered new sounds. She staggered, hardly able to walk, out onto the fairway. Mac, Hines and the others were jumping in the air, punching their fists in exaltation at having survived the contact. Pip turned away from them and stumbled back among the trees.

She knew what would happen next and told herself that her subordinates could not see her like this.

She fell to her hands and knees, her fingers gripping the dried, dead grass. Her body retched. Only some mucus dribbled from her cold, trembling lips. She waited. Finally, the retching ended and she gasped in air. She waited for some saliva to collect in her mouth and then spat out the acid.

Pip dragged herself to a sitting position at the base of a tree. She extracted her canteen and rinsed her mouth before drinking some water.

Mac appeared through the trees. "You okay, cap?"

She nodded. "Sure. Get everyone else ready for a return to billet."

Mac's gap-toothed smile showed as he replied, "Aye, cap," and left her.

She waited until she believed he was out of earshot and asked, "ETA on the medivac unit?"

"Approximately five minutes and thirty-seven seconds."

"Is the battlespace still secure?"

"Affirmative."

"Why me?"

"Please expand or specify your question."

"Why me? Why don't I die?"

"The answer requires examples using several mathematical specialist areas related to probabilities and will take at least fifteen minutes to deliver. In addition, it will require a level of concentration that you may find demanding given your current location and condition. Would you like to proceed?"

Pip shook her head. "No." Her breathing slowed and tiredness crept into her limbs once again as the adrenalin subsided. She told herself it didn't matter. Like Pratty on the shuttle, or Crimble in Spain, or those Spanish specials ops' guys, or all those less fortunate than her in so many engagements since the beginning of this awful war, this time she'd lived. Again. Somehow.

She decided she needed to talk to someone who would understand. Someone who really knew her. She said, "Contact Forward Observer Martin Phillips, Royal Observer Corps."

Her Squitch replied, "Forward Observer Martin Phillips was killed in action this morning."

Pip considered the super AI's words. "Say that again," she requested.

Her Squitch repeated the information.

And then she cried.

Chapter 14

14.02 Friday 3 August 2063

At most sitrep meetings with his generals, Terry hardly noticed their individualities. The NATO forces deployed for Operation Repulse included soldiers from the remains of the armies of every European country, as well as many Americans, Antipodeans and Canadians, as well as from each Home Country on the British Isles.

But at this meeting, every accent grated. For the first time, Terry noted the spoken errors the Europeans made using English as their second or third language. Something he had for years been able to dismiss as irrelevant—even faintly racist to acknowledge, let alone be offended by—now caused him a frustration that had no outlet.

The catalyst for Terry's vexation had been the commander of the Polish First Army, General Pakla. The Pole burned with a passion for vengeance that Terry thought bordered on an obsession that might affect the man's martial professionalism. On the other hand, without Pakla's support for Operation Repulse at the critical meeting almost a year earlier, they might not have achieved what they had in the last twelve months.

Now, Pakla's face stared out from the main screen in Terry's private office in the War Rooms, full of anger and passion but, this time, for the wrong reasons. The Polish general cried, "I lost over five hundred of my best troops to this 'innovation' today morning and you say that this is 'not so bad'? I think, field marshal, that you prefer to—how do you say it in English?—play this down."

Terry shook his head and replied, "Absolutely not, general. But I do believe it is important to acknowledge the incredible work done by the teams at Aldermaston. The first Falarete to fail to destroy an enemy Spider was logged at twenty-one minutes past seven this morning. Within an hour, those teams had established the cause: the enemy had begun modulating the frequency of the shielding around its Spiders, meaning that the Falaretes' nets simply bounced off the target.

"However, although random in selection, the modulations were limited to a comparatively narrow range. In less than an hour, the teams had developed a countermeasure, which could be piggybacked via the SkyMasters, that rebuilt part of the Falarete's systems so that, on contact, the netting would also remodulate and destroy the Spider. Now, that countermeasure was fully implemented to all deployed Falaretes in less than two hours. And that was a truly remarkable achievement." Terry sensed the atmosphere shift a little in his favour.

Another thumbnail rose up to cover part of the screen, displaying the oval, severe face of General Sir Patrick Fox. His head tilted as he said, "If you'll excuse me, field marshal, I do believe we should also accept that the issue with the Falaretes was compounded by increased deployments of the enemy's ACAs at the strategic level. However savage the enemy might be, he is unfortunately not stupid. Rather than simply introducing this innovation to the Spider to defeat the Falarete, he simultaneously instigated a vast pincer movement on two fronts in Europe, to force us to divert our Scythes. It is worth considering these latest casualties in this strategic light. This morning, the enemy made a concerted effort to not only stop Repulse dead in its tracks, but actually with the intention of reversing our armies altogether. In this respect, his efforts have been a complete failure."

"Thank you, general," Terry said. Fox's image shrunk back to a thumbnail along the lower edge of the screen. Terry said, "General Pakla, I hope you can see there is nothing to 'play down' here. Quite the opposite, in fact. On all fronts we have suffered just under five thousand casualties. The computers claim that our forces will still achieve all of their R-plus-three objectives less than four hours behind schedule."

Pakla's elegant Slavic face moved out over the screen, his Slavic features creased in apparent concentration. He said, "My point, field marshal, is not how quickly or well we handled the situation, but why we failed to anticipate it from the start. Operation Repulse holds much risk and danger for every single soldier, and as their commanders we are responsible to support them to the best of our abilities. The enemy might have failed today. But so did we."

In the row of thumbnails along the bottom of the screen, Terry saw a few heads nod in agreement with the Pole. Terry refocused his thoughts before speaking. Fatigue from the lack of rest over the last three days suffused each disc in his spine and bled out across his back. His breaths came hollow and light, as though an illness were just beginning.

He said, "As you no doubt saw in various updates over the last few months, the enemy might come up with several improvements or adjustments to his munitions and tactics. We give each of those developments a probability rating based on things like how much benefit the enemy would enjoy, both strategically and tactically; how long it would take to neutralise or develop countermeasures to the development; the enemy's own estimates of our ability to respond to a development; as well as several other factors.

"In this morning's counterattack, the fact remains that the enemy's computers should've told him we would be able to deploy a countermeasure quite quickly. That is why this particular issue was ranked as unlikely to be deployed. Nevertheless, the enemy elected to proceed with it anyway, possibly in some kind of double-bluff hope of catching us unawares. Whatever the reason, we did all we could in the circumstances, general."

The French general, Abrio, said, "There is also another issue I think we are missing here." His head enlarged on the screen; round, forlorn eyes set in a bony face. "It is, we can say, a good thing that we suffer not many casualties as we might have. But I look at how many of his ACAs the enemy was sending today. And I have big concerns."

Terry glanced at the cold, empty tea mug on his desk. He wondered why Simms hadn't organised a refill, until he recalled that his adjutant was off duty.

Abrio went on, "Our new ACAs may be better, but look how many of the enemy's Blackswans and Lapwings they had to face this morning, eh? Despite all the things our intelligence reports tell us, our armies are still in great danger, no? I read reports telling us that the Terror of Tehran is getting ready to invade India. My staff and others whose opinion I trust inform me he must be mad if he truly is planning—"

"Yes, absolutely," the German General Keller called out in support.

"—to try to expand his empire even further. I must confess, field marshal, I am of the opinion that this will not happen. If Operation Repulse continues to progress as it has so far, then the casualties we absorbed today may be very small compared to what we will face if the enemy chooses to return his full attention and assets back to Europe. Do you agree?"

Terry shook his head. Operation Repulse was going according to plan and he found the faintly morbid tone from his generals in their fractured English to be disagreeable. "No, general. Our intel is sound on the build-up of forces on the enemy's eastern border, which must, logically, mean fewer forces for our armies to face. And it's not our role to speculate on the sanity or otherwise of our opponent. However, I do agree that the weight of assets we face needs to be reduced if Operation Repulse is to succeed. I hope to have news on that for you all in due course. Now, let's move on to assess tomorrow's R-plus-four objectives."

Terry fought to focus as the meeting continued. Each thrust of the operation, Attack Group East and Attack Group South, had dozens of localised fronts with specific challenges: from dense urban environments through to forest and open land. Confirmations of supporting deployments were sought and given; the super AI was consulted and confirmed timings and locations and risks.

But all the time, Terry's tired mind drifted to the top-secret operation on which so much depended. He realised that they should be underway by now.

Chapter 15

06.22 Saturday 4 August 2063

C olour Sergeant Rory Moore threw himself off the hull of *HMS Spiteful* and plunged into the Mediterranean Sea. The water chilled his skin. When his head came clear of the gentle swell, he jabbed the carabiner clip into the belt around his waist. The straps connecting him to the two equipment cylinders undulating on the water either side of him became taut to confirm his connection to them. He glanced at the others and, not seeing any obvious signs of distress or other problems, he drew in a breath and began pounding the water in a strong front crawl to overcome the inertia and commence towing the cylinders to the shore.

He switched to breaststroke to allow him to gulp in more air when his head rose above the water. However, concern crystalised when he realised that with each slight rise and fall of the waves, the shore changed its location slightly. He decided on a general direction and stopped trying to confirm or deny his suspicions. He swam on, his arms and spine feeling the weight of pulling the cylinders. The sounds of other limbs splashing close by reassured him that his comrades were also making progress.

Ten minutes later, the swell softened and the waves pushed him close to the shore. The light increased as the sun rose to his left, illuminating a vista of low sand dunes. Finally, he stabbed down with one leg and his toes scuffed sand on the seabed. He pulled a few more strokes and then came to a stop when he could stand and the waves sloshed around his midriff. His chest heaved and water lapped up his back, the waves pushing him forwards in encouragement.

He peered at the empty beach looking for any sign of movement. He saw none. Then, a dark figure splashed out of the surf and crouched on the beach. Rory recognised the slim form of General Hastings, who arrived ahead of Rory as he was the only team member not towing cylinders.

Rory strode forwards through the waves and up onto the beach. He'd hoped the general might assist him with pulling his cylinders ashore, but when he turned around to look, the general was hurrying around the edges of the dunes, securing the landing area. Rory heaved on the lanyard and laconic waves rolled the cylinder noses onto the sand. He pulled and the weight of the cylinders tripled when he had to drag them clear of the water. With some relief, he unclipped the lanyard.

Out in the water, the other three team members made their way to shore with differing degrees of success. Harry Dixon, probably the fittest of all of them, had got close enough to get his feet on the seabed. Rory splashed into the surf. Without words, Harry unclipped his lanyard and together they pulled Harry's cylinders onto the shore a few metres from Rory's.

They stood in silence and watched Nick Bird breaststroke through the waves with what Rory considered to be painful slowness. Rory waded out and grabbed Nick under the arms when he realised how tired the navigator had become.

"Get off me, you great lump," Nick gasped.

"Shut up, you tart."

"That was hard bloody graft."

"That's what we trained for. And I told you to shut up."

When they were almost out of the surf, Rory let Nick go. Nick unclipped his lanyard and handed it to Rory. The navigator staggered a little way up the beach and collapsed with a sigh of relief.

Rory pulled Nick's cylinders to the shore and returned to look at the team's navigator. Rory crouched next to him and asked in a lowered voice, "You okay?"

Nick's narrow torso rose up and down. He said, "Yeah, more or less. All that time in the sub made me sloppy, I reckon."

"Nah, mate," Rory said, aping Nick's London accent, "you're just a right lazy bastard, that's all."

"Piss off."

Rory smiled and stood, the camaraderie acting like a shield of armour now that they had finally arrived on enemy territory. A tap on his shoulder made him turn to see Harry. The captain nodded out to sea. Rory followed Harry's gaze and saw the last team member, the Irishman Declan Gardner, still at least thirty metres from the shore and not making way.

Harry nodded again and ordered, "Fetch."

Rory hissed, "I'm not your fucking dog, Harry."

"It's why you're on the team. You're the beefcake and he needs help. So, go get him."

"Right, I'll bring him in and you bring his cylinders. Deal?"

Harry's expression changed. He glanced again at Declan. "No, I'll bring him in. You pull his cylinders."

"Okay."

Both men ran into the waves. Rory opted for breaststroke for better breathing. They reached Declan in moments. Exhaustion had all but overcome the Irishman. Harry reached him and unclipped the lanyard, which Rory took and clipped onto his own belt.

Five minutes later, all of the men lay on the beach breathing heavily. General Hastings returned and motioned them to sit up and form a circle. They did so. He spoke in a lowered voice, "Good news, chaps. Our immediate area is secure. There is no need for us to swim further along the coast. We should now assemble our kit, before the sun gets very much hotter."

Over the following ninety minutes, the five men worked together in the manner for which they had spent weeks training. Rory lugged the heaviest equipment from the cylinders while Declan reconstructed the motorbikes. Harry and the general organised the munitions: the novel sonic mines, the concept of which Rory found impossible to grasp, and the old-fashioned pistols they decided to bring more as a martial comfort blanket rather than weapons with which they might actually defend themselves if they ended up in a tight corner. Nick prepared a navigation set for each team member, consisting of paper maps and a small metal compass.

As the work progressed, Rory's confidence grew. They all knew that this was the riskiest part of the mission. If a patrolling enemy ACA should chance on them, Operation Thunderclap would be over very quickly. On the other hand, Rory's concern was tempered by the general's insistence that those scans of captured warriors' brains suggested the enemy did not ordinarily trouble itself with such precautions. This was for two reasons: the open North African desert was now so inhospitable that without sufficient supplies or a water replicator, no human being could last longer than seventy-two hours; and two, the knowledge had begun to become an accepted 'urban myth' among the enemy's population that the implants they were all given at birth would kill them if they strayed beyond the Caliphate's borders.

Nevertheless, Rory found the absence of modern tech discombobulating. Without a lens in his eye offering streams of data, without his Squitch providing information and instructions, and without the sense of being one element in a highly organised military construct, a sense of looseness, of not really belonging, crept along his shoulders and chilled his spine.

On the other hand, he reflected how this manner of waging war must have seemed to those squaddies in the previous century and earlier, with little more than a man's own courage and morality—plus the threat of punishment—to make him face the enemy. Contemporary tech like super AI, the lens, and smart bullets gave modern soldiers a far stronger sense of being part of a very powerful whole.

While the others helped Declan assemble the Triumphs, Rory hefted each empty cylinder and carried it along the beach. He left them at intervals of five hundred metres, each with its unique designation number uppermost. When they returned to rendezvous with the *Spiteful*, these would then act as guides if they ended up slightly off course.

A final aspect of such a low-tech mission had been that, while on the submarine, each of them had trained the others in their individual specialisms. Declan had taught them how to assemble the Triumphs and explained how they worked.

Nick Bird had described the methods for getting them across six hundred kilometres of desert to Tazirbu. Rory recalled being dumbfounded by the concept of dead reckoning: using speed and time to calculate distance between fixed points manually, without a computer or satellites or any kind of modern comms. Fortunately, the target lay almost directly south. Unfortunately, several slight detours would be required due to the presence of treacherous areas of the desert that would slow their motorbikes down.

Finally, and with sweat soaking his fatigues, Rory shovelled enough sand to cover the majority of each cylinder. He returned to the team to find Declan completing the assembly of the fifth and final Triumph.

The mechanic tightened the bolts holding the exhaust, which with its enhanced baffles would reduce but not entirely eliminate noise. He stood and, wrench in hand, checked over all of the other connections, from the handlebars and their ridiculously antiquated cable controls to the split-pins in the bolts holding the chain and rear wheel in place. Declan looked at the others, sweat also dripping from his face and soaking his combat shirt, and nodded. Harry and the general then loaded all of the most important equipment: the sonic mines and the water, into the pillion bags on each bike. One minute later, each bike stood at a rakish angle, resting on its stand, fully laden with the weapons and supplies the team needed.

Hastings indicated that they should converge in front of him. They did so. The general said, "Very good work, chaps. Now, we move to the next phase: Bird as navigator will lead, then Dixon, Moore, Gardner, and I will bring up the rear. Remember to keep checking those round mirrors poking up from the handlebars to keep an eye on the rider behind you in case the line needs to stop. Now we've arrived, I'm sure none of us wants to stay here a minute longer than we have to. We've got to cover, more or less, six hundred kilometres to get there, do the job, and then six hundred to get back. We've got all the kit we need and we are absolutely trained to complete this mission as planned. Any questions?"

Silence followed the general's question, which did not surprise Rory. The team had spent weeks testing and training and supposing 'what if' at every opportunity and with every item of kit. Now the mission had begun, none of them needed to bring up again the two central issues that no amount of planning could account for: what if the sonic mines didn't work, and what if the ACA plant was in fact too large to destroy?

"Very well, gentlemen," Hastings said with a frown of determination. "Let's get our moisturisers on and get to the bikes."

The men stood and each went to his allotted motorbike. Rory took a small package from the pillion bag, tore the top off, and extracted the tightly packed material. He placed it on the top of his head and rolled it down to cover his face. This itched his skin but all of them understood the need for a complete face covering, unless they wanted to get their heads sandblasted on the journey.

Then, he took out a small steel flask and a thin tube. He connected one end of the tube to a small port on the head covering and the other to the top of the flask. Finally, he stuck the flask in his breast pocket. While they travelled, the moisturiser would collect the sweat from their heads and the vapour in their exhalations, and convert it to drinkable water in the flask.

Rory sat astride the Triumph, flicked the kick-starter out and stabbed down with his leg. The engine came to life. When all five motorbikes were running, the general waved his arm. Each rider set off in the allocated order. Rory pulled in the clutch handle, flicked the gear lever with his foot, and revved the engine. The thrill of actually being in control of his method of transport still made his skin tingle. For all of his life, modes of transport had been controlled by super AI. He could recall episodes from his childhood where older relatives lamented the passing of vehicles controlled by humans; but, ultimately, it was a question of safety.

He trailed Harry in front of him and kept glancing in his mirror to make sure Declan was following. As they sped away from the beach and into the hot interior, Rory considered that Operation Thunderclap had begun as well as it could have. The only thing that hadn't gone right was Declan struggling to swim, but the team had worked properly in that situation. Rory began to feel that they might just be able to pull this off.

Chapter 16

09.13 Saturday 4 August 2063

Sergeant Daniel 'Davy' Laidlaw of 22nd Special Air Service Regiment trod with care along the Parisian backstreet. The detritus of occupation littered the road: broken glass, smashed ceramics, shrivelled animal carcasses. The digital overlay from his lens offered several data streams, the most important of which was the green circle that flashed in the bottom-right of his view, denoting that no threats were present.

Davy loved the Regiment, but detested jobs like this. He wished the Regiment operated the way it had after it was formed, like fighting the enemy behind the lines and similar missions to support actually winning a war. This job, like so many in this conflict, was reconnaissance—supposedly very important, but still low-risk work. And how could any member of the legendary Regiment get satisfaction from that?

The voice of the squad leader sounded in his ear, "SkyMaster now down to two-zero. If there's a raghead's pube stuck to a toilet seat within one klick, we'll know about it."

Davy disliked frivolity on a mission, no matter whether fighting would be involved or not. Archer never missed a chance to crack a joke, but this objective was no lark. Their briefing had come from TT himself, hence the unlimited air support above them. The liberation of Paris was an important political as well as military goal—an achievement to show the whole world that the Caliphate had failed and that Europe would once again be free. While Davy was just a soldier who wanted to fight, if his superiors impressed upon him the significance of an objective, he would give his all to carry out their orders.

"Davy, on your right. You're looking for an entrance door consisting of two glass panes and a standard lever-handle of silver-coloured metal. There may or may not be a sign in French on it."

Davy answered, "Roger," happy that Archer had packed it in with the smartarse answers. He moved nearer to a façade smashed up local shops on the ground floor of a five-storey row of elegant French tenements. With the dedicated SkyMaster just two hundred metres above them, there was little any remaining enemy could do. They should have ample advance warning if one were hiding in ambush. And if such an enemy were stupid enough to think they might engage in urban warfare, the supporting Scythes would soon disabuse them of it.

Between the damaged shops, his lens flashed directions towards a nondescript doorway that in fact was the entrance to a maintenance area for an adjoining Metro station, the closest public access to which protruded a further ten metres along the street. A light and fresh breeze made a piece of paper trapped under some debris flap back and forth, the sole movement in Davy's field of vision. The air smelled clean with just an occasional waft of something unpleasant. Davy didn't look too closely at the rubbish.

Davy approached the doorway. His lens indicated that he needed to turn the handle downwards, and since the city's super AI had long since been destroyed, no identification protocols or other restrictions would prevent the door from opening.

"About to reach the door now," he said.

The response came back, "Roger that. Brick and Mongrel are coming up behind you. When you're inside, you're looking for an access shaft, thirty metres, straight down."

"Roger."

He grasped the handle and turned it. There came a click and he pushed. The door moved a few centimetres and then jammed.

"Got an obstruction."

"So give it a shove," Archer said.

Davy pushed. He stepped back, shouldered his Pickup, and pushed with his left shoulder. The door shifted, the cause of the obstruction a dried and stiff animal carcass.

From the street behind Davy, Mongrel said, "Any drama?"

Davy replied, "Negative. Domestic animal that couldn't escape."

"Roger."

Davy entered and brought his Pickup back into his arms in silence. Ambient light enhancement in his lens showed a small area mostly clear of debris compared to the street. The digital image overlaying his surroundings indicated an escalator to his right. He advanced and descended with care. With each step, his boot clumped down heavily on the escalator's treads. Although immobile, the escalator was unobstructed. He reached the bottom and came into a broader area. His lens listed the equipment in recesses in the walls, including power junctions and stores for spare parts, mainly mechanical for the trains and other areas of the adjoining Metro station. The air here carried a taste of corroded metal.

He reported, even though Archer and the others were seeing everything he saw, "Am in the maintenance area now. Little debris."

"Any signs of bodies?" Archer asked.

"Negative. Judging by the dust, no one's been here in quite some time." Davy sensed the weight of the silence that greeted his observation.

Archer said, "Okay, there on the floor, at two o'clock, is the access hatch."

Davy answered, "Roger." Again, he shouldered his Pickup. He knelt down at the circular hatch with a wheel mechanism and wondered if he'd descended into a submarine. He brushed his hand over the dust and grasped the wheel.

Archer said, "Anti-clock to open."

Davy heaved but it would not move.

Archer offered, "Need some WD–40?"

Davy ignored him. He sucked in a breath and pulled on the spokes of the wheel with as much strength as he could muster. There came a dry metallic squeal and the wheel turned.

Archer said, "Bravo. It should open after one complete circuit."

"Roger." Davy pulled on the spokes until the wheel stopped. He stood, bent over, and pulled again. With a hiss of air, the circular hatch lifted on a single hinge.

Archer said, "You're gonna need your torch for this next part."

Davy pulled a palm-sized torch from his webbing and shone it down into the darkness. The light-enhancement feature in his lens lit the descent clearly to reveal an empty shaft. "Nothing doing," he reported.

"Proceed with caution. It's thirty metres straight down to the bottom, so don't slip."

"Ha-fucking-ha," Davy whispered.

"We heard you," Archer replied.

Davy clipped the torch into a mounting for it in the rim of his helmet. He patted himself down to check for any protrusions from his kit that might get snagged. He sat and lowered himself into the shaft. After ninety seconds of measured descent, he reached the bottom.

"The entrance is behind you," Archer said.

"The door is open," Davy replied.

"Go in."

Davy pushed and the heavy metal door yawned wide with a foreboding whine. His torch lit up a tunnel in front of him. He stepped over a high flange and reported, "I can see three bodies."

"Roger," Archer said. "We're seeing them, too. Take a closer look, please."

Davy approached the nearest partially decomposed corpse and said, "Male; Caucasian; has a massive head injury." He wondered what those on the other end of his comms were thinking and saying to each other. Archer had told him at the start of the mission that this feed would be going through to all kinds of VIPs.

Archer asked, "Any distinctive features?"

Davy leaned in closer so they could see as well before replying, "Doesn't look like it. The clothes have rotted, possibly due to the earlier stages of decomposition."

"Are strong odours present?"

"Negative. The air is stale." Davy stepped forwards and arrived at the next body. "This cadaver has massive damage to the chest cavity." He leaned nearer to the head, almost skeletonised, and added, "I can make out some markings on the skin on the head and neck. Yes, I can see a spider's web tattoo."

There came a pause. Although these details meant nothing to him, Davy sensed he was delivering important information.

As if in confirmation, Archer said, "Okay, we think we've ID'd these two."

Davy said, "There's a third corpse." He advanced further along the shadowed tunnel. "I can't tell whether this one was female or male, but I can't see any signs of injuries."

"Roger that. Wait one."

Davy stopped. His lens displayed a map of connecting tunnels that were part of a vast network under the city, built the previous year before Paris fell to the enemy. Despite the establishment of the most secure comms possible during construction, nothing had been heard from any of the hundreds of people who'd taken shelter just before the enemy overran the city. This mission's objective was to find out what had happened.

Archer spoke, "Listen up, Davy. You've got Brick and Mongrel heading down the shaft to join you now. Charlie and Delta squads have entered the complex at locations to the east and north of you. Your Squitch has maps of the entire complex now. Make to rendezvous with the other squads in the central admin section. Keep your weapon ready in case you come across any Spiders."

"Are we expecting to find some?" Davy asked with irony. He stared at the small green circle still flashing in the bottom-right of his view, wondering if it would ever detect any danger.

"Maybe a few. We need to get the forensics boys down there as soon as possible, and they're relying on us to make sure they'll be safe. So, crack on, please."

On hearing a noise behind him, Davy turned to see Brick and Mongrel enter the tunnel, their torches illuminating the three cadavers who, if the briefing before the mission had supposed correctly, were part of the reason all of the other members of the resistance in this underground warren died.

Davy nodded to the other two and said, "Come on, let's get this place secured. Who knows, maybe then Brass will give us some proper fighting to do."

Chapter 17

17.29 Saturday 4 August 2063

Crispin Webb hurried to collect the field marshal from the lift that carried the most important soldier in the western world up to the third floor of Ten Downing Street. Despite adopting a demanding fitness regime after his heart attack the previous year, Crispin's breaths came in short gasps at the prospect of a second difficult meeting following on from another.

Less than half an hour earlier, the boss had had yet another testy call with that absolute flake who occupied the White House. Crispin swore that fate was playing games with him. The long-awaited deployment of NATO troops to the European mainland had begun and everything had been going well, at least from the political perspective. Fewer soldiers were holed up in all of the bases, easing the potential for civil problems when they left their barracks for a drink in the nearest town. The endless news from the continent—from military gains after bloody clashes to images of poor, ragged survivors—meant that people were less focussed on all of the local supply and reconstruction problems.

The future had at last begun to take on a positive hue. The boss had led England through one of the darkest periods in the country's history. If the war might even be concluded as a relative success, everyone involved would make a lot of money in the following years. In anticipation of a light at the end of the tunnel, the previous night Crispin had slipped into a working-class place south of the river and spent a couple of hours chatting to a gorgeous young man who'd lost a great deal to the war. Nothing happened, but they'd arranged to meet again this evening, in a couple of hours. And Crispin was determined to ensure something would indeed happen tonight.

He reached the lobby in which Sir Terry would arrive. Crispin's lens told him that the field marshal had just entered the lift six storeys below.

But then today happened. A mere five days into the operation to free Europe, NATO soldiers entered Paris. They located the lair that the city's now-certainly-dead mayor, Nicolas Favre, had garnered so much publicity when building to house a 'resistance' à la World War Two. But everyone in it was dead and had been dead for at least a year. Samples were taken and within hours the boffins at Aldermaston confirmed that the enemy had used a lethal and fast-acting nerve agent.

And for Crispin, the proverbial shit was still hitting the fan, and the fan was spraying it all over Downing Street—on turbo.

The lift arrived and the doors opened. Field Marshal Sir Terry Tidbury exited and said, "Well?"

Knowing the old soldier didn't use a lens, Crispin indicated to his left and said, "They're in the conf—"

"Thank you, Mr Webb. I know where it is."

Crispin hurried after the smaller man, unnerved more than usual. Sir Terry had a brittle calmness in his demeanour that, to Crispin, exuded greater potential danger, not less. For the first time, the small but powerfully built man carried with him an element of suppressed rage.

Crispin hurried to keep alongside the field marshal in the narrow corridor. He stammered, "I thought you should, er, know that the boss—er, the PM—has had a call with the White House, and, er—"

"Spit it out, man."

"The American military are unhappy about you postponing—"

"And you think I am unaware of that, Mr Webb?"

"No, I only wished to brief you before the meet—"

"Thank you. I will keep it in mind."

They reached the conference room. Crispin stepped ahead and opened the door to show the field marshal in. Crispin followed him, reflecting that if this meeting didn't end quickly, he'd miss his date. And he missed going on dates.

"Terry, thank you for coming," Dahra Napier said, rising from her seat at the small table. "I wanted to discuss the latest news from Paris. I assume you know, yes?"

The room darkened when clouds outside the two ornate Georgian sash windows obscured the sun. This made the room seem to shrink. Crispin sensed a kind of focussed anger radiate out from the field marshal. The other cabinet members sitting around the table did not appear to relish the prospect of having to try and mollify the head of the armed forces of what remained of the free world.

Liam Burton, defence minister and himself a former soldier, reacted to the field marshal's arrival. He echoed the boss, "Yes, thanks for coming, TT. I'd like to congratulate you and everyone involved on how well Repulse has gone so far."

Crispin admired Burton's soft-spoken compliment. He offered, "Can I get you something to drink, Sir Terry?"

The field marshal looked at Crispin and said, "No, thank you." He turned to the boss, "I am aware of our allies' frustration, PM. But this is very unwelcome news."

The boss said, "Please, sit down, Terry."

The field marshal did so and the tension eased. Crispin had suggested to Dahra that they should've used the larger conference room one floor below, but she'd insisted this would be enough—around a smoked glass table that could seat up to six, with barely enough room to push the chairs back.

The boss said, "President Coll insisted that I speak to you directly to impress upon you the importance of maintaining our ad—"

"This is unacceptable, PM. If you, as my political superior, have lost confidence in my ability to command our joint forces, then you must sack me. It really is as simple as that."

Crispin froze. He had no idea the field marshal would say such a thing.

The boss immediately backtracked, saying, "Of course I'm not going to sack you, Terry. How could you even suggest such a th—?"

"Because I am the most senior officer in the field. And the military decisions to be taken are mine alone. I may, and any able commander would, consult my generals and other ranks, including specialist advisers and such like, before I give an order. But—and I cannot stress this enough—political interference will only lead to military atrophy and failure."

The boss's features hardened. She said, "This is not interference, absolutely not. But I must insist that I am able to ask questions and raise doubts when our allies come to me with such issues."

Terry clasped his hands together on the table and hunched his shoulders. "And you may. But you cannot question my operational decisions. I have decided to pause current operations until we can assess the full impact of the enemy deploying lethal nerve agents in the battlespace."

"I see."

"I hope so, PM. The Spiders my troops discovered in the underground base of the Paris resistance had, as we conjectured when we lost contact with them a year ago, been loaded with a gas-based agent that killed those occupants within a few seconds. As my troops advance, they have to clear thousands of settlements, from hamlets and villages to vast metropolises, any of which might hide such dormant Spiders, still loaded with active nerve gas and just waiting."

Foreign Secretary Charles Blackwood tugged at a cufflink and said, "But global condemnation will be complete. The Terror of Tehran has made a huge mistake using such weapons. It's as bad as if he'd used nukes."

Terry's eyes flicked over to Blackwood. He replied, "But the enemy used them solely because he wasn't expecting to be found out. He never presumed we would regain territory. In addition, we can take it as all-but-certain the same fate was inflicted on the underground resistances in Berlin and Warsaw."

"Indeed," the boss agreed, eyes cast down.

"But to return to your original point. My American subordinates have given me their frank and honest opinions of my decision. Their main counterargument is that if the enemy intended to make full use of these weapons, they would already have been deployed to hinder or even thwart Operation Repulse."

Burton asked, "Could you give us any indication of how long this pause will be?"

"No."

Blackwood's handsome face didn't flicker.

Terry looked at the boss. "If that will be all, PM?"

"No," Dahra replied in an echo of Terry's answer. She tucked a strand of auburn hair behind her ear and asked, "I would like to know your opinion on what we should do if the Caliphate does, at some future point, use more of these banned weapons?"

"Develop and deploy our own."

"Are you serious?" she said, aghast.

Crispin heard the shock in the boss's voice and thought it was a dumb thing for her to say.

Terry replied, "We have mothballed facilities, PM. Aldermaston used to be used exclusively to render such munitions safe years ago. But if the enemy uses them against NATO troops, you can depend on me to push that we should repay him in the same coin."

"Very well."

"Is that everything, PM?"

"Yes. Thank you again for coming up here, Terry."

The field marshal nodded to her, and then to the men. He stood and said to Crispin, "I can find my way out."

The door closed behind the field marshal. The men swapped concerned glances.

Dahra's eye twitched and she said, "Monica? Glass of white, now, please."

Blackwood said, "We need to leverage this in the global media. We have to put more diplomatic pressure on those countries that have been ambivalent over the Caliphate's belligerence."

Now the discussion had moved on to a subject on which Crispin knew something, he spoke. "If I might suggest something, PM?"

Dahra nodded.

"I think the angle we need to push here is fear."

"Meaning?" Burton asked.

"Who's next?" Crispin offered with a shrug of his shoulders. "Much of the rest of the world has been indifferent to what's happened to us, and I really think the story itself won't change that. But if the Caliphate is prepared to use these kinds of weapons when it really didn't need to, what about everyone else?"

Dahra said nothing, but Blackwood murmured, "Makes sense."

"Right now," Crispin went on, "the global focus is on the brinksmanship between the Caliphate and India. There have even been riots in some of the Indian border cities who know they'll be the first to get barbequed if the Caliphate does invade."

The boss threw him a withering look at his choice of words.

Crispin continued, "We must make sure they know that banned nerve gas weapons will also be coming their way."

The boss said, "And China as well."

Burton added, "We'll submit a motion at the UN, won't we?"

Dahra said, "We will, not that it'll make much difference."

There came a soft tap at the door. Monica opened it, wordlessly delivered the boss's glass of white wine, and exited.

Dahra lifted the glass and concluded, "Very well. Crispin, make some calls to the press office and media contacts, and start making things happen. God knows we could use all the international aid we can get to feed the refugees and rebuild here, never mind the rest of Europe. This episode could help in that direction. At least some benefit from the suffering of those poor people."

The boss sipped her wine. Crispin glanced at the two men and the sense of the meeting's natural conclusion came to him. Dahra stood and said, "Thank you, gentlemen. I think that's enough for today. Let's all try to get some rest, shall we?"

As Crispin followed the others out of the conference room, he checked the feeds in his lens and began selecting contacts. Oh yes, just a few calls to make and then he would be free for the night. And he vowed to do everything he could with that young working-class lad.

Chapter 18

00.01 Sunday 5 August 2063

Rory became suspicious of the knocking sound from the engine of his Triumph Bonneville when, according to Nick's estimates, they must have been fewer than fifty kilometres from Tazirbu. The majority of the journey had passed without incident. Nick had been obliged to make several unscheduled diversions, usually around geographic features such as prominent rock plateaus or to take account of low mountains that weren't where they were supposed to be on the team's paper maps. But bringing everyone to a stop and informing them of these minor changes allowed the team brief breaks to sip water and relieve themselves.

They'd spent much time on the submarine discussing risks of detection. For example, normal operational procedure when behind enemy lines would demand they take all traces of their presence—including bodily waste—with them. However, the nature of this covert mission was such that any detection would be immediately fatal. In addition, the climate in the interior of the North African desert now meant few, if any, nomadic tribes remained. Therefore, they'd agreed that continual movement would be the key to minimising the small risk of discovery, and ditched the more stringent protocols.

At the last stop half an hour earlier, Rory whispered to Declan that the engine might be making a strange noise; one of the symptoms of potential trouble of which the Irishman had warned them. Declan had told him to wait until they were running on smooth terrain, and if the noise persisted then, Rory should cause an unscheduled stop and Declan would take a closer look.

As it transpired, events overtook them. They were traversing a flat, rocky plateau riven with treacherous wadis, their speed slowing as a result. Then, without warning, the knocking in the engine turned into an abrupt screech and the back wheel of his motorbike locked rigid. Rory pulled the clutch in and the skidding rear wheel began rolling again. He yanked on the brake lever on the handlebar and dabbed his foot down on the foot brake. He slowed gradually so Dixon would see him fall back, and Gardner behind him would slow down as well.

When the whole team had stopped, Rory kicked out the stand and got off the motorbike. All of them gathered at Rory's machine. Viewed through his own ancient night-vision goggles over the moisturiser, the others looked like uncertain green monsters wearing theirs. He rolled the moisturiser up his head and whispered, "My bike is definitely knackered."

Declan looked the machine over. He pushed his own face covering up and asked, "What happened?"

Rory related the sequence of events.

Declan looked at the others and said, "That'll be that, then. This never would've happened with a Harley, so it wouldn't."

Hastings said, "We need to hide the bike. Moore, you ride pillion with Dixon. Come on."

Dixon cautioned, "Watch your step. Walk slowly and carefully. Last thing we need is an injury."

Hastings waved an arm to the east and said, "Looks like there's a decent wadi over there. Let's ditch it and crack on."

As rehearsed in training, Nick, Declan and Harry reached into the pillion bags on Rory's bike and extracted the kit for which each of them had responsibility. Rory put the motorbike into neutral and pushed it, struggling to make out smaller depressions in the ground as he walked under the dome of stars above. A few minutes later, he reached the edge of the wadi and stopped, breathing easily despite the effort.

Hastings said, "I believe this should do."

"My display suggests it's only about five metres deep," Harry said.

Rory asked, "Do we have to follow it down and try and bury it in these rocks and shale?"

Silence followed. Rory kicked the stand out so he could let go of the bike. He removed the last thing of value from the pillion bags: his water containers, and set them on the ground.

"Affirmative," the general finally answered. "Although movement is key to this operation and the likelihood of discovery before we complete the mission is low, we still need to take reasonable precautions."

Nick said, "Right, let's chuck it over the edge and get on with it, then."

Rory kicked the stand back for the final time and vowed that if he survived the mission, he'd do everything in his power to get his own motorbike and enjoy the thrill of being in control of a motorised vehicle. He pushed the Triumph as hard as he could. It rolled over the lip of the wadi. There came a dull thud and then a scraping as the motorbike bumped and slid gracelessly down a few metres before jamming on an outcrop.

Rory and Nick descended with care into the wadi. Rory needed all of his strength to lift the bike over the outcrop before letting it fall into sand at the bottom of the wadi. In moments, he and Nick used their small hand-shovels to toss sand over most of the bike.

When its wheels and engine were covered, with only one handlebar sticking out, Nick said, "C'mon, that'll do."

"Yup," Rory said, wiping yet more sweat from his face.

Both men clambered back up the side of the wadi.

"Good," Hastings said when he saw them. "Let's resume, just as we trained for in this kind of situation."

Everyone pulled their masks back down their heads and put their night-vision goggles back on. Rory collected his water supplies, wondering how on earth it was possible for any army to have fought campaigns without water replicators, and followed Harry. Nick and Declan removed the pillion bags from Harry's motorbike, so Rory would be able sit on it. They adjusted the straps and slung Harry's bags on their backs as rucksacks. Rory's own water containers hung from the rear metalwork of Harry's bike.

All of the team members remounted their bikes. Rory threw his leg over behind Harry and put his hands on Harry's waist.

"Don't get any funny ideas, Mister gay Royal Engineer," Harry advised over his shoulder.

As Harry kickstarted the bike, above the roar of the engine Rory shouted back, "I'd only shag a Royal Anglian if I wanted to give him a dose of the clap."

Harry yelled back, "So, my luck might be in, after all."

Despite the banter, Rory disliked riding pillion and felt aggrieved that his bike had been the first to fail. However, once in motion again, the desire to face the approaching danger overrode all other feelings.

An hour passed and a new, brighter glow grew in Rory's night-vision goggles. Nick stopped the team to let them know, with more than a hint of satisfaction, that they had reached the multilane autonomous highway which, if they turned right and followed, would take them to Tazirbu. Rory's foreboding eased. They had covered the most dangerous part of the journey: the unknown six-hundred-odd kilometres to the target.

Forty-five minutes later, Nick again brought them to a stop. They dismounted their bikes and drew together to whisper. Nick rolled his moisturiser up his face and said, "Two things. First: those dark shapes up ahead are part of the ACA production plant."

The general turned his head in that direction and said, "I'm glad to see we didn't bring too many sonic mines."

"And second," Nick went on, "I don't know about the rest of you, but this bloody moisturiser mask ain't working."

Rory took the small container from his breast pocket to find it empty.

"Would you look at that?" Declan said of his own flask. "Not a single drop."

"Mine's empty," Harry replied in dejection.

"So, what's gone wrong?" Rory asked the others.

"We tested this quite thoroughly," Harry said defensively. "It worked fine in up to forty-five-degree heat back in Blighty."

Nick squeezed the mouthpiece and offered, "I reckon the filter's packed up."

"Chaps," the general said, "the moisturisers were aids. We had to wear full-face coverings to protect us from the sand in any case. But these were not designed to actually keep us from dying of thirst. We have our water supplies, and they shall be sufficient to get us to the end of the job."

"Yes, sir," Declan said. "But these things were supposed to give us more room for manoeuvre if we got delayed for any reason. Now, time is going to become more critical, is it not?"

The general ignored the question and ordered, "Bird, Dixon and I will reconnoitre the plant now. Moore, remain here with the bikes; Gardner, scout about and find a passable lying-up point. If we do not return by sunrise, hide yourselves and the motorbikes in the LUP till sunset, then return here without the bikes, obviously, to rendezvous. We still have four hours of darkness, so we need to aim to identify sites for the sonic mines. Any questions?"

Along with the others, Rory shook his head.

"Very good," Hastings said. "Well done so far, chaps. Despite two small setbacks, the potential for which we adequately factored into our calculations, everything is proceeding according to plan."

Rory watched the three men disappear into the night. He and Declan spent an hour methodically radiating out from their location to find a suitable lying-up point. The Irishman discovered a broad plateau of shale and sand that dipped over ten metres at one end into a sheltered, shallow cave. They marked the meeting point and took the bikes and equipment to the LUP.

As the eastern edge of the night sky paled into deep blue, the general and the others returned. They reported only that the ACA plant was a vaster complex than they had appreciated. The general seemed to consider this development a serious intel failure.

Day broke and the temperature rose. Riding through the night had been almost pleasant, but within a couple of hours the desert heat again became punishing. Rory tried to sleep when it was his turn, but struggled as he constantly sweated.

Then, just after midmorning, a vast, loud siren blared out across the city of Tazirbu, which lay to the team's south on the other side of the highway.

"Right-ho," Nick said to the others, "now it's time for prayers, lads."

None of them laughed.

The air suddenly split with a flurry of hisses. In unison, the men of Operation Thunderclap leapt to their feet, scrabbled out of the LUP, and ran up the bank of shale. The hisses continued at regular intervals. For a terrifying moment, Rory thought they'd been discovered and this was the prelude to an attack. But even then, common sense told him they would already be dead if that were the case.

Rory caught his breath when he turned to the west and saw that the noise was made by a wing of aircraft leaving the ACA production facility. All of the men stood and watched. Wing after wing launched, speeding north, towards Europe.

On Rory's left, Nick spat, "And I'll bet you a pound to a pitch of shit where those bastards are heading to. Fuckers."

Hastings gently chastised the navigator with, "Steady on, Bird. Look at the advantage. We now know at least one part of the facility we need to strike."

The launches continued until nightfall. Rory estimated that over three thousand ACAs left the plant in that time.

Chapter 19

18.51 Sunday 5 August 2063

" The Englishman, reporting from Beijing. This data-pod contains three sub-topics. First, to answer your previous question. I don't know if anyone at MI5 actually bothers to pay any attention to Chinese media, but if they did, they'd know how much shit is flying around about now. No, of course the Chinese government did *not* give the Third Caliph permission to use weapons of mass destruction. We've seen this through his entire conduct of the war so far, not least when Israel threw all of its nuclear weapons at him and his conventional ACAs swatted them aside.

"My contacts in the lower echelons of the civil service and the intelligence agencies both claim—and I cannot verify this as yet—that various factions in the government are getting pissed off with each other about how to react. Rumours coming back from Tehran talk about the Third Caliph seeing the discovery in Paris more as a show of determination to ensure the infidels duly suffered what they deserved, blah, blah,

blah. However, ultimately there may not be much the Chinese government can do about it because of sub-topic two.

"You also need to realise that the absolute lead story is the Third Caliph building up his forces on his border with India. Again, the Chinese are finding it difficult to influence events. Ansh Dasgupta in Delhi is not going to take even a micron of shit from Tehran. My contacts also report concerns in the government here that Dasgupta may even start a shooting war and blame the Third Caliph for it. This would not be too difficult given the proximity of the opposing forces on the border. I don't usually give opinions in these reports, but I would speculate this might be close to the truth. Dasgupta is in trouble in the polls and he's got to hold an election next year—remember, India is one of the last countries in the world to still hold reasonably free elections. He then comes under pressure from the hawks in his own party to do something—*anything*—to get their polling numbers up. And there are not many things better than having a good old ding-dong with the nearest bloodthirsty regime. This leads to sub-topic three.

"Any open conflict between the Caliphate and India is almost certain to see an exchange of nuclear weapons. Indian intel intercepted by the Chinese acknowledges the Indian military's deficiencies. These include the fact that the Third Caliph will invade with battle-hardened troops from the Europe campaign and the expectation that India's inferior ACAs will be outnumbered about three to one. Amazing that Dasgupta would covertly attempt to spark a war just to stay in power, if that war were to lead to massive loss of life in his own country.

"Finally, before I finish and send this off in the diplomatic pouch, you guys in England really need to understand how unimportant you are in a place like China. Yes, the Third Caliph using a controversial chemical weapon to wipe out those centres of resistance has angered the government, but the Third Caliph has been doing pretty much as he pleases for a while now, and the Chinese can't just rein him in anymore. In any case, you can bleat about the injustice of it to the world's media all you like, but these crimes are already dropping out of the headlines—after as little as thirty-six hours—in the countries that really matter.

"Oh, and thanks for approving my expenses for last month. Appreciated."

Chapter 20

07.33 Monday 6 August 2063

Mark Phillips reclined in his monitoring pod at 3rd Airspace Defence in London. He monitored a sector of northern France for enemy air activity, and was also in command of fifty other monitoring posts around England.

His body trembled from time to time, as though a chill breeze had crept in from outside. The past weekend had been the worst of his life. On Friday, his older brother Martin had been killed in action. On Saturday, he spoke to his sister, Maria. He'd never heard her sob so uncontrollably before, and it terrified him. Afterwards, she pointed out that from the five of their family who had been alive in January 2062, now only the pair of them remained. Mark hadn't known what to say, so he apologised. From all of his discussions with his friend, Simon, he recalled that Simon advised apologising could help even when something wasn't his fault.

On Sunday, Lieutenant Rose Cho called him into her office and explained that Airspace Defence had experts who could help him cope with grief. Mark had politely declined and requested only that he remain in post. At that meeting, with a superior officer he'd grown to trust, he realised that he had to keep these emotions within himself, in private; that they were not for the British Army to pick over and dissect, however well-intentioned their efforts. Besides, coping came more easily with the distraction of monitoring enemy air activity.

A red-level comms icon flashed in the lower left of his view. Mark always tried to avoid talking to those in subordinate locations, preferring to use automated codes. But sometimes he could not.

A bright and excited female voice came to his ears, "Hi. Control? I've got a situation developing."

Mark answered, "This is control. Please allow and advise."

"Roger."

Mark's view of northern France abruptly zoomed in on the city of Tours and swung about to face south.

The woman, identified as battlespace monitor Corporal Donna Butler, said, "I've got a SkyMaster that's tracking sixty-four wings of—"

"Yes, I can see," Mark broke in, failing to keep the irritation from his voice.

Butler's voice dropped and lost its enthusiasm. She said, "Squonk says they must have originated from North Africa, which means they could be different types of machines."

"Ah, right. Good work, corporal," Mark fumbled, realising his responsibility to respect his subordinate. The view around him lowered in altitude and took on a shallow, three-dimensional aspect. Data streams splayed out around the approaching enemy machines.

With a hint of sarcasm, Butler went on, "As I'm sure you can see, sir, their G-10 sigs are higher than normal Blackswans or Lapwings—"

"But they are still Blackswans and Lapwings because they're following similar inbound flight paths and altitudes on their attack paths."

"Actually, sir, that might be a ruse."

Mark stopped, realising the clever corporal was right.

Butler added, "Scythes will engage them in ten seconds."

Mark watched digital lines emerging from behind him as they drew towards the oncoming enemy ACAs. He withdrew further to get a more comprehensive overall picture as the contact developed. The enemy spearhead over Tours was the vanguard of sixteen such spearheads across northern France. As those waves of enemy machines came into range of the SkyMasters, other operators began flagging the same differences in readings.

Corporal Butler unnecessarily said, "Here we go."

When the Scythes and the enemy ACAs converged to within ten kilometres at the highest altitudes, there began an aerial battle of unparalleled complexity.

Mark whispered, "Jesus," as dozens of autonomous combat aircraft suddenly rose, dived, pitched and yawed to every point on the compass. His eyes struggled to follow more than a few of the digital lines as they weaved a web of absolute chaos in the sky. Each side's super AI fought to gain any advantage to increase the possibility of scoring a laser hit on the other's machines.

Corporal Butler exclaimed, "It looks like mayhem."

Squonk announced: "Information: enemy ACAs are performing better than previously and must therefore be benefiting from increased power."

"Specify," Mark demanded.

"The battlespace is too dynamic to sustain—"

"So speculate," Mark yelled, appalled at the implications for NATO troops on the ground.

Lieutenant Rose Cho appeared in a thumbnail in the bottom-left of his vision. She said, "Attention, all operators. A red-level advisory will shortly go out to all NATO units."

Squonk said, "The most probable conclusion is multiple enhancements to their muon-based power units."

Butler voiced what Mark was thinking, "They analysed our Scythes' aerodynamic performance and extrapolated what we've done, and have improved their ACAs in the same way."

Mark had to choke back an expletive. He watched the digital chaos in the air in silence. The seconds ticked by. He knew that the Blackswans and Lapwings should've been falling out of the sky by now. But they were not. The Scythes were using up power and, much worse, time, to reach and engage the enemy's enhanced ACAs. And even when the Scythes could hit them, the Lapwings and Blackswans were absorbing more laser hits. At lower altitudes, the percentage of successful Falarete hits fired by the few X–9s in theatre dropped.

A familiar dismay began to envelope Mark, similar to that which he'd felt on Friday, when the Falaretes had stopped working. NATO had solved that issue in just a couple of hours, but this new development promised to need more time. His heartrate accelerated. He knew the name for this feeling: frustration. The battle in the sky over northern France would play out as the computers dictated—and he would remain impotent throughout. The gamer inside him, that part of him he thought he'd got under control, taunted him. Mark hadn't been able to do anything to stop his older brother getting killed, and now Mark would not be able to do anything to stop more NATO troops on the ground from being killed this morning.

Chapter 21

10.15 Monday 6 August 2063

Corporal Edward 'Ned' Smith huddled with the rest of his squad in the ruined basement of a school. Narrow windows at the tops of the walls let in little light, their glass either broken and obscured by debris or dirty with grime. In the sky outside, a lone Lapwing had taken command of the airspace above the town of Anderlecht.

Captain Joel Harding, crouching opposite Ned, yelled into the middle distance, "No, Squonk will bring the tanks back for fire support, but we are boxed in here. We need a Scythe. Where the hell are they?"

Ned's eyes flicked over the other squad members watching the captain trying to get them out of this outrageous situation. He leaned over to his pal, Squid, and said, "Typical, eh? The day we resume ops, and the ragheads pitch up with better kit."

Squid's beady eyes looked back and he muttered, "TT could've given us a longer break."

Opposite them, Captain Harding nodded and said, "Uh-huh. Well, that's just great." Harding's chiselled jaw jutted in frustration. He lifted his head and addressed all of them, "Okay, lads. No drama. We just need to sit tight and we'll be fine."

As if to confirm that the Lapwing had other ideas, the sounds of hissing and thumps of falling masonry made everyone tense in anticipation of the remaining building squashing them like bugs.

Ned coughed some dust out from his throat and elbowed Squid. "Something's gone well wrong, I reckon."

Squid looked out from under the rim of his helmet, incredulity on his dirty, sweat-stained face. "Cor, you're a right Sherlock, you."

"My Squitch is not saying shit," Ned complained, a feeling of being cheated forming in his offended mind.

"No one's Squitch is saying anything, dummy. It's how they're protecting us."

"What you talking 'bout?" Ned said. "We could get flattened any second and you think staying here is helping?"

"Like the drill sergeant told me back in Blighty, I don't think nothing. I just do as I'm told. And so should you."

Ned glanced at the captain and the other six of the squad crouching among the broken machinery and pipework. There came the sound of more falling masonry from outside and more dust blew into their dungeon. All of them began choking and coughing and cursing.

"Steady on, lads," Captain Harding said.

Ned eyed the captain between coughs. He tried to contain his frustration. The whole point of the battlefield management system was that each soldier knew what was happening and the best course of action available. It shouldn't be used to keep soldiers in the dark, as though they were fighting in some earlier war. And Ned did not wish to be buried alive because a computer thought it was for the best.

When he'd spat most of the dust from his throat, Ned addressed the captain, "Sir, I think we might be better off outside. If that Lapwing blasts this building directly—"

"Your opinion is noted, corporal. Thank you," Harding replied, the look on his face deepening the creases when he frowned. His head tilted and his eyes narrowed. "Roger that," he said. He looked back at Ned and said, "Seems the super AI shares your opinion, corporal. We're to make a run for it back to the start line."

Ned stood and said, "That's more like it."

The rest of the squad also got up when Captain Harding stood. Harding instructed, "Right, we're going to have to be on our toes now, lads. We can get back to the start line in no time. You remember the canal to the east?"

Ned nodded along with the others.

"Right, we've got a squadron of tanks coming back. They'll give us cover—"

"So where are the Scythes?" Squid asked.

Harding shook his head and replied, "Not supporting the advance, that's for sure. Look, Squonk isn't telling me all that much—" he broke off at the sound of a couple of derisory scoffs. "Really, you think—? Anyway, doesn't matter now. Let's move out before we're buried. And stay on the ball—getting lasered is a horrible way to buy it. Lead the troops out, Corporal Smith. I'll bring up the rear."

"Follow me," Ned said. He shouldered his Pickup and grasped his Falarete, his hand closing all the way around the tube. He led the squad out from the basement and up a narrow staircase. He emerged into a dark, windowless corridor. He kicked some upended boxes littering the floor out of his way before reaching the large double doors through which the squad had entered fifteen minutes earlier.

Ned waited and watched additional data streams form and update. These confirmed a Lapwing in the sky above the town and the squadron of autonomous Challenger tanks along the canal. As the seconds passed, the tanks began going offline.

His Squitch said, "On exiting the building, turn left and head west as indicated," before adding ominously, "Caution: you are entering an active battlespace."

Ned asked no one in particular, "Why does this stupid thing tell us pointless shit like that?"

From behind him, Squid offered, "Because it knows we're as thick as shit?"

"Speak for yourself," Ned replied, before heaving in a deep breath to steel himself.

From behind him, Captain Harding shouted, "Let's go before it finishes the tanks."

Ned pushed the doors open and the hot, dry air hit his face. He turned left and hurried along the outside of the school, bent over and staying as close to the wall as possible. The stomps of other boots on broken masonry told him the rest of the squad followed.

His Squitch gave him the position of the Lapwing in the sky and the Challengers' location relative to the squad's. He picked up his pace, eager to get to the start line of the morning's advance. The feeling of being cheated intensified. Ned had been recruited while gaming—and the lying bastards who convinced him to join up said life in the British Army was no different. But it was. Sweat stung a cut on his forehead and seeped into his eyes, forcing him to blink continuously, which in turn caused problems with his Squitch and the data streams it displayed.

He reached a junction of smashed up bungalows in front of a damaged two-storey apartment block. His display told him to turn left and, ten metres afterwards, to turn right to keep leading the squad west. Then there came a series of crumps and Ned realised that the tanks must have—

The roofs of the bungalows in front of him exploded with a deafening crash when thousands of red slate tiles were blasted into the air. Ned dropped to the ground, hurting his elbows and knees. The heat increased at least ten degrees before abruptly whooshing away. Smoke coiled and a new cloud of dust made him cough.

His Squitch said, "Danger: a Caliphate Lapwing has targeted your location. Seek cover immediately."

Various curses and shouts rose up behind him.

Captain Harding urged, "Stick together, squad. Let's backtrack to the school."

Ned stopped listening and asked, "Where are the tanks?"

His Squitch replied, "All tanks in your vicinity have been destroyed. Seek cover immediately."

"Fuck that fucking bullshit," he spat, his emotions boiling in the heat.

"Excessive profanity may be reported to your superior officer."

He began running towards the damaged apartment block. "Where are the fucking Scythes?" he demanded.

His Squitch ignored the question and repeated, "Seek cover immediately."

Ned ran down a narrow alleyway between two bungalows, dodging flaming fences and the remains of a garden shed that crackled furiously, matching his rage. Determination lent his legs more energy. He'd had enough of being cheated, of being lied to by the poxy British Army, and being attacked by this shit-bastard enemy. He didn't need his Squitch to tell him the Lapwing's trajectory. Its last pass had been to finish off the tanks, and it managed to get a few shots in close to the squad. Now, it swung about out of view and was about to come back to burn them all to cinders.

A gust of wind blew the smoke in front of him to one side, revealing the broken walls of the two-storey apartment block. In his ears, Captain Harding urged the squad to stick together and retreat in orderly fashion back to the ruined school again due to the threat.

Ned was done with retreating.

He arrived at the nearest smashed wall. Twisted and bent steel rods stuck up from the shattered concrete pillars. In between them the walls were made of old-fashioned breezeblock with render on both sides that hung off in thin slabs. He needed to gain height, and the ridge of the broken wall, which ascended at roughly forty-five degrees, offered the best option. He put his Pickup on the ground and clambered up to balance on the sill of a smashed window. In one fluid movement, he leapt onto a steep ridge of fractured breezeblocks, grasping a bent steel rod jutting out of the concrete pillar in front of him. His Falarete swung about in the air in his free hand.

"Seek cover immediately."

"Shut the fuck up immediately," he hissed.

Ned climbed higher along the ridge of the broken wall, grabbing a steel rod poking out of the next concrete pillar. He tried not to look down at the masonry, glass shards and other debris into which he'd plunge if he slipped. The indicator in his lens denoting the approaching Lapwing flashed red as the machine closed in on him and the squad. With no time to spare, Ned let go of the steel rod and balanced precariously while snapping the Falarete tube open and placing the rear half of it on his shoulder. For once, his Squitch assisted him, activating and aiming the weapon. With the black dot of the Lapwing growing, Ned pulled the trigger. The shot popped out of the tube with a brief hiss. Ned discarded the redundant tube, and then grabbed the steel rods with both hands before he lost his balance.

There came a screech from low in the sky close to him. In reflex, he ducked as the air pressure warned his primaeval senses of mortal danger close by. The tumbling, out-of-control Lapwing missed Ned by a metre and smashed into a building behind him. When the noise and falling debris subsided, Ned turned and saw the blackened ACA embedded in a bungalow on the other side of the road. Innumerable pieces of glass, tile, brick and render continued coming back down to earth with waves of tinny crashes.

He breathed out a foul curse and, with care, made his way back down the ridge of the broken wall, nearly losing his balance when a steel rod bent completely over as he put his weight on it. He recovered himself and continued down, muttering, "Bastards. Bloody sick of being cheated… Lied to… Every bloody bastard lying and cheating and always trying to get one over on me… Bloody world's full of them… Sick of the lying, cheating bastards…"

He was still mumbling curses when he jumped off the window sill and landed back on the ground. He recovered his Pickup, stood upright, and dusted himself off. Only then did he notice the rest of the squad standing in the road, staring at him agape.

Ned asked defensively, "What you all looking at me for?"

Squid took a pace forward, gestured at the smoking ruins of the Lapwing and said, "Do you know what you just did?"

Confusion grew inside Ned. "Yeah, so?"

Captain Harding let out a guffaw and strode up to Ned. He also indicated the enemy machine and said, "That's a VC right there, Corporal Smith."

"Why? I was only doing what we're s'posed to do, right?"

"You bet," Harding said. "Just what we're supposed to do."

"Good. Can we go back to the start line now? I'm getting well hungry."

Chapter 22

16.48 Monday 6 August 2063

Terry Tidbury embraced his taller and slimmer American friend, and said, "Welcome back to the UK, Suds. It's been a while."

General Studs Stevens stood back a step and replied, "It's great to be back, field marshal. Although, I gotta say that if you weren't SACEUR and could court-martial me, I would kick your sorry ass for some of your recent decisions, you know?"

Terry's smile faded and he asked, "You still don't beat about the bush, do you? Did the pause on ops really go down so badly over there?"

Suds exclaimed, "Are you kidding me?"

Terry said, "My first obligation is to defend NATO lives. I absolutely will not expend my soldiers' lives without a damn good tactical or strategic reason."

"Earl, you think I don't know that?" Stevens asked rhetorically with his arms outstretched.

"Besides which," Terry added, "we resumed after only thirty-six hours. Once I concluded that his use of chemical weapons didn't extend beyond those centres of resistance, Repulse restarted."

Stevens looked around the War Room and asked, "Can't we go someplace a little easier on the eye?"

Terry called out, "Simms?"

From behind him, his adjutant replied, "Yes, Sir Terry?"

"I'm going topside with my guest for a little while."

"Very good, sir."

In silence, both the soldier and the airman ascended from the War Rooms to the Whitehall building above, and then exited into the dry gardens that gave views over the Thames. The grass lay yellow and brittle; the trees stood dry, branches bare from the heat.

"Rebuilding sure is going really good, Earl," Stevens said, staring into the distance at the sprinkling of construction replicators laboriously reconstructing parts of the shattered city.

Terry took in the recovering skyline and ignored the observation. "The enemy finally hit us with something better this morning."

Stevens turned to Terry. "Wanna talk it over?"

Terry smiled at the Americanism, as though the issue were something trivial. He replied, "It wasn't unexpected, I suppose. But it's nearly stalled Repulse and might even reverse it."

"No kidding?" Suds said, a note of incredulity in his voice.

Terry nodded towards the river and said, "Let's walk. No, I'm not kidding, Suds. As you might expect, his strategy and tactics were very clever."

"But did he hit us with new machines?"

"No, upgraded power units in his existing ones."

"A workable solution till he can bring new ones to the fight, I guess."

Terry murmured his agreement. "Very 'workable'. Our defences are straining under this development."

"How about casualties?"

"Increasing as the computers forecast. His tactics today were smart, Suds. Two pincers to draw off our main ACAs. Then he saturated almost the entirety of both fronts."

"The computers ceded air superiority?" Suds said, aghast.

"Only in a few sectors, but where they did, they had no choice," Terry countered. "Once our main forces had been depleted with diversion, it was enough for the enemy to deploy individual machines to certain sectors to force our troops back."

"So, we don't have enough machines?" Suds asked.

"Or perhaps the enemy has too many?"

Suds stopped walking and turned to Terry. "And what's that supposed to mean, field marshal?"

Terry stared into Suds' face. The look of curiosity creased the scar above the airman's right eye. Terry knew he could trust his friend, but op-sec was op-sec. He said, "There is a secret mission in support of Repulse."

"No shit?"

"No shit, Suds. And it simply has to succeed."

"How will you know if it does?"

"Oh, we'll know."

"Sure."

"But if it fails—and as today showed, there's not much time left—then Repulse is certain to be reversed."

Chapter 23

20.55 Tuesday 7 August 2063

As the time to make the attack approached, Rory sensed the tension increase in inverse proportion to how much everyone's water supply dwindled. Although the moisturisers were only to assist the team, their failure had narrowed the time available to carry out the attack if any of them wanted to get back to the rendezvous with the *Spiteful* before dying of dehydration.

Although the wet-bulb temperature—the combination of heat and humidity beyond which the human body simply shut down—did not rise to a level to threaten any of them, the forty-five-degree daytime heat gave Rory's pink skin a constant sheen of stickiness he could not alleviate.

The cooler nights offered some respite. During the previous one, from August 6 to 7, all of the team members had left the LUP to reconnoitre the plant. Rory had gone with Harry Dixon to establish how to knock out what they deduced was the building in which the enemy's ACA power plants were either manufactured or assembled. On their return, Nick Bird and Declan Gardner insisted they'd identified the final assembly building, from which they'd witnessed the multiple launches the previous day.

Now that darkness had fallen and the temperature had begun a gradual drop from its furnace-like heat, all five men gathered in the LUP for a final briefing before conducting the attack. Surrounded by the four remaining Triumphs and their kit, the darkness in their hiding place deepened.

"Right, chaps," Hastings began, stroking his pencil-thin moustache with the knuckle of his index finger, "does everyone have his proper compliment of sonic mines?"

Murmurs of confirmation emanated from the others. Rory looked at the ground in front of him, on which sat the strange devices that were supposedly powerful enough to destroy the entire facility. Black slabs fifty by fifteen centimetres, ten centimetres thick, and weighing a hefty two kilos.

"Now," Hastings went on, "it's taken us a tad longer than we'd hoped, but we're still on schedule. I will leave the LUP first as I have the most ground to cover. I will go north, then west, then track south for a kilometre to the building we suspect is the armaments plant.

"Dixon and Moore, you follow twenty minutes later. Go to the northernmost perimeter and set your mines as close to the largest building as you can. That is where the finished ACAs leave this facility.

"Bird and Gardner, you have the least distance to your target. Therefore, you will leave the LUP last, twenty minutes after Dixon and Moore. You go to the eastern perimeter and set your mines at the power unit production building. And if we're lucky," Hastings added with obvious relish, "that should go up like a powder keg."

Rory shivered as he realised the time had arrived. He recalled the original summons to travel to see the general and Heaton's mocking joke. It had led him here, to be with these comrades in the middle of enemy territory, about to attempt something vital to the war effort.

From his pocket, Hastings held up a small, bottle-shaped device between his right index finger and thumb, just visible in the dimness. He said, "This is the trigger that will start the shaft inside the sonic mines rotating. It operates on the now-defunct frequency modulation waveband—another calculated risk. Although, if any of the enemy does happen to detect the brief burst of radio waves, he shan't know what it portends. The shaft inside each mine is set to a gradual acceleration that will give me thirty minutes to evacuate the immediate area."

Rory sensed doubt among the others, although none of them asked the question if half an hour would be enough for the general to get clear.

Dixon said, in his plumiest accent, "I should think that will be ample time for you to reach a safe distance, sir."

Hastings nodded, "Quite so." He put the trigger back in his pocket. "Despite Moore having to ride all the way back as pillion on Dixon's bike, we will still stick to our original evac plan. Bird and Gardner, place your mines, return here, get your bikes, and be on your way. We will hear you leave; thus, if you have a problem, we'll be able to deduce that.

"Dixon and Moore, ditto. Place your mines and come back to the LUP. I will do the same. I want the first pair to have a good head start before you two leave. I shall wait a further thirty minutes, then return to the plant on my bike, detonate the mines, and follow you out."

"Piece of cake," Dixon said.

Hastings continued, "As Bird is the navigator, he and Gardner will find an alternate route back to the rendezvous at the coast. Dixon and I shall endeavour to retrace our steps, more or less, on the route by which we arrived here. Let's get prepared."

Rory went back to his kit and grabbed his night-vision googles now full darkness had descended on the LUP. He and Harry Dixon organised their kit in silence, which, Rory reflected, was easy given how often they'd rehearsed those parts of the operation that were predictable.

All five of them stood ready. Hastings asked again, "Any questions?"

Nick said with a smile, "If this all works out, you are buying the beers when we get back to Blighty, ain't you, sir?"

A determined smile creased the general's face and he replied, "It shall be an honour to invite all of you as my guests to my club in Kensington on our return."

Nick gave the others a look as though he'd won an unexpected prize.

Dixon leaned towards the general and said, "I'm not sure the Twenty-nine will be very pleased—"

Hastings frowned at Dixon, shook his head, and tutted. Dixon became quiet. The general eyed all of them in turn and said, "Men, we've come a long way to carry out this raid. The enemy, we can be fairly certain, is doing all he can to harry our comrades in Europe. It is now up to us to throw quite a large spanner in the works. Whatever happens in the next few hours, this mission is the priority—not any single one of us."

Rory just wanted to get on with it, but he understood the need for the general's peptalk.

Hastings concluded, "We've trained for this. And we're ready." He collected his kit and left the LUP.

No one spoke as the minutes passed by. Any apprehension Rory felt was tempered with relief that the mission had reached its key phase. Finally, the time came for Rory and Harry to leave the LUP.

Rory collected his own kit and nodded to the chipper cockney Nick Bird and the dour Irishman Declan Gardner. "See you at the rendezvous."

Rory and Harry emerged out into the open and proceeded to their objective without speaking. After a further twenty minutes of trudging over shale and sand, the two men approached the target. In his mind's eye, Rory replayed memories of the discussions the team had held during the weeks of training and the days on the submarine. They all accepted that traditional military tactics like camouflage and silent movement held almost no benefit if the enemy detected them. Besides which, crawling along on their stomachs to keep the lowest profile would've been completely unworkable given the distances they had to cover.

But now, trying to traverse the sloping shale and rock towards a huge enemy building in the starlit desert night, made Rory feel as if a Spider could descend on them at any moment—and he had neither Squitch to warn him nor Pickup to defend against it.

Off to his left lay the city of Tazirbu. He eyed it in curiosity. Bright green hues emanated from it. He asked Harry, "Is it me, or is that place noisier than it was last night?"

Harry stood still and tilted his head. He replied, "You might have a point, there. Perhaps, though, it just seems louder because of our change in location?"

"Maybe."

"The LUP deadened all sound. Now, we're on-mission so our senses are heightened and we're seeing the city from a different angle."

Rory didn't answer, unsure if Harry's observations were credible. They went on. The shale became sand and the going became heavier. Rory could see only shades of dark green through the goggles. The desert remained silent and the air warm from the day's heat absorbed by the ground.

At length, they reached the perimeter of the facility, a chain-link fence. Harry took out his wire cutters, but Rory stopped him when inspiration suddenly struck.

"Maybe we don't need to cut them? Maybe we can dig under it?"

Harry shrugged, jabbed the cutters back in his webbing, and began scooping out handfuls of sand from the base of the fence. Rory joined him, but after a moment it became clear that whoever built the fence had considered that eventuality.

Harry whispered to Rory, "We just have to trust the intel. It said they only have barebones security to keep unauthorised locals out. They can't even imagine an attack from outside."

Rory nodded his agreement.

With care, Harry opened the jaws of the cutters, placed them over a link of the fence, and snapped them closed. The metal cut with a dull snap.

Rory held his breath. Nothing happened; no alarms, no searchlights, no shouts of concern. "Fuck's sake, let's get on with it," Rory hissed, extracting his own cutters.

Quickly but with methodical precision, Rory snipped up one side of the fence while Harry did the same next to him. Then, they cut towards each other. They created a gap large enough for each to crawl through and pushed the severed part of the fence down into the sand. Harry crawled through first; Rory followed.

Bent over, they ran for the nearest building. Rory scanned in front of them but spied no blobs of green brightness to signal a warm body that might see them. The building they reached was constructed of sheer metal sheets, corrugated vertically.

"Back here in sixty seconds—go," Harry whispered. He ran to the south.

Rory ran in the opposite direction. He counted twenty paces, stopped, took out a sonic mine, and placed it at the base of the metal sheet. He flicked some sand on it to hide it. He stood, ran, and repeated the placement of four more mines, relieved at the lessening weight he had to carry. With the last one lightly covered in sand, Rory turned and sprinted back. At set distances, he noticed small depressions in the metal and wondered what they were for. He quickly decided he didn't give a shit.

Harry arrived at their starting point just before Rory. "All done?" he asked, panting.

"Yes," Rory replied. "Can we fuck off now?"

Harry smiled. "Jolly good idea."

They withdrew to the chain-link fence and crawled through.

Rory asked Harry, "Should we pull it back up—?"

"Shit, hold everything," Harry uttered.

Still heaving for breath, Rory looked back towards the building. Bright green shapeless masses had appeared and were moving towards their position. The unidentified people were still some distance away, but they proceeded inexorably in Rory and Harry's direction.

Rory lay flat on the sand and whispered to Harry, "I threw some sand over my mines to hide them."

"Good idea."

"Did you?"

"No."

"Twat."

The minutes passed. Rory watched the green bodies advance. Aping Harry's posh accent, he whispered, "If those buggers spot those mines, we'll be for the chop, old boy."

Harry whispered back, "Ha-fucking-ha, peasant. Now decide what you prefer."

"What?"

Harry reached down and extracted his semiautomatic pistol. He showed it to Rory.

Rory understood. He did the same as the Royal Anglian and said, "When the fight's over, they'll still display our bodies for the global media like they did with those unlucky SAS guys back in '58."

"I should think so," Harry replied. "But we'll be dead so I don't expect we'll be too bothered, wouldn't you say?"

Rory observed, "They're getting closer."

The bright green blobs walked along the side of the building. Slight variations in brilliance when they passed each corrugation denoted their rate of approach. Rory's heart thumped harder when he realised how this had to end. If those enemy guards were soldiers and they were equipped with even modest modern technology, he and Harry stood no chance of escape. It was one thing to cross vast expanses of wholly inhospitable and unpopulated desert in the hope that sheer scale would allow them to evade detection, but two NATO soldiers lying next to a cut fence around the enemy's most important munitions facility were certain to be discovered, modern tech or not.

The guards stopped. Rory heard their mutterings. One of them took a few paces away from the others and urinated, the sound of the stream landing in the sand unnervingly loud. He re-joined his comrades and the conversation resumed. Minutes passed. The guards became more animated in their discussion. Rory swapped a confused glance with Harry, feeling certain that Harry was thinking the same thing.

Finally, the guards withdrew, plodding away from the NATO soldiers with an agonising slowness but still debating in loud voices.

Rory turned to Harry and whispered, "What the fuck were they doing? Were they patrolling or what? My guts are in knots."

Harry whispered back, "Probably they're supposed to patrol around the whole place, but didn't feel like it for whatever reason."

"I dunno," Rory said, "that city feels… agitated. Maybe they've got other things on their minds than just tedious stag duty?"

"We shouldn't speculate. Let's get back to the LUP."

Rory followed Harry bent over as they scurried away. The sand became shale and they jogged upright, lighter without the sonic mines. Twenty minutes later, they reached the plateau, and hurried down the other side and into the LUP.

"And what the devil are you two still doing here?" the general demanded, sitting on his motorbike.

"Sorry, sir," Harry replied. "We were delayed by the presence of patrolling guards."

Hastings scoffed and said, "I can see they didn't detect you, so can I also assume the mission has not been compromised?"

Harry nodded and replied, "Yes, sir. You can."

Rory said, "Those guards must've been hanging around longer than it seemed. Although it felt like hours to me."

The general put his hands on the handlebars of his Triumph and said, "Well, the sonic mines have been activated and are building up to critical mass. So, I think it would be prudent to retire to a safe distance, gentlemen."

Harry had already begun pushing his motorbike, and on hearing the general's words, Rory placed his own hands on the back of the seat and gave it a shove. When clear of the LUP, the engines on the two bikes roared into life and carried the three soldiers away.

General Hastings flagged Harry to stop when, by Rory's reckoning, they'd covered about twelve kilometres. They alighted the machines and stood facing the distant ACA production plant. To the east of that dark mass on the horizon, the city of Tazirbu glowed brighter than it had when they'd been approaching it, and the hour was getting late. Rory wondered about the significance of this.

"How much longer, sir?" Harry asked.

"Any minute now," the general replied with understated confidence.

"Do you really think those sonic mines could cause so much damage as we expect?" Rory asked.

Hastings replied, "They have to. If Operation Repulse is to succeed."

Rory shivered despite the heat.

Minutes passed.

Nothing happened.

Harry asked the general, "Is it possible that the mines could've detonated without our being aware of it at this distance?"

Rory glanced at Hastings to see a thoughtful expression on the man's face. The general stroked his pencil-thin moustache with the knuckle of his right index finger and said, "No. They are a type of munition that either works frightfully well or does not work at all. And it is clear they have not detonated."

"Shit," Rory muttered.

"Can we ascertain what might have gone wrong?" Harry asked.

Hastings shrugged and replied, "Either the mines or the trigger. The mines have been sealed since manufacture; therefore, if the problem is with them, there is nothing we can do."

Rory offered, "A bit unlikely that all of the mines would malfunction at the same time, isn't it?"

"Very much so," the general agreed. "Which leaves us with the trigger."

Harry asked, "Did you not get some kind of confirmation that the signal had been received by the mines and the shafts had started rotating?"

Hastings shook his head. "No. The type of frequency modulation the trigger uses doesn't work like that. In keeping with everything else on this mission, frequency modulation is quite thoroughly outdated."

Rory glanced at the other men, aware that he was the outsider. Harry had known the general for years, and now Rory sensed that he was watching both of them from a distance.

Hastings shook his head and said, "No, it must be the trigger. Has to be. Perhaps I was too far away when I fired it?" He paused and then ordered, "Dixon, you and Moore leave the area, return to the rendezvous, and meet up with Bird and Gardner there. I will return to the facility and see if I can correct the problem."

Harry said, "Sir, if I may, two heads might be better than one, here. Moore can take my bike and I can ride pillion with—"

"No," Hastings broke in. "I will do this alone."

"Very good, sir," Harry replied at once.

Harry's swift acquiescence surprised Rory, until he realised that that was how a professional subordinate should behave.

Hastings made to get back on his motorbike. "Right. Good luck, chaps. See you at the rendezvous."

Harry stuck his hand out and said, "Er, sir, would you like some extra water in case you're delayed for any reason?"

"No, thank you, captain," Hastings replied. He kicked the lever on his bike down and the engine started. Without another word, the general accelerated back towards the enemy's ACA production facility.

Rory waited a space of time he deemed respectful and said, "Right, we'd better get going, eh?"

Harry turned and stared at Rory. "Oh, we're not going anywhere."

"I think the general's orders were quite specific."

"Yes, but I'm not leaving here... yet."

Rory didn't know how to react. Harry Dixon was a snob, but a pretty okay one. And up to now, the sense of teamwork among all five of them had overridden any personality frictions.

Rory decided to compromise. He asked, "How long are you prepared to wait?"

"That depends. If the place goes up, we'll be out of here like... what is it you lower-class-types say? 'Shit off a shovel', yes?"

Rory let out a mirthless chuckle. "Yeah, something like that."

"Yes, if the general succeeds, we shan't wait for him. But if nothing happens? I don't know."

"We need to agree a time limit, Harry. We can't wait another day; we don't have the water."

"Fair comment." Harry looked at his wristwatch. "It's a half an hour to midnight. Let's give it another hour."

"That will mean riding in the morning daylight. We'll miss the morning rendezvous and have to wait it out for when the *Spiteful* next comes up at seven in the evening."

"I know."

Rory sensed the feeling of conflict growing and wanted to diffuse it.

Harry suddenly said, "It's only that I don't want to abandon him just yet."

"'Abandon'? I'd say that out of the five of us, he's the one most likely to make it out of here."

"The general's not a young man anymore."

Rory didn't answer. He turned away and gave his comrade space. Time passed. Rory counted out the first twenty minutes. The night was cooler than the previous one, and the dazzling array of stars in the sky glittered with the promise of a different future. Rory kept on pacing in a circle around Harry and the bike. He thought and considered and wondered where all this would—

"My god, look," Harry announced, his chiselled jaw open in wonder.

Rory spun around to peer at the horizon. He thought his eyes deceived him. At this distance, the buildings looked like tiny dominoes slumping over, one sagging onto its fellow and knocking that one over. He strode back to join Harry close to the Triumph. The minute shapes toppled and threw up billows of dust and sand. Rory stared agape, realising that the destruction must be vast. Clouds of debris rose high into the desert night, obscuring the entire area where the plant had been.

"And more, over there," Rory said, indicating the city next to the facility. The brightness increased so Rory lifted up the night-vision goggles. He was glad he did so, for the sky above Tazirbu abruptly exploded in a blinding orange glare that, incredibly, made the plumes obscuring the facility look modest by comparison.

Rory muttered, "That's some seriously pissed off ragheads, right there."

Harry laughed. "They sowed the wind," he hissed in vindictive jubilation.

"What?"

Harry looked at Rory with a sudden frown. He repeated, "They sowed the wind."

Rory knew Harry alluded to something but couldn't think what. "Whatever," he responded.

Harry tutted and replied, as though explaining to a simpleton, "And they shall reap the whirlwind."

"If you say so, captain."

"God, you're such a pleb."

Rory saw his smile reflected on Harry's face. "I think we should leg it," he said.

Suddenly, the rock beneath their boots trembled and then shuddered. Terror gripped Rory when he thought it was some kind of earthquake. Harry's arms snapped out and grabbed Rory's shoulders. Rory grasped Harry's elbows. The tremor lasted six seconds and stopped. Stillness returned and the surface under Rory's feet felt as stable and immobile as it should. The two men let go of each other.

"Come on," Harry urged. "We've a long way to go." He climbed on the Triumph, flicked the kick-starter out and started the engine.

Rory got on the bike. The machine bit when Harry engaged first gear. The engine revved, Harry turned the wheel, and Rory took a last glimpse of the remains of the ACA production plant and the now-destroyed enemy city of Tazirbu.

Chapter 24

23.55 Tuesday 7 August 2063

Serena Rizzi fought to control her emotions. Although she, Liliana and Tiphanie remained safe from the violence that raged outside Father's huge palace, she sensed how the recent weeks of civil unrest had begun to coalesce here in Tehran.

From the first-floor window of her servants' quarters, the horizon glowed with the orange of distant fires. Her gaze drifted down to the gardens, a beautifully laid-out forest of tall palms and citrus trees up-lit by soft yellow lights in the ground. She could make out shadowy figures among them—guards who hurried to the outer wall, their boots squeaking on the marble pathways. Reflexively, her right hand touched the sheath strapped to the inside of her left forearm, hidden by her *abaya*. It contained a stiletto blade in case Kasro or Hormoz or Aziz or any other of the 'men' attempted to sexually assault her.

Now, eighteen months since Caliphate warriors had kidnapped her from her beloved Rome, Serena had at last gained some level of fluency in Farsi. She still utilised the

Italian translations that resolved digitally in the air next to the speaker due to the implant, but she used these for confirmation—not to understand.

A familiar voice spoke from behind her. "There you are."

"Could you not sleep, sister?" Serena replied without turning around.

Liliana's waifish form arrived at Serena's side, concern on her young face. "Who do you think is causing it this time?" she asked.

"I am not sure," Serena replied. "I only hope, as always, these disturbances are in support of the Third Caliph and not against him."

Liliana let out a scoff. "There are not enough weapons being fired for it to be any kind of uprising against his evil empire."

"I am glad you are taking more interest in our surroundings, sister," Serena said with a smile.

Liliana looked up and replied, "Tiphanie has helped me understand. In some ways, she is very clever."

"Oh, yes," Serena agreed. "She has not been here as long as us, but her command of their language is as good as mine."

Liliana sighed and said, "I cannot make any progress with it, sister. I struggle so much to remember the sounds the symbols represent—"

"Hush," Serena said. "It does not matter. Each of us has skills that can support the other two. And together, we can—"

Footsteps padded into the room. Tiphanie came up to the others at the window and, with a shocked smile on her face, hissed, "You will not believe what has happened."

"Oh?" Liliana said.

Tiphanie smiled mischievously and replied, "I was eavesdropping outside Father's bedroom. He and his wife were arguing—"

"You should be more careful," Serena insisted.

The glint in Tiphanie's eye concerned and excited Serena. The Frenchwoman had grown to exude a liking for danger that Serena thought might help in the future, a far cry from the timid creature who Ahmed had found to assist them nearly a year ago.

Tiphanie replied, "There is little risk, sister. Father is often worried, and his wife always tries to make him think he is wrong. And I believe he is cleverer than that."

"So, what did you eavesdrop?" Liliana asked with a mix of curiosity and fear.

Tiphanie paused and looked behind them. The room was quiet and still but for the three European slaves. She said, "There is news of a huge earthquake from the west of the Caliphate, in the desert."

Serena frowned and asked, "How is that possible?"

Tiphanie said, "I do not know if it is possible or not, sister. I only know what I heard. I only had a few seconds, after all. But the agitation sounded severe to me. Father's wife was most upset."

Liliana asked, "Did anyone see you?"

Tiphanie shook her head.

Serena said, "So, is this 'earthquake' the reason for these riots tonight?"

"I do not believe so," Tiphanie answered. "I still think too many warriors are here. They cause—"

"You there," cried a new voice.

Tiphanie turned and stopped at the sight of Ahmed, suddenly standing in the doorway, his black *kandora* hiding his form. He stepped forwards and hissed, "Despite my protests, your exalted owner insists you slaves must be spared. Leave here and go to the cellars in the east wing."

Serena asked, "Is this house in such danger?"

An accusatory finger shot out and Ahmed said, "Do not dare to question your owner's orders, slave." He turned and hurried from the room.

"He seems more concerned than usual," Liliana said.

"Come along," Serena urged. "This is not the first time Father's house has been close to danger in this backwards, medieval place."

The three western women gathered the folds of their *abayas*. Each returned to her bed and small, ill-made drawer. Serena tidied her things and stopped at the door to hurry Liliana and Tiphanie. Together, they strode across the hall to the servants' lift. It arrived and the chrome doors opened with a whine.

"Oh, it's you," said a startled Aziz, the young cook on whom Serena had expended much effort to cultivate as a source of information.

Serena led the others into the lift, which could hold ten. She addressed Aziz in his own language: "Did you not expect us to come from the slaves' quarters?"

The doors whined closed and the lift jolted downwards.

Aziz replied with breezy confidence, "Not at all. We all know how Father dotes on his favourite slaves, so I assumed you would have already left."

Serena caught the implied accusation and asked, "What do you mean, 'favourite slaves'? We are but three among a staff of thirty or more."

Aziz tilted his head and leered. He said, "You should be careful. If the lady of the house were to hear of the rumours—"

"Shut your mouth, puppy dog," Tiphanie said in French.

Aziz's face dropped in anger when he understood the translation.

Serena put her hand on Tiphanie's arm, feeling the clenched muscle there, and said, "There are no rumours, Aziz."

The lift shuddered to a stop and the doors opened. Serena waited for Aziz to exit, then flashed Tiphanie a look urging caution before following the young cook.

The narrow, dark corridor in which they found themselves opened out into a poorly lit cavern with smooth walls and the smell of clean metal. This was the palace's garage, a vast space full of autonomous vehicles. She led the others towards a more brightly lit area at the far end. Most of the palace staff milled about there, muttering and shuffling in apparent concern. A hint of jasmine carried on the air.

Serena ignored the odd glance of disdain from the female staff and the lingering looks from the men when they arrived at the group.

Ahmed emerged at the front. He motioned to someone with a bony finger. A boy Serena recognised from working the grounds fetched a circular container. Ahmed stepped up onto it. He turned and addressed those present, "Listen, all of you. There is a possibility that we will have to leave here."

Gasps of shock echoed among the group. Serena noted that an Italian translation had not resolved in the air next to him, thus deducing that he must have instructed the computers not to translate for the European slaves. Serena smiled in grim satisfaction at Ahmed's failed attempt to hide the truth from her.

The old man continued, his right shoulder lifting up when he spoke, as if he were trying to morph into a hunchback. "Our exalted Third Caliph has passed a decree to introduce greater restrictions on travel for the majority of Caliphate subjects. Therefore, we can shortly expect the fuss in the streets to end."

Ahmed coughed into the sleeve of his black *kandora*, and Serena was grateful for the pause. She struggled to translate his words in her head, and anger at herself flashed inside when she realised how much she still relied on the Italian translations.

Ahmed went on, "However, our illustrious Father has asked that we remain here until we are certain any danger has passed. In addition, and as some of you may have heard, some kind of natural disaster has befallen our blessed Caliphate this night. It appears an earthquake has struck a city in the central district of Sahara Province. Many subjects have perished, and we should pray for their souls to find peace in Allah's embrace."

Serena hid a smile at the bad news that Ahmed believed she could not understand. She noted how stilted his enunciation became when mentioning this apparent earthquake, and decided his naturally vicious nature meant he found it impossible to show a sympathy he could never feel.

Ahmed finished with, "Tea will now be served," and stepped down from the container.

Serena spun round to see Liliana staring up at her with her face creased in confusion. Tiphanie wore a scowl, and Serena guessed that the Frenchwoman had not been able to follow everything. She drew them close to her and whispered, "I will tell you later. Let us wait for everyone else to go first and then get some tea, if any remains."

Chapter 25

01.56 Wednesday 8 August 2063

The gentle vibration of the slate under his right hand took time to penetrate the depth of Terry Tidbury's sleep. Awareness encroached slowly before accelerating. Terry lay in the darkness and allowed his senses to return. He reflected how precious the act of sleeping had become. Pre-war, he never gave it much thought. But now, any block of sleep went deep into his limbs. He felt as though his muscles had atrophied and his bones were made of lead.

He tapped the slate to stop it vibrating. Maureen's gentle breathing continued by his side, and he endeavoured to leave the bed without disturbing her. Joints creaked when he sat up, and he wondered if he shouldn't yield to Simms's occasional suggestion to increase the frequency of his medical examinations. But then, whichever doctor had the misfortune to be on duty would try to persuade Terry to have some of those blasted nanobots put in his body to monitor things. And Terry regarded nanobots with a similar disdain as the lens.

Three minutes later, Terry stood at the work surface in his kitchen, the door to the corridor closed so he could speak normally with no risk of disturbing Maureen. Bubbles of water in the glass kettle flicked and flashed and grew as the liquid heated. His heart cantered in his chest while he waited. The kettle boiled. He made his tea and sat at the breakfast bar. He took the first sip. The hot, malty liquid activated his body like a machine that had been switched on.

"Contact the War Rooms," he instructed.

The screen next to the breakfast bar glowed and blinked. The tired face of his adjutant, Simms, appeared. "Good morning, Sir Terry," he said in a voice that tried to suggest that everything was business as usual.

Terry gave him a tight smile and said, "What's happened?"

Simms replied, "Several seismic monitoring stations around the world are reporting the occurrence of an earthquake in North Africa. The quake measured seven-point-six on the Richter scale."

"There is no doubt?" Terry asked.

"None whatsoever," Simms confirmed. "Else, as per our arrangements, I would not have awoken you."

"Indeed. Did the earthquake happen as we expected?"

"The event had a duration of six-point-zero-two seconds, sir, and even as we speak, news outlets are questioning the veracity of the numbers. No such kind of earthquake has ever been recorded before, and certainly never before in the middle of the North African desert."

"Summarise the speculation."

"Entire guesswork, sir. From huge conventional missiles to nuclear weapons to false-flag operations by the en—"

"What has the enemy said?"

"No official statement yet, Sir Terry."

Terry lifted the mug of tea and sipped in thoughtful consideration. He said, "So, Hastings actually pulled it off?"

"Er," Simms hesitated, "the general did quite a bit more than that."

"Oh? How so?"

"I took the liberty of contacting Professor Hill, the head of Seismic Monitoring in Florida, who was involved in assessing the tsunami that caused so much damage to America last October, primarily to verify what Squonk was telling us."

"And?"

"And according to him, not only the ACA production facility, but also the entire city of Tazirbu, has been levelled."

"Destroying the city and its population does not necessarily aid us militarily. Although," Terry added on reflection, "flattening that as well as the objective should give our enemy something to think about. An 'act of god' comparable to the tsunami he caused last year."

"Quite so, sir."

Terry took another pull on the mug of tea, which tasted even richer. He said, "Very well. Simms, give the con over to one of the LGs until I get to the War Rooms later in the morning. Go and get some rest."

"Very good, sir."

"Any news on Hastings and his team, yet?"

"No, sir. We shan't be sure until the *Spiteful* returns to England."

"Hmm. So, let's hope for the best for all of them. I should like to buy the general and his team a drink on their return."

Simms nodded and the screen went blank. Plunged back into darkness, Terry watched the residual outline of the screen dance on his retina as he cast his eyes about the kitchen. The image faded and the dark outlines of real objects materialised. He said, "Squonk? Speculate on the success of Operation Thunderclap and its impact on Operation Repulse."

The super AI spoke from somewhere above him, "Based on currently available data, the sonic mines performed at one-hundred-and-seven percent of anticipated effectiveness—"

"Why so high?"

"The most probable cause was specific atmospheric conditions that enhanced the ultra-low sound waves' destructive capability."

"Continue."

"The ACA production facility has certainly been destroyed. The most accurate estimate is that it will remain inoperative for between five to ten weeks. However, it is also highly likely that the facility will be reconstructed to produce the enemy's next generation of ACAs."

"I don't doubt it," Terry muttered. "Can we stay ahead of them in weapons' development and production?"

"The destruction of the facility at Tazirbu has put the balance of probabilities in the favour of NATO forces."

"Take all possible steps to refine and, where possible, advance the timetable for Repulse."

"Confirmed."

Chapter 26

10.56 Wednesday 8 August 2063

"Christ Jesus, Harry. We don't have time for this," Rory exclaimed.

"You did the dead reckoning—"

"We followed the map and until the last twenty klicks, and we were bang on the money. And even I'm not capable of fucking up dead reckoning over a lousy twenty klicks." Rory stomped away from Harry, who was sitting on the bike, and approached the blue water of the Mediterranean, the overpowering heat lessening a fraction with the slight sea breeze.

"Let's head east," Harry insisted.

Rory spun around and replied, "I really think the nearest cylinder is west."

Harry's shoulders slumped and Rory abruptly caught the impression that the captain might be feeling worse than he was letting on. The ride across the desert had been draining even though they'd benefitted from the experience of the outward journey. They'd needed to make fewer diversions and they'd also taken fewer breaks. Rory rode the bike for nearly half of the journey, nudging Harry awake when the captain's body sagged onto his own.

Rory approached Harry and said, "You look just about on your chinstrap, captain."

Harry waved an ineffectual hand, "Nearest cylinder's east," he insisted. He sat bolt upright on the bike and said, "Feeling a bit rum, actually, old chap." He put both hands on the handlebars and steadied himself.

Fear grew inside Rory. They could find the cylinders and then make the rendezvous, but not if one of them were injured or incapacitated. The heat had been outrageous; their water was almost gone, but they'd stuck to their schedule, no dramas. The mission had become extended, but no more than they'd trained for, and not as bad as the worst-case scenario they'd war-gamed in training.

Thirst clawed at Rory's throat and his limbs ached. He had a permanent headache from the relentless burning sunshine and his skin was sticky with a constant sheen of dull, warm sweat that made him despise the heat causing it. He looked at Captain Dixon and said, "You Royal Anglians really need to learn to be proper soldiers. Let me ride the bike."

"Ha, ha, pleb," Harry replied, but the humour had gone out of his eyes.

Rory helped Harry move back to the pillion seat and mounted the machine. He kicked-started the engine.

Rory pulled Harry's arms around his waist and yelled, "Hold on, okay?"

"Yes, peasant," came to Rory's ears and the Royal Engineer smiled. He kicked the bike into gear and revved the engine. He turned the bike to the west. Harry's head lolled against Rory's shoulders but the man's grip around Rory's waist remained firm. Rory silently promised that never again would he despoil the name of the Royal Anglian regiment.

After fighting to keep the Triumph upright on the sand and just as he was beginning to lose hope, in the distance the cone of a cylinder poking out from a dune came into view. Rory checked his excitement lest it transpired to be a mirage or some piece of debris, but as the bike chugged nearer to the object, relief lent Rory a fraction more strength.

"Okay, we're good, Harry. We've found a cylinder."

"Said they were east and I was right, wasn't I?"

"Absolutely, old chap," Rory replied.

"Don't get too smart, pleb."

Rory opened the throttle and sped along the expansive beach. He stopped at the cylinder, dismounted and stomped through the sand. He checked its unique designation number to confirm it was the westernmost of all of the cylinders. The fourth cylinder from this end was the agreed rendezvous point, from where they would swim out to the *Spiteful*.

He got back on the motorbike, noting that his comrade seemed better. Rory said, "Not long now, fella. Two klicks along this beach and we'll meet the others."

Harry just patted Rory on the shoulder and clasped his arms around Rory's waist. Rory motored along the beach. He couldn't wait to be reunited with the others. He was certain the renewed camaraderie would ensure they'd all make it back to the submarine.

He rode past the protruding nosecone of the second cylinder, and then the third. The beach curved to the south and they arrived at the fourth cylinder.

It was deserted.

He stopped the motorbike, dismounted and peered from where they'd just come, doubting if he'd counted the correct number of cylinders.

Harry got off the bike and then sat back down on the seat conventionally rather than astride. He sighed. "You're sure this is the fourth one?" he asked, sounding like a drunk.

Rory turned back and forth, staring along the beach, desperately hoping for any sign of the others. He left Harry and trotted inland. He scrabbled up the nearest dune, his boots sinking in the fine, dry, hot sand. But at every point on the landward compass, there was no movement.

He galloped down the dune and returned to Harry. He said, "We're on our own."

"Bugger."

"We've still got a few hours before the rendezvous," Rory offered, trying to stay positive.

Harry shook his head. "Bird and Gardner should've been here by now."

"Maybe they were quick and made the seven o'clock rendezvous this morning?"

Harry shook his head. "No way. Too many obstacles, diversions."

Rory replied, "Reckon so. Nick and Declan would've had to cover the distance from Tazirbu without a break or any diversion to have arrived and got to the sub in the morning."

Harry said, "And I do believe the general has also bought it."

"Why?"

"Something you don't know about, I'm afraid."

"Oh?"

"The trigger. He didn't like the frequency modulation method of starting the mines' rotation. So, he had a signal booster added as a last resort. A failsafe, if you like. Problem was that it meant the mines would go off in less than a minute and he'd not be able to get clear."

"But then why did you offer—?"

Harry smiled ruefully. He looked askance at Rory, his head lolling. "That's why I offered to go with him. To keep him from using it and giving the main method another try. But he knew the whole mission was reaching a point where it might fail." Harry gave a shrug and summarised, "We were delayed. We had too many obstacles. And those blasted moisturisers packed up. I knew he was going back to make sure we didn't fail… and, true to the man, he didn't fail."

Rory protested, "But we're not even in our worst-case scenar—"

"We are beyond it, you pleb," Harry broke in with what Rory thought was a supreme effort. "Look at us. We're out of water."

"Almost."

"And whatever's happened to Nick and Declan, they're also out of water. Only they're not here, at the coast, but somewhere in there," he nodded his head behind him, "thousands of square kilometres of inhospitable desert." Harry's head lolled again.

Rory said, "Save your energy, Harry. We've got to get through the next few hours and reach the sub. I'm not giving up on any of them." Rory looked inland, to the blazing furnace of the North African desert, and heard his words ring hollow. He took out the last of the water and salt tablets, took a sip enough to swallow two tablets, and gave the rest of his water to Harry.

When Harry had drunk the water and taken the tablets, Rory pulled him inland. He found a nearby depression behind a low dune and decided to call it an LUP. He extracted both BHC sleeves from his and Harry's trousers, and pulled them open. He covered Harry first and then himself, the silver material hopefully throwing a fraction of the overbearing heat back out into the sky.

Rory's headache worsened. He dozed and his dry lips cracked when he woke with a start, thinking he might have heard the distant roar of a motorbike. But it always turned out to be the sea breeze blowing grains of sand on the BHC sleeves covering them. He willed the others to come to him, while on some deeper level he accepted that they would not.

Somehow, the agonising waiting passed. One hour before the rendezvous, he wanted to get into the water. He nudged Harry, "Come on, time to rock and roll."

Harry came to and said, "Right. Yes, give me a minute."

"How are you feeling?"

"Still pretty rum, actually. Is it time to go for a swim?"

"Yes. Can you?"

"If the water will relieve this blessed heat."

Harry moved and Rory was reassured by the last vestige of defiance in the man's eyes.

Harry said, "Shouldn't we bury the bike?"

Rory threw him a withering look and replied, "If you want to, captain, go ahead and I'll say fuckety-bye now, then."

Harry gave Rory a smile that was only half-grimace.

"Wait here," Rory told him. "I'll be back in five."

Rory returned to the nearest cylinder, removed the cone, and upended it. From the protective packaging and other detritus, he found two of the harnesses they'd used to tow the cylinders from the submarine to the shore.

He returned to Harry and said, "Come on, Captain Dixon. Time to catch our ride out of this open-air oven."

"All right, old chap. I'm not a complete cripple," Harry said when Rory made to help him up. Together they reached the waves. Even the sea felt like warm, watery treacle. Rory put one harness around his waist and helped Harry with the other.

"Think I won't make it, eh?" Harry said.

"We need to swim the better part of two klicks in an hour. And the only thing we've got going for us is that we weigh less than we did on the way in."

"How do you always keep being able to get the positives out of everything?"

Rory chuckled and replied, "Because I am a Royal Engineer. And with the harness, if you try and let me down again, I'll drag you along myself."

Harry's face suddenly lit up. He croaked, "Race you," and ran into the waves.

Rory shook his head and followed. His concern that Harry would dehydrate increased. He knew he could not pull his comrade any great length through the water. At the outset, however, Harry surprised Rory by making good progress. The lanyard that connected them was long enough that each could make his own way. But as time passed, Rory pulled ahead. The shore lay far behind them when the lanyard first became taut. Rory stopped swimming. The waves undulated but he could not make Harry out. He pulled the lanyard and coiled it around his shoulders to maintain tautness.

He reached Harry. The Royal Anglian flailed and gasped for air.

"Stop it," Rory advised.

The man made no response. Rory cupped a hand under Harry's chin and began the standard rescue stroke, pulling his delirious comrade through the water. Panic gripped him. With the gentle swell buffeting both of them, he lost sight of the coast and couldn't be sure in which direction he headed. His world became a wet, directionless, undulating, agonising struggle to keep both of them afloat.

A dull metallic thump came to his ears. He craned his head painfully to see the black mass of *HMS Spiteful* bearing down on them no more than twenty metres away. Rory's strength deserted him. He heard the flop of a cargo net being thrown down the side of the submarine's vast hull. The sounds of splashes and shouts reached him.

Arms grabbed his torso, strong and determined. A coarse voice demanded, "We're expecting five of you. Where are the others?"

"Didn't make it," Rory muttered, relief at their rescue flooding his exhausted body; regret at the team's losses flooding his exhausted spirit.

Three hours later, Rory had recovered and sat in the same wardroom in which the general had held his final briefing a mere seven days earlier. But Harry remained in sickbay. Alone, Rory had the room to extend his legs, not needing to wedge them under the table with the faded walnut veneer. He grabbed the jug of water on the table and poured a glass of the cold water. He glugged it down and the chilled sensation in his chest refreshed him immeasurably. He stared at the skin on his forearms, dry and free of sweat for the first time in days.

The door clicked open and a tall, diffident woman stepped over the flange, ducking a little so her Royal Navy cap did not snag on the doorway. She introduced herself, "Executive Officer Pettifer," and stuck out a slender hand.

Rory leaned forward, too tired to stand, shook her hand and said, "We've met."

The woman's narrow face creased in momentary confusion. She said, "Ah, yes. Corporal Moore. I thought I recognised the name on the manifest."

Rory couldn't be bothered to correct his rank for her. He replied, "You got me and a pal out of Spain eighteen months ago when all this shit kicked off." He noted her nose rise slightly at his profanity, but didn't care. "You were the chief petty officer then."

"I recall," she said, sitting in a chair on Rory's left. She lifted and dabbed at a handheld screen. Without looking at him, she asked, "Would you like some tea? Something to eat?"

"Not right now, thank you. How long can we wait for the others?"

Pettifer looked at him. "The captain has allowed two days. We'll surface four more times at the agreed hour. Then—"

"You don't have to say it," Rory broke in, not prepared to discuss the obvious with this woman. He remembered the interrogation she'd put him and Pip through when they'd escaped Spain at the start of the invasion. Then, from his four-troop team, he'd lost Pratty, blown to bits on the transport, and they'd had to leave Crimble in the care of the kind locals, amputation the only option for his rancid arm.

Pettifer asked, "Do you feel up to answering a few questions?"

"No. And I mean it, this time."

"Very well," Pettifer said, standing. "If you need anything else, the chief purser will help you. Once we are underway—whether or not we retrieve anyone else—we'll hold a full debrief."

"How's Harry doing?"

Pettifer glanced back from the doorway and replied, "He's only in sickbay. You should go and ask him yourself."

The door closed and Rory muttered, "And fuck you very much, XO." He poured and drained another glass of the gloriously chilled water. He stood, reinvigorated, and left the room. He used his lens to navigate to the sickbay, halfway up the *Spiteful*'s conning tower. He pulled himself up the narrow metal ladders, his muscles aching, and ignored the lingering glances from the other crew members.

He stepped over the flange and entered the sickbay. He waved aside the momentary concern of the submarine's only doctor and indicated he felt fine. The doctor nodded over to the far bunk.

Harry lay there, covered in a white sheet. Through split lips, he croaked, "How's it going, peasant?"

Rory smiled and replied, "They're going to give it a couple of days."

Harry shook his head and replied, "Waste of time. The general's bought it, no doubt about it."

"Maybe not?" Rory offered. "And Declan and Nick could be waiting on the beach up there right now. We don't know."

"That blasted desert is too big and too hot. If their bikes let them down in addition to the moisturisers, they'd not last more than a few hours. And remember, they left well ahead of us."

"I don't think we should just give up hope."

Harry scoffed and said, "Hope is one thing; realism is another."

Rory watched Harry's pained expression. He slowly began to share the captain's despondency. Nick and Declan had left hours before them and might even have already been aboard the submarine. The fact remained that any delay they'd suffered must have carried only negative consequences. But yes, they'd wait.

Harry coughed and said, "You know what?"

"Yeah?"

"If I ever get back to Blighty and survive this bloody war, I'm going to write a book about this operation."

"Why?"

"So they'll be remembered, peasant."

"Fair enough. What will you call it?"

Harry's forehead creased in thought. He said, "Do you recall the final briefing before we left this sub?"

"Sure."

"What was it that Declan said? Something about sightseeing?"

Rory smiled. "Yeah, I remember."

"That's what I'll call my book: *Sightseeing in Tazirbu*."

Chapter 27

12.37 Tuesday 14 August 2063

Geoff Morrow hurried along the deserted street in a northern suburb of Paris. The midday heat made his scalp itch and he tried to recall when he'd last had a shower with proper shampoo and soap. His flaccid conscience admonished him by noting the death and destruction that lay all around the district of Sarcelles, and that he really should be grateful he still lived.

His relief at escaping Sergeant Savage of the Royal Marines was tempered by a familiar sense of isolation. His self-imposed task of recording every last victim of this war always seemed more gargantuan when he was alone.

A contact icon flashed in his lens. Geoff raised it. His editor at *The Guardian*, Alan, barked, "Where are you?"

Geoff minimised the icon, needing to see the debris on the street in front of him. He answered, "Rounding the park on the west side of the cemetery."

"Okay, you need the residential block on the south side."

"Yeah, I know," Geoff replied, wondering why Alan had taken such a keen interest in this assignment.

"Hurry up, Geoff," he urged. "I need more feelgood content."

"People getting fed up with endless burnt and mutilated bodies, are they?"

"Remember who pays your wages, Ge—"

"Give it a rest, Alan," Geoff said with a sigh. He stepped out into the street to go around the burnt and rusted hulk of some kind of autonomous vehicle. He told Alan, "On the way back from the front, I caught up with things and there's a load of positive news coming out now. They've reopened the first road from Calais to Paris. Thousands of refugees are coming back, and they're helping to clear up this bloody mess."

"Just get to the person the stringer gave us and leave your lens on live. There is still some competition for readers and viewers in the international press environment, you remember?"

Geoff didn't reply. He turned left onto the road, called the *Rue Jean Zay*, that ran along the southside of the park. At the junction, he made eye contact with a pair of young French soldiers. After staring at him for a second, they nodded their approval and the smaller female gave him a thumbs-up. Ahead of him, a pile of rubble splayed out over the road and into the damaged houses opposite. Dull green weeds and other dry growth evidenced the passage of time.

Geoff veered to the left to go to the rear of the building, a four-floor, tan-brick structure that still had its original red slate rooftiles. He followed a low mechanical noise. He arrived to see a small Axpan construction replicator patiently sifting and sorting, its appendages unconcerned at the enormity of the task of rebuilding the block.

"Hello?" a voice called.

"Hi," Geoff answered.

A thin man with black hair similar to Geoff's emerged from an undamaged doorway. Suspicious eyes regarded him, until the man verified the journalist's credentials. At the same time, the name 'Pierre Caron' resolved in Geoff's vision. Pierre stuck out a hand and asked in heavily accented English, "Do you have the special pack?"

Geoff tapped the small rucksack he carried over one shoulder in confirmation.

"Good," he said. "Mme. Petit is resting in the common area over there." Pierre indicated before walking off in that direction.

Geoff followed, asking, "Is it just you and her here?"

"*Non*. But with the 'eat of the day, most try to keep inside."

They entered the building and the smell of aged plastic invaded Geoff's nose. He said, "That little construction replicator is going to take a while to get through the work out there."

"We are not in a rush."

They arrived at a wider set of dirty doors that used to be cream coloured. Pierre said, "Let me make sure she is not sleeping."

As soon as the small Frenchman pushed the doors open, Geoff heard an exclamation.

Pierre turned back to him with a resigned expression on his face. "You can go in," he said, and walked off, leaving Geoff to catch the door.

The journalist entered to see a small, wizened woman peering at him with squinted eyes, sitting in an armchair with thin cushions and wooden arms.

"Ah," she exclaimed, "you are English, yes?"

Geoff approached her and crouched. He answered, "Yes, Mme. Petit. Thank you for meeting me."

Her face scowled in mock seriousness. "Did you bring what you promised?"

Geoff opened his rucksack and took out a small British Army GenoFluid pack. He offered it to the old woman and explained, "This is already pre-programmed and will help you."

Thin arms streaked in purple varicose veins under pallid, wrinkled skin trembled as she took the pack. She laid it on the small coffee table beside her. She said, "Thank you. Pierre tells me it is very busy now we are taking our countries back."

Geoff hesitated and then pulled a surprise out of his rucksack. He said, "I hope you don't mind, but I thought you might like this."

She took the small cardboard box and exclaimed, "Channel No. 5. Thank you."

"I don't know if you like it—"

"I do. It is very thoughtful. It has been a such long time..." she held the box to her nose and inhaled. She put it next to the GenoFluid pack.

Relief suffused Geoff and he knew he'd gained at least some of the old lady's trust. His desire to get the story burned. He watched Mme. Petit's wrinkled face and rheumy eyes, and wondered if she'd been beautiful when young. The skin sagged from her face and neck, and Geoff found it remarkable that he crouched in the presence of a person born as long ago as nineteen eighty-eight.

When he could hold back no longer, he asked: "Could I ask you, mademoiselle Petit, how did you survive? How did you manage through eighteen months of war and occupation? How did you live through it all?"

Her face frowned and Geoff wondered if he might've offended her. She said, "Firstly, I am a 'madame' not a 'mademoiselle'."

"Sorry," Geoff said while twitching his eye to ensure every word would be heard and recorded in London.

She became thoughtful. "You know," she began, "every autumn I buy a few sacks of potatoes from a local farmer who sells them cheaply. When the war began, I still had three sacks left, and divided them up to last a year. By then, of course, the potatoes had all grown long roots, but even these were quite tasty when boiled properly with salt and dried herbs. When they ran out, I boiled a handful of dried oats once or twice a week until I saw our wonderful French soldiers in the street a few days ago."

"Did you not think of trying to escape when the war began? And why were you left here to begin with?"

She paused and sighed. Geoff sensed an indescribable sadness well up from within her frail body. She said, "My son, Gaston, and his family, they urged me to go with them to the shelter in the centre of the city."

Geoff probed, "Why didn't you?"

"Because I knew the mayor did not want this new 'resistance' to have any elderly or very young children. I thought that if I were with them, they would be refused entrance. And as Gaston's children were adults, all five of his family would get in without me, but probably not with me. But at least we said a proper farewell, I'm grateful for that. I never expected that they would perish and I would survive. Life can be strange, sometimes."

A lump formed in Geoff's throat. He tried to retreat behind his veneer of journalistic cynicism, but could not. Mme. Petit's eyes, watery and rheumy, exuded regret, exhaustion and understanding.

Geoff swallowed down his emotion. He cut the link to London so he had some privacy. He placed his leaden hand on the old woman's wrinkled skin and promised: "They will all be remembered. Gaston and his children and all of them. There will be a record of everyone who was lost to this war."

Her eyes focused on Geoff's face and she replied, "Thank you, young man."

Chapter 28

11.18 Saturday 18 August 2063

Colonel Trudy Pearce analysed the digital map on the screen of her mobile command vehicle as it bumped through fields less than ten kilometres from the German border. In a few moments, she would reach the last known location of her beloved Dan, logged on 5 June the previous year.

Trudy congratulated herself on her subterfuge. Marta and the others remained at the main forward command post twenty klicks further west, while she elected to monitor one of the day's advances from closer to the action in a single-seat vehicle. While certainly unorthodox, her actions did not break the letter of the regulations. Besides, she thought with a satisfied smile, her notoriety still carried some weight among the ranks, and notoriety in war remained a valuable commodity.

Her vehicle slowed as it shadowed the morning's advance. She watched the super AI coordinate all of the military elements so they worked together seamlessly. Once the Scythes had cleared the target area, autonomous tanks advanced followed by flesh-and-blood troops. The tanks and the troops were all armed with Falaretes, and mobile Falarete fire teams and autonomous launchers bristled among the advancing units. It all worked as a modern army should, provided the enemy played his part and produced no surprises.

Since Operation Repulse had begun eighteen days earlier, the enemy had delivered only two shocks: the first when the enemy modulated the frequency of the shielding protecting its ACAs, and for a terrifying few hours, the Falarete had been rendered useless. A countermeasure had been rolled out in mere hours. And the second was the upgrading of the power units in its own Blackswans and Lapwings once the enemy's super AI must have deduced what NATO had achieved with the Scythes. But in this case, a massive earthquake in North Africa had reduced the enemy's ACA supplies.

Nevertheless, with each day and every hour, NATO forces advanced such that reversing the operation seemed impossible to Trudy.

Her thoughts returned to her personal objective. She said, "Squonk, overlay my personal target onto the current map."

"Confirmed."

An indicator resolved, showing Dan's last location.

"What is the terrain like there, at Hill 121?"

Squonk replied, "A shallow valley leading up to a building on the summit of Hill 121."

"Type?"

"A former chateaux."

"Okay. Stop the vehicle and wait here. Let's give those tanks and troops some time to secure the hill."

"Confirmed."

In a few moments, Trudy thought, she'd have the confirmation she sought. Icons on the map flitted and shimmered along the screen as NATO forces advanced eastwards on a front tens of kilometres long. She withdrew and zoomed the view as she fancied, admiring the geometry as each element of the advance played its role.

Presently, however, a depression developed in the line of advance. The depression became a bulge as the line moved forwards everywhere except for a small section—exactly at Hill 121.

"Squonk, what's the problem at that hill? Why has the advance stalled there?"

"An enemy ambush has taken place."

"Really?" Trudy queried in surprise. "And how did that happen?"

"Enemy warriors concealed themselves from airborne recon and opened fire when NATO troops advanced into open ground."

"Hmm," Trudy said. With a sweep of her hand, she zoomed the line and saw the troops belonged to the Ox and Bucks, 2nd Battalion, one of dozens of long-disbanded British Army regiments reconstituted after the vast expansion in preparation for Operation Repulse. She said, "So, now the Scythes on that part of the front have destroyed them, yes?"

"Negative."

Surprise gave way to confusion. "And why not?"

"The enemy warriors in the building are offering to surrender. NATO Rules of Engagement strictly prohibit the killing of enemy combatants who are offering to surren—"

"Shut up," Trudy ordered, appalled at the super AI's response. She enlarged the screen again to note the name of the commanding officer. She barked, "Contact Major Wilcox, now."

A gruff, strained voice filled the vehicle. "Good morning, colonel. If you don't mind, I have quite bit on my pl—"

"You have a problem, major," Trudy replied tersely. "The rest of the line is already advancing and your delay will expose their flanks. You must remove the obstacle."

"I've also got dozens of casualties, colonel. The RoE don't allow the Scythes to fire—"

"Have the enemy actually surrendered?"

"No, of course not. They ambushed us and shot my troops up, hid, and when the Scythe came in for a pass, it didn't fire because a few of the fuckers—pardon me, ma'am—had run out the back with their hands in the air. The Scythe has made two more passes with the same non-result. Now we're stuck, and I need medics in that field of fire—"

"But if the enemy attacks again, the Scythe will—"

"Yes, but they haven't, so it's a stalemate, colonel. We're stuck."

Fury burned inside Trudy. She muted the connection and said, "Squonk? Override the RoE, bring the Scythe back in, and destroy that building."

But the super AI remained unmoved, "Negative. Rules of Engagement can only be amended by the Security Council on a motion of a solider, sailor or airperson with the rank of general or equivalent."

Trudy swore, although the answer hadn't been a complete surprise. She unmuted the connection and said, "Major Wilcox, I order you to send a squad to remove those enemy from the battle. Or do I have to drive up there and do it myself?"

"I'll assign fire teams now."

She terminated the connection and said aloud, "Which is what any capable commander would've done five minutes ago... Squonk? Bring a Scythe into the area, ready for when it's needed."

"Confirmed."

"And give me any visual or audio available."

Truncated grunts and the breaths of a tired soldier bounced off the vehicle's interior. There followed a series of shouts and orders and confirmations. As the two fire teams closed in on the chateaux, Trudy realised that one of the main concerns of Operation Repulse was coming to pass. Major Wilcox dithered because of the increasing aversion battlefield commanders had to taking casualties. Even now, listening to the chatter as the fire teams approached the target, she picked up on an underlying resentment that they should have to put themselves in harm's way at all. This affected all soldiers in battle to a degree, especially when they could see the bodies of comrades who might just as easily have been themselves. But that was why majors like Wilcox were expected to spur their troops on, not to dither.

She asked herself if Operation Repulse was in fact going so much to plan that the troops were beginning to lose any sense of the obligation to fight, relying instead on the machines to do the important work of killing the enemy.

Suddenly, the chatter became urgent. Enemy warriors were sighted in damaged windows and the upper balconies. There came the sound of rapid gunfire, followed by claims, counterclaims, and deductions of hits.

"Squonk? Confirm active enemy fire from the building."

"Confirmed."

"Please destroy the building now."

"Confirmed."

"Clear the windows and take me closer to Hill 121."

The maps and other mission data vanished, replaced by the very real bright sunshine outside. The vehicle resumed its journey, bumping over a dead brown field and dried grass. It crested a ridge and turned right to bring it onto a dirt track. This gave Trudy a clear view of the target on the further side of the shallow valley. She nodded in satisfaction when, under volleys of invisible laser shots, everything combustible ignited. She zoomed the image: elegant chimney stacks exploded; the grey slate-tiled roof erupted into thousands of pieces; glass and render on the sides of the building split and flew into the air.

Flying alone and not as part of a wing, the Scythe used the pirouette manoeuvre, where it flew over the target in a rapid, low circle, rotating and pitching its body so the laser played constantly on all sides of the chateaux. In less than a minute, the building's roof timbers, glowing orange and spewing grey smoke, collapsed into the blackened shell. Gouts of debris spurted out from every window and doorway as the internal floors gave way, and the whole building was reduced to a four-walled crackling furnace.

"Major Wilcox?"

"Yes, ma'am?"

"Are your fire teams safe?"

"Yes, ma'am. But I've got a lot of casualties in the—"

"I can see that. You should've stormed the building sooner."

"Yes, ma'am," came the cautious reply.

"Why didn't you?"

"It was an ambush. My main concern was with saving lives."

"Your main concern should've been with holding the line."

Wilcox's voice rose: "Then the bloody Scythe shouldn't put the lives of those bastard ragheads ahead of our advance, should it, ma'am? Whoever decided those RoE has obviously never been on the wrong end of a raghead's rifle, especially when the crafty little bastard is pretending to surrender. Wouldn't you say so, ma'am?"

Trudy reined in her frustration and conceded that Wilcox had a point. She replied, "I'm approaching the base of Hill 121 now and will let you have the battlefield GenoFluid packs in my vehicle. Please send someone to meet me and take them."

"Roger that. Thank you, ma'am."

She terminated the communication. Her vehicle entered the valley and descended into the field in front of the burning building, where most of the NATO casualties lay.

"Squonk, what is the current state of the advance on this part of the line?"

"Stabilised. Units of the 6th Battalion, Oxfordshire and Buckinghamshire Light Infantry, have closed the line, which continues to advance."

"Any notable delay to the R-plus-eighteen objectives?"

"Negative."

Trudy watched the chateaux continue to burn as her mobile command vehicle trundled further into the field. She told it to stop. The heat of the day hit her when the door opened and she exited. A familiar regret and sadness deepened her breaths as she stared around at the NATO casualties caused by a particularly cowardly unit of warriors. She wondered why that group had chosen to make a futile stand, but had done so in a way that ensured the deaths of several dozens of NATO troops. She realised she'd answered her own question. She made up her mind that this situation must not be allowed to happen again.

A junior rank trotted up to her and introduced himself. She lifted the metal plate at the rear of her vehicle and the young man scooped up the GenoFluid packs. He thanked her and hurried away, muttering instructions to the other teams to identify and prioritise the injured.

Trudy returned to her mobile command vehicle, finally free to complete her own mission. The journey resumed, uphill to the other side of the chateaux, to an outbuilding that must've seen many uses over the years. On the screen, digital indicators described the second wave of the advance. These included support units bringing with them all of the rear area equipment, including ground and air vehicles laden with ammunition, food, water and construction replicators, and the troops and other ranks to ensure everything functioned. In time, these units would themselves move on and be replaced by a third wave of support elements. Thus was Europe being reclaimed.

The mobile command vehicle rolled to a stop and Squonk announced, "You have reached the coordinates of the last known location of Lieutenant-Colonel Daniel Milnes, 104 Royal Artillery Regiment, posted missing-presumed-killed-in-action on 5 June 2062."

"Oh, Dan," she said reflexively, a lump in her throat. She exited the vehicle and the heat beat down stronger than in the shallow valley. Twenty metres behind her, the shell of the chateaux hissed and crackled, smoke billowing into the sky. In front of her, there rested the bleached remains of an autonomous troop transport.

She paced with care around the site, her boots losing grip in the barren, sandy dirt. The blackened, dead trunk of aged oak stood sentinel over the transport. The white metal body had broken and twisted gaps that offered only blackness when she peered at them.

"Speculate cause of destruction."

Her Squitch answered, "The damage is consistent with multiple shots from an enemy Lapwing."

"So, the occupants burned to death, yes?"

"Negative. Exposure to the heat from the laser of an enemy Lapwing in such type of vehicle will cause the human body to lose consciousness from extreme pain before the body can combu—"

"Enough," Trudy broke in. "Who else was in the vehicle?"

"Lieutenant-Colonel Milnes' adjutant, Captain Goodfellow, air defence specialist Sergeant Kibby…"

Trudy listened absentmindedly as her Squitch listed the troops who had also died in the ATT with her beloved Dan. Her imagination offered a suggestion of the thousands of other NATO career soldiers who'd made the ultimate sacrifice in a war they did not provoke and which no one foresaw.

"And now the armies are full of volunteer civies," she said aloud. "Overweight gamers and baristas and lawyers who think they can make some kind of difference, when even majors like Wilcox are struggling to motivate their troops to take the necessary risks."

Her Squitch said, "Caution: enemy warriors are in the vicinity."

"What?" she said. "Where?"

The super AI didn't reply. An indicator flashed in her lens, noting that behind her, a few metres from the burning chateaux, two wounded enemy warriors lay immobile.

Trudy turned on her heel and paced towards the inferno. As she looked, one of the walls collapsed inwards with a heavy, resigned sigh and sent up a plume of sparks and smoke. The indicator settled over two prone figures, blackened but crawling away from the building. They made a pitiful sight. Both warriors lay flat on their stomachs. Steam drifted from their backs. Their limbs struggled to propel them forwards, away from the danger. They were engrossed in their fight for survival and entirely unaware that they had been seen.

Trudy withdrew her pistol from the holster on her waist. She aimed it at the head of the nearest warrior. She pulled the trigger. The pistol declined to fire.

Her Squitch said, "The injured enemy combatants pose no threat to your safety."

Trudy replied, "Override, by my order, Colonel Trudy Pearce."

"Confirmed."

She aimed again and pulled the trigger. The weapon fired. In satisfaction, Trudy saw a chunk of the warrior's skull flip over, exposing the whiteness underneath. He sagged and remained still. She moved her arm and fired at the second warrior. There came a puff of pink mist from his black mane. His head sagged and his legs twitched for a few seconds.

Trudy turned, re-holstering her weapon. She gave the ATT that represented Dan's final resting place a lingering look. Her chin trembled and her eyes moistened. She murmured, "Darling, we will be together properly again very soon. I only need to continue for a little while longer. I don't expect it to keep us apart for very long."

She climbed back into her mobile command vehicle and strapped herself in.

Her Squitch advised, "The override command will be escalated to your superior commander."

Trudy recalled her notoriety among the ranks ever since she'd dealt so effectively with those hostage-takers on the south coast of England in July the previous year. She said, "Of course. It makes little difference. If they'd survived and we'd evac'd them, they would only have died when we scanned their brains for intel. It's not like they were ever going to live, anyway. Now, let's go."

The vehicle trundled away from the burning remains of the chateaux.

Chapter 29

11.01 Monday 20 August 2063

Rory stood outside the door to the colonel's office, wondering if the tremble in his left leg represented nerves or that his sea legs had yet to reaccustom themselves to dry land. He tapped his knuckles on the panelled door.

"Come," echoed faintly through the wood.

Rory turned the handle and entered the expansive office. Colonel Doyle was already striding towards him, steely eyes shining out from a friendly face.

Rory closed the door, stood to attention and saluted. The colonel stopped, returned the salute, and said: "At ease." He shook Rory's hand and said, "Welcome home, Sergeant Moore. Come and sit down."

Rory waited for the colonel to sit on one side of the large, ornate desk before sitting in one of two chairs opposite him.

"Firstly," Doyle began, "let me say how proud the regiment is of your exploits."

"Thank you, sir."

"Obviously, we all regret that Hastings and the other two team members did not return with you."

Rory said nothing, suddenly aware of how Operation Thunderclap must have seemed to those not involved in it. To the colonel, Hastings and Nick and Declan were just three more soldiers lost to this war.

Doyle went on, "Nevertheless, the contribution that mission has made to the war effort is difficult to understate. Now, however, we need to consider your future. Have you given it any thought?"

Rory shook his head. "None whatsoever, sir. At least, not yet."

Doyle didn't miss a beat, "I have. I think, to begin with, you might benefit from some leave to rest properly. Obviously, thereafter you should move to a non-combat role. For example, I require an adjutant. You might like to consider that. After some time, when you're ready, we could arrange a lecture tour for you. We rely a great deal on goodwill from the US, and of course you'd be quite safe on the other side of the Atlantic."

Suddenly, the four walls of Doyle's office closed in on Rory. He realised he could not follow the path of becoming Doyle's trophy, paraded wherever the colonel wanted. The trembling in his leg returned. He said, "Thank you, sir. But I think I would prefer to be placed back on combat duty."

Doyle's eyebrows rose. He said, "Sergeant, you have done more than enough—you had done so even before Thunderclap—that you need never be in mortal danger again. Indeed, have you considered the rewards and opportunities that will await you at the end of this war? You have most certainly earned them."

"But the war isn't over yet, sir."

"For you, perhaps it should be?"

"I spoke to Sergeant Heaton on my way here, sir. They're on the line supporting the Polish First Corps in Germany. I'd rather like to get back to my pals in my old squad."

Doyle sat back in his seat in apparent consideration.

A desire that Rory could not name burned inside him, but which crystalised in an irony: he believed safety lay in returning to his company on the front line, not trying to avoid danger by moving to a non-combat role. Ever since his deep clean at the Advanced Medical Research Establishment the previous year, he'd felt as though he had a physical edge, an advantage that had so far allowed him, among other things, to survive the brutal heat of the North African desert.

Oddly, the prospect of not being in danger terrified him.

Doyle queried, "Are you certain that is what you really want, sergeant?"

"Yes, sir," Rory answered at once, disinclined to reveal his true feelings to a CO whose motivations, Rory now realised, might not be entirely selfless.

"Very well. I approve your request, but only on the strict understanding that you come back to these headquarters in one piece. And that is an order. Clear?" Doyle added with a half-smile.

"Yes, sir," Rory answered.

Doyle stood and said, "Squonk, reassign Sergeant Moore back to his previous company in the Royal Engineers. His secondment to the Royal Anglians is at an end."

"Confirmed."

Rory also stood and accompanied the colonel to the door. Doyle said, "Just also remember, young man, that if you get over there and have doubts, you still have a choice. You need only contact me directly and say the word."

Rory didn't like the cautious tone in the colonel's voice. He asked, "Thank you, but I don't think I will, sir."

"An advance is not the same as a retreat," Doyle advised, voice lowered. "All that time you spent withdrawing under the enemy's onslaught, things had a certain... reliability? We knew where we were heading and what we had to face. Now, our troops—the majority of whom are recruits with little or no combat experience, not at all like the career soldiers we had a year or more ago—have to reclaim territory constantly. And the evidence of the enemy's unlimited atrocities is not easy to endure day after day."

"I see, sir," Rory said, not at all sure he did see.

"Good," the colonel replied with a smile. "Just so long as you know, you only need to call me."

"Thank you, sir. I'll keep it in mind."

The colonel opened the door and Rory left with a nod. When the door closed behind him, Rory exhaled and walked over to the high windows on the opposite side of the corridor. The parade ground below him was deserted apart from an autonomous gardener deadheading the roses and flicking the withered blooms into a metal basket on its back.

A notification icon flashed in his lens. He raised it and read his new deployment orders. He heaved a sigh of relief. He would rejoin his company and would never have to get on a submarine again. Memories of old friends resurfaced in his mind's eye.

He said, "Squonk? Contact Captain Philippa Clarke, 103 Squadron."

He waited. An audio link opened.

"Rory? Is that you?"

Rory smiled. "Yes. How are you doing, mate?"

"Never mind me, where have you been? You've been out of touch for weeks."

"Yeah, I have to be careful otherwise the bloody super AI will block us."

"Right."

"But have you heard of any earthquakes in the news recently?"

"Only the one at that place inside the Caliphate. One of their ACA plants… wait, you're not say—"

"Maybe," Rory broke in. "Maybe not. Where are you?"

"Germany is probably as much as I can say."

"I'll be around soon. Coffee?"

"Yes."

Rory ended the connection, the weight of the relief that Pip still lived forcing him to put a steadying hand on the window in front of him.

Chapter 30

16.23 Monday 20 August 2063

Maria Phillips leaned against the side of the field operating theatre and wished she had the energy to go on. High above her, the mountains of the Spanish border loomed dark and grey and forbidding. The casualty clearing station on the russet, barren field in front of her was a hive of activity. Medics and surgeons and doctors fought to repair and limit and reverse the damage inflicted by enemy ACAs and warriors, in addition to injuries both minor and critical caused by the vagaries of chance that any warzone offers to the unwary.

For the last three weeks, Maria had performed her work with a growing sense of the closeness of death that bred a feeling of ultimate futility. She placed the beginning of this sensation with the loss of the injured soldier called Zander. Then, her best friend Nabou died. A few days later, the super AI in her field surgeon lens had delivered a sterile message lathered in faux remorse that her brother, Martin, had been killed during an enemy counterattack.

In the days since, she'd kept a tally of each casualty she'd failed to save. She'd held the hands or the shoulders or the heads of fifty-seven NATO troops who, for more reasons than she could remember, had succumbed to their injuries. Some had arrived on transports already unconscious, and her role had simply been to monitor their demise. For others, she was the last human with whom they had contact; to whom they spoke; who they touched. Some offered prayers. Some begged her for help. Some entrusted messages to her that she personally had to deliver to their loved ones.

But, in the end, they all died.

She looked at her hands. She turned her forearms over and back again. A growing pain burned inside her head. She tried to concentrate, to focus on the daily sitreps that her superiors issued. These insisted that Operation Repulse continued to go according to plan. In twenty days, all of the daily objectives had been achieved. The democracies were taking Europe back, but at a terrible cost.

She pushed herself off the wall and began walking to the canteen. The heat had dried her throat and she needed to drink. A comms icon flashed in her lens and she smiled as she raised it. "Hi, Jamie," she said.

Jamie's handsome face resolved in a thumbnail in the lower-left of her vision. "Hi," he said. "How's my favourite person in the whole world whose first name is 'Maria'?"

"Fine, more or less," she replied, wishing she could feel how she used to, before all the deaths.

"Are you very busy?"

"Not too much. We're coming up to a big push soon. You?" she asked, wanting to get the focus off of her. "Are you all healed now?"

"Nearly there, thanks to you."

"No, it's not."

"You saved my life."

"No, Jamie. The bots in the GenoFluid pack saved your life."

"You made sure. And without you, they'd never have had the chance, so I blame you," he argued with a grin.

"Okay," Maria conceded, the canteen looming ahead of her; her thirst forgotten. "Have you accepted the new posting?"

"Yes, my CO convinced me I'd done my bit and deserved a posting behind the lines, at least for a while."

"Good," she said, not wanting to articulate the wish that all of those who knew her brother should survive as long as possible, so that, somehow, Martin's memory would also survive.

"But," Jamie went on, "I'm going to organise special travel arrangements so I can come out there and take you to dinner. Deal?"

Maria smiled again, the feeling on her face so alien after so much pain. "Deal," she replied.

Jamie's smiled vanished and he said in a level voice, "I mean it, Maria. Stay safe."

"Okay," she whispered.

The connection ended and the warmth of positive emotion vanished. Maria asked herself how there could be a space for such feelings while the war raged all around. Certainty enveloped her that none of them had yet endured the worst this conflict yet had to offer.

Chapter 31

14.00 Wednesday 22 August 2063

Mark Phillips, 3rd Airspace Defence, reclined in a different monitoring pod from his usual one and put the headset on. He waited while Squonk confirmed his identity and allocated a sector of the front to him to monitor. Once again, he was assigned to Attack Group South and a one-hundred-kilometre section of the front in southern France.

"Okay," he muttered to himself, "R-plus-twenty-two, here we are." He allowed his eyes to acclimatise to the digital deployment of tens of thousands of NATO troops and the hundreds of towns and villages they had to clear. In the vanguard, the SkyMasters burned through enemy jamming, which allowed Scythe ACAs to advance, destroy the defences, and gain domination of the airspace. Then, the autonomous tanks moved up, working seamlessly with the Scythes to eliminate any remaining threats. And only then, when the machines had cleared the ground as much as possible, did NATO troops advance to retake possession.

A familiar voice called in his ears, "Babyface Phillips? I'm so glad I'm your supervisor again today, so I can once more have the pleasure of observing how pathetic and hopeless you are."

"The redoubtable Captain Shithead," Mark replied. "Well, sir, I'm afraid to inform you that I might need to take some sick leave."

"Oh? Has your local dog shelter finally decided to have you put down?"

"No, sir. I believe that I have contracted piles. Although I have named the most irritating one 'Captain Shithead' in your honour, sir."

"Yes, but if you've got piles, how on earth are you going to be able to think?"

Mark opened his mouth to utter another rejoinder but stopped when the numbers in his display changed in an unusual manner.

Captain Shithead added, "Given that you keep your ridiculous excuse for a brain in your arse."

Mark observed, "The joke really wasn't that good to begin with, sir."

"And you think you're—?"

"Look at Sector Sierra 10-A. The numbers aren't right—that's not normal."

There came a moment's silence before his superior answered, all trace of sarcasm gone. He said, "Squonk is not flagging it. The variation is still under three percent relative to the enemy's tactics to date."

"Yes, but it shows the enemy is defending with fewer ACAs than is normal."

"There could be a number of reasons for that."

Mark didn't reply, wondering what the motivation for the change might be.

Captain Shithead offered, "The most likely explanation would be a tactical withdrawal to muster more ACAs at a prepared line of defence in the future."

"Request access to the relevant data on all sectors of the front."

"Granted, Babyface. Keep me informed."

"Yes, I'll be around to spell it all out for you, sir," Mark replied, but his superior had already terminated the connection.

"Squonk?" Mark said. "Extrapolate from the drop in the number of enemy ACAs in sector Sierra 10-A and compare with all other sectors."

"Confirmed."

"Well?" Mark demanded, struggling to hold on to his patience.

"The reduced number of enemy ACAs currently defending against NATO advances is reflected across the length of the front to within a margin of less than one-thousandth of one percent."

"And that must be by design, not accident. Speculate the reason for this drop?"

"The most probable cause is a strategic husbanding of reserves given the recent destruction of one of the enemy's main ACA production plants."

"Okay," Mark said with slow enunciation, realising he'd also have to spell it out for the not-so-super artificial intelligence. "Speculate where any such defensive line might be located. What I mean is that, if the enemy is holding back using its available ACAs, then it must have a plan to slow our advance down at a particular location. If so, where is it?"

Mark's digital view of his sector on the front line withdrew until the entire line of Attack Group South wriggled across southern France. Then, flashes of pinpoint lights glinted at hundreds of locations in what remained enemy-held territory, across northern Spain and Italy. But none developed into any kind of cohesive whole. An ironic smile formed on Mark's face as his hypothesis gained evidence.

In the absence of Squonk replying, he said, "There is nowhere that the redeployment of the enemy's limited resources might form a line that would slow or otherwise hinder the advance of Operation Repulse, is there?"

"Affirmative."

"Oh, Captain Shithead?"

A comms link winked into existence. "Found your miniscule penis yet, Babyface?"

"No, and please stop projecting your own inadequacies onto me—"

"Now, you're really going to—"

"We don't have time for this. I believe the enemy has changed tactics in a way that will certainly cost NATO lives, sir."

There came the slightest pause before his superior demanded, "Explain."

Mark knew from experience that he had to guard his emotions. His friend, Simon, always told him that to get results, he had to maintain a dispassionate demeanour. He said, "The only logical explanation for the drop in deployed ACAs is that they will be used to attack us in a novel manner."

"Okay, so what 'novel manner' might that be?"

"I'm not sure, sir. But I think we should issue an advisory to all field commanders."

"An advisory about what?"

Mark paused. A trembling began and he knew it could lead to a descent into panic. He regulated his breathing before answering carefully, "I am sorry, sir. I don't know for certain."

Captain Shithead said, "I'm so tempted to rip you a brand-new arsehole for this, but I think you've got a point."

"Perhaps an advisory for the advancing troops to use as much caution as possible?"

"That's sound advice at any time when there's a war on, Babyface."

"We should issue something, sir. Those missing Spiders must be somewhere—"

"Shit."

"What?"

"Check Leanne's sector, Bravo 7-D."

With a wave of his hands, Mark did so. His view zoomed down to the French town of Poitiers.

At the same time, a light female voice sounded in Mark's ears, "Attention, everyone. I've got an unanticipated Spider detonation on the western approach to today's objective. Squonk doesn't know how it happened."

Mark listened to Captain Shithead question their colleague in a tone of voice not dissimilar to how he spoke to Mark, only without the foul language. The issue soon became plain: the retreating enemy forces had left Spiders behind to act like mines against the unwary approaching NATO troops.

Mark kept his own counsel as the discussion expanded when more of the team noticed this novel development on their own sections of the front. Mark comforted himself with the knowledge that he was safe in central London, while the advancing NATO soldiers now had to attune to a new threat.

Chapter 32

18.34 Wednesday 22 August 2063

Senior Tech Janis Bagget sat at the horseshoe table and watched with concern as Louis Reyer hobbled into the conference room. The Englishwoman, Emily, helped their ailing leader to a seat. The thin Frenchman collapsed his telescopic cane and put it on the table in front of him with a sigh.

He glanced at Janis and said, "I think we are running out of time."

Janis met his gaze and replied, "What we need to agree is more of a formality. If the ariel dynamic specs from the army haven't changed, then the thousands of options can be narrowed down quite easy." She added, "We could've had this meeting remotely."

Reyer waved a hand in dismissal and said, "I look worse than I feel. And the doctor tells me I must keep moving."

With an index finger, Emily dabbed at the table surface in front of her. In the middle of the horseshoe there resolved a holographic image of a serrated globe, an orb made up of circular slices. The globe became translucent, revealing a smaller globe within, like the nucleus inside an atom. A multitude of elegantly curved linkages connected the central globe to the exterior one. Lists of numbers and other data appeared around the image.

"Thank you," Janis said. "This unit meets the army's requirements, professor. The output levels are as high as we dare given the limits of the 3-D ultra-Graphene body that's going to house it."

"Pity," Reyer mused. "If only they appreciated just how powerful we could make this unit, if it were unencumbered by the limitations of the machines it must power."

"The spec said it has to allow the ACA in which it's housed to maintain battlefield supremacy against anything the Caliphate can develop for at least eighteen months."

Reyer spoke while staring at the image. "That would depend on which aspect of its own weapons the Caliphate decides to enhance. How many initial designs did you begin with, Janis?"

Janis recalled, "Several hundred. But those were just the muon-catalysed versions. If the enemy decides to go for something completely different, like we nearly did at the beginning—"

"You mean the lepton?" Emily broke in.

"Uh-huh, for example," Janis said. "Then they'd have thousands more potential power unit designs to consider."

"But, like us," Reyer said, "they will proceed with what their computers tell them will be best overall."

Janis pinched the bridge of her nose and replied, "Sometimes, I think this whole pointless war is just second- and third-guessing by the computers."

Reyer chuckled and said, "Do not discount the human element."

"Anyways," Janis said, the urge to conclude the issue after so much effort burning inside her, "we need to relay this to Ample Annie and Squonk so they can get on with finalising the armaments and body. But yeah, professor, we're done. This is the power unit that's either gonna win this war or—"

"Do not say that," Reyer broke in with a raised hand. "We were correct with the first-generation Scythes, and I believe we are correct again now." He cast another glance at the hologram of the new power unit before lifting himself to his feet with his hand on the table. Emily also stood, concern creasing her face. Reyer pressed a button on the top of his walking aid and it pinged down to the floor. He concluded, "Thank you, Janis. If all this goes well, we may even be able to have a day off on vacation." He turned to Emily and said, "Let us continue to the canteen. I have not done enough steps for today, yet."

Janis said nothing while Emily paced alongside Reyer as he hobbled from the room. Alone again when the door closed behind the others, Janis stared at the holographic image, recalling all of the work it had taken to refine, to stabilise output delivery, to maximise the directional thrust against airflow resistance.

"Muffy?" she said, referring to NASA's super AI. "Give me an image of the power unit inside the current design for the next-gen NATO ACAs."

"Okay."

The globe shrank and the outline of a sleek ellipsoid encased it.

"Show me the business-end. Where are the outlets for the thrust?"

Highlights shadowed the relevant sections. Muffy said, "Further detailed data is restricted at this time."

"Makes sense. Okay, I've seen enough."

The hologram vanished, and with it, Janis's reason for working such long hours over the preceding weeks.

She stared at the empty space wondering what she would do next. A sudden thought stuck her. "Show current open tickets."

Muffy replied, "Specify range."

"Everything," Janis replied, seeing no reason to limit herself.

The empty space in the horseshoe filled up with a list of data. She scanned these open tickets, which were requests submitted by anyone in NATO, from the lowest-ranking soldier to generals, and from all of the quasi-military and supporting units following the armies across Europe. All carried flags to denote their level of urgency. Most asked for improvements to existing equipment—increasing the power of a laser or the magazine size for the Pickup—and most carried flags denoting no or little urgency.

Janis saw nothing that piqued her interest. She said, "Filter to urgent only," expecting zero returns because any ticket regarded as urgent meant lives were being lost in real time due to the issue.

One request sat suspended in mid-air.

"Enlarge." She instructed. She read the ticket. It explained that the enemy had begun leaving behind dormant Spiders to act as mines and kill unsuspecting NATO troops.

"That should not be possible," she said aloud, one eyebrow raised. She scanned the rest of the data, saw the name of the person responsible, and said, "Contact senior tech Roy Parker."

"Okay," Muffy replied.

The image of a bearded man resolved and covered the data. His eyebrows frowned in the harried expression of a person who had many demands on his time. "Er, what?" he began in a frustrated English accent that was nothing like

Emily's. "I mean, thanks for reaching out, Ms... Er, Bagget, but I'm not really—"

"The open ticket is also on NASA's super AI, Mr. Parker, or can I call you 'Roy'?"

"Not sure this is a job for the JTDC. We're working on it, thanks all the sa—"

"I'd really like to help out, if I can."

The discomfort on Roy's face lessened a fraction and he paused. He said, "Right you are. Tell you what, then, here's a challenge for you: we need a gizmo that will be able to detect dormant Spiders before they can hit flesh-and-blood troops, but which does not use non-replicable kit. Any ideas? Oh, and by the way, the lives of our troops are actually at stake here, Janis."

Janis ignored the man's frustration. She said, "I have an idea of the pressure you're under. I headed the team responsible for refining the 8C power unit in the Scythes, so I can tell you things will work out, eventually. But first, how are the Spiders able to hide like that to begin with? The Scythes should detect and neutralise them almost without effort."

Roy sniffed and shook his head. "The Scythes and all of our other kit depends on each Spider being in contact with its Blackswan, whether it's in the body of the Blackswan or already released. The SkyMasters and Scythes track either the linkage or the 3-D ultra-Graphene when it is charged and seeking targets."

Janis said, "But if a Spider shuts down so we can't see it, then it can't see any targets. So, how the heck can it know when to detonate?"

Roy nodded and replied, "That's the sneaky bit. It sends out a UHF pulse, like old-fashioned radar. This is tricky to spot given all the jamming and burn-through going on around the battlespace. All a dormant Spider needs is a single return from one pulse to predict where our troops will be at a given time, to maximise the chances of scoring a kill, which, by the way, they're doing really bloody well."

"So, we need to reset our 'gizmo' to detect those pulses," Janis said, somewhat stating the obvious.

"Yup, right," Roy nodded. "Only problem is, by then, it's too late. Do you want to see the cam-footage of what these dormant Spiders do to a squaddie when a single pulse is missed?"

"No, that's okay. Thanks."

"Thought so. It's not pretty, Janis. These are men and women literally getting blown to tiny pieces. By the time the heat's gone, there're just bits of meat and bone—"

"Can you show me what your super AI has come up with so far?"

"Sure. This is the best we've got up to now."

Roy's face vanished, replaced by a four-legged, metallic android that stood twenty centimetres tall. The image rotated and then the legs curled up and withdrew into the body in a miniature imitation of the enemy's Spider.

"Looks neat," Janis observed with approval.

"Yeah," Roy agreed laconically. "It only weighs three-and-something kilos, so when it's retracted like that, the squaddie can carry it in their kit. The idea is that they chuck it out ahead to clear an area. The widget—we don't have a name for it yet—emits the same sig as a squaddie's kit. The Spider won't know the difference, so the idea is to use this gizmo to flush the dormant Spiders out before the troops move in."

"But it doesn't have any way to take a Spider out if it finds one, right?"

"Right. Its job is to convince the Spider it's a squaddie, so the Spider attacks."

"Sure. And given that the Spider's pulse has to be so low so it avoids detection, that part is sure to work."

"But there's a problem," Roy said.

"Uh-huh. That dual-sensor component can't be replicated."

"So, do you think the JTDC can help?"

Janis hid her frustration. The data proved the device could not be constructed from replicable components only. She didn't need Muffy to confirm it. She said, "Sorry, Roy. To work, it's going to need to be manufactured."

Roy's head slumped. "Thanks," he said without rancour. "I suppose it's useful to have someone as high up as you confirm it."

"Your super AI already insisted, yup?"

"Yeah. Makes me sick, to be honest. If we could replicate this thing, all of the leading troops would be kitted out with it in just a couple of hours. Now we've got to manufacture the bloody thing, it's going to take days to get it to the front lines."

Janis shared his concerns. She said, "Maybe the generals will pause ops?"

"Not a choice I'd like to have to make," Roy said with a scoff.

"You bet," Janis agreed.

"Thanks for helping."

Janis shook her head and replied, "I didn't do squat. Sorry and good luck over there."

Roy's face vanished. Janis remained in her seat, rereading and analysing the data to confirm what the super AI had established. She sighed, satisfied nothing more could be done to change the requirement to use parts that had to be manufactured.

Her mind came back to her place in Reyer's team now that the power unit for the next-gen NATO ACAs had been signed off. She would still have work to do, mostly consisting of instruction training for the aerospace engineers further north. But first, she decided, she would go back to New York, to visit her sister, Janet. She'd make the journey for no other reason than to spend a few hours at Janet's graveside and tell her big sister of all that had happened. Janis missed her sister.

Chapter 33

10.33 Saturday 25 August 2063

Terry Tidbury fought to control his anger. The sense that he might actually lose his temper—for the first time since he'd been a much younger man—both concerned and fascinated him. Then again, the genesis of his frustration was also a novelty: the unwelcome sensation of losing control.

Outside the windows of his autonomous Nissan Shuttle, the English countryside sped past, a brown, sunburnt patchwork interspersed with small areas of verdant green under the blazing blue sky, like tiny glimpses into a richer past from a dried present.

The smooth female voice of the vehicle addressed him, "Sir Terry, your heartrate is higher than normal. Would like to hear some appropriate music that might help calm you—?"

"No, I would not," Terry broke in.

The vehicle stayed silent only for a moment before it announced, "Sir Terry, your adjutant wishes to contact you."

"Fine."

"Would you prefer to talk to him on—?"

"Put him on the screen."

Simms's face resolved in front of Terry. He said, "Good morning, sir."

"What is it that can't wait until I arrive in seven minutes' time, Simms?"

His adjutant's thin eyebrows drew together and he said, "The Chiefs of Staff meeting might be more problematic than usual."

"Who's causing trouble today?"

"General Pakla. The Polish First Army's casualties have increased since the enemy introduced his new tactic of leaving dormant Spiders. I have considered the situation and thought we might prepare options in case Pakla becomes… shall we say, excessively vocal? …during the meeting."

"Very well. Thank you, Simms."

His adjutant nodded and disappeared.

Terry kept his eyes focused on a distant church spire as the countryside rushed by, until the rising verge of the motorway hid it. Simms would've been told, or found out through contacts, that Pakla might be planning to ratchet up the pressure on Terry to pause or slow the advance until the countermeasure, now named the 'Pathfinder', could be deployed in a few days. Pakla, the Polish general whose enthusiastic support had so helped Terry during the darkest days of 2062, now threatened to turn that support into opposition.

Despite the anger that made his heart beat harder and faster in his chest, Terry still understood that he could not allow any challenge to his authority. Most of his generals, while being militarily competent to a greater or lesser degree, lacked sufficient charisma to bend others to their will. And now, with Operation Repulse more than three weeks old, Terry's main concern centred on his generals' lack of ambition; a reluctance to prosecute Repulse to the maximum extent lest they incur more casualties than absolutely necessary. But Pakla was different. And wars were seldom won by commanders whose first priority was to minimise casualties.

The Shuttle veered gently to the east, where it left the M25 and joined the M3 heading towards central London.

"Time to destination?"

"Four minutes, Sir Terry."

"Contact General Pakla, Polish First Army."

There came a moment's silence. Pakla's elegant Slavic face resolved on the screen. In a neutral tone, he said, "Good morning, field marshal."

"General Pakla, I've reviewed the overnight situation reports and I am anxious that the Polish First Army is taking more casualties than NATO is incurring in other sectors. How would you assess morale among your frontline troops?"

Pakla's forehead creased. Terry wondered if the general suspected that anything were amiss.

Pakla replied, "Thank you for your concern, sir. I believe morale is very high. I have thousands of Polish men and women fighting to reclaim their homeland. This is not a new experience for us Poles. And they cannot wait to get home."

"I don't doubt your or your troops' commitment, general. But I am aware that some might feel we are taking casualties that could be avoided, mainly due to the enemy's innovative tactic of leaving Spiders in a near-dormant state to attack unsuspecting troops as they advance."

Pakla seemed to consider his response before answering. He said, "Some might say, field marshal, that a pause until the new *zbawy* becomes available to deal with this threat would be a good idea."

"And others might say that military operations are often subject to unpredictable events that oblige one or both sides to fight harder to gain their objectives. Do you think we should pause the advance?" Terry asked, intentionally using the plural 'we' instead of 'I'.

Pakla nodded, his upper lip pinched. With a trace of sarcasm, he said, "Well, *we* paused Operation Repulse eighteen days ago, when *we* discovered that the Paris resistance were slain by nerve gas. Then, as I recall, it made sense to pause, to evaluate. But now, with more troops getting killed because of another cowardly move by the enemy, it makes no sense to pause. So it would look like."

Terry bit down on his emotion, loathe as always to explain himself. Nevertheless, the tactical imperative now was to keep the Pole onside. Terry said, "The enemy's confirmed use of a banned weapon of mass destruction was a strategic issue of the utmost importance, general. As I noted at the time, if this war were to expand to involve those kinds of weapons, we needed to reassess the situation at the strategic level. However, this latest development is a tactical problem. Extremely unwelcome—yes; an increase in the danger our troops face—absolutely; but a reason to pause the operation?" Terry shook his head and said, "No."

Pakla's face reddened. "But these additional casualties are not necessary, field marshal," he protested. "My soldiers are dying for nothing. Never mind the moral argument of the loss of life. I will need as many of my troops as possible to reclaim Poland. Already we see those vultures in the Kremlin watching—"

"But general, I cannot pause Repulse for such a tactical consideration. Today, we have two key advantages that are aiding our forces in Europe. One, the destruction of the enemy's ACA plant at Tazirbu. However, our intel cannot give us any hard-and-fast data on how soon the enemy will be able to rebuild and get that facility back into operation. Our computers insist it will be rebuilt and likely retooled to produce his own next-gen weapons. Every single moment that plant is out of action, we must push on and reclaim as much territory as we can.

"Two, the enemy's current standoff with India. As long as those two superpowers keep staring each other down, a substantial portion of the enemy's resources are tied up there. As with the plant at Tazirbu, we don't know how long that situation will continue, so we must, again, take advantage as much as possible."

Pakla shook his head and said, "I thought our new weapons would have the advantage for more time."

"Not at all. General Pakla, however painful at the tactical level, we cannot allow this issue with dormant Spiders to limit or hinder our overall strategy. Every part of NATO and civilian support is working to deliver the Pathfinder countermeasure as soon as we can. But until then, we must continue to meet the operation's objectives. There is simply too much at stake. But I want to be crystal clear here: your troops are not 'dying for nothing'."

The daylight outside the Shuttle suddenly vanished when the vehicle dipped and entered the bowels of the Ministry of Defence building in central London.

Terry watched Pakla's face. The Pole frowned in consideration, and then he said, "Yes, it can be easy sometimes to lose sight of the strategic picture."

Terry concluded, "Understandable when each of us has so many issues to deal with and decisions to take, general. We'll talk more in a little while."

Pakla nodded and Terry stretched forwards to press a square on the screen and terminate the connection. He exhaled and waited for the Shuttle to park itself. When it had, he exited the vehicle and took the stairs up one floor to the War Rooms. On entering the main area, his adjutant strode up to him.

"Welcome, Sir Terry," Simms said with his usual diffidence. "Where would you prefer to attend this morning's Chiefs of Staff, sir?"

Terry glanced around at the screens, taking in the headline numbers and the attitude of the staff present. When satisfied that Simms had everything in order, he replied, "My office, this time."

"Very good, sir. Tea?"

"No. Come with me." Terry led his adjutant into his private office and closed the door. He said, "Thank you for the advance warning about Pakla."

Simms nodded his acknowledgement but said nothing.

Terry said, "I spoke to him from the car and explained the problem to him."

"A prudent move before the meeting begins, sir."

Terry shook his head and allowed himself the rare luxury of venting. He slapped the back of his chair and hissed, "Really, Simms, it's as though these generals think they can be averse to casualties. When did any army win any war without losing troops, eh?"

"This is modern warfare, sir," Simms answered in a measured voice. "It was only two years ago that our accepted military doctrine insisted the machines would do all of the fighting and our troops would mainly be required to take possession of territory."

"Yes, but these generals should have long ago been disabused of such a notion."

"Perhaps, after the somewhat traumatic retreat across Europe and the much-vaunted Scythes, our mid-level commanders expected a return to a more doctrinal type of warfare?"

"Ridiculous," Terry dismissed with a wave of his hand. "Besides, we have enough problems with discipline in the ranks. Plenty of volunteers are only too willing to get their revenge for all the destruction since February last year. We're having to court-martial numerous lower ranks for what amounts to the murders of PoWs. No, the problem here is that too many commanders are becoming complacent. I must try to rile them up at the meeting."

"Indeed, sir."

Terry sat at his desk and spun around to face the wall screen. The meeting would begin in one minute. He turned to Simms and said, "Actually, I will have that tea now, thank you."

Yes, sir. Just one other thing?"

"What is it?"

"When you have the time, the prime minister would like to meet you to discuss the same issue—"

"No, absolutely not," Terry said raising his hand. "If I have to explain current tactics to that woman and her fellow politicians, I may very well lose my temper. Tell her I'm too busy, and fill up any spaces my diary until the Pathfinder is deployed."

"Very good, sir," Simms replied with a half-smile. He closed the door.

Terry turned his attention to the large screen as thumbnails of his generals appeared along the bottom and down the sides. He muttered under his breath, "I dare any of you to tell me we need to pause Operation Repulse."

Chapter 34

14.44 Thursday 30 August 2063

Serena Rizzi poured the boiling water into the ornate, silver teapot. The dry tea leaves swirled and twisted under the impact. The elegance of the teapot seemed to represent Father: not understated, but also not flamboyant. He'd asked for two glasses to be on the tray, so Serena assumed he had a guest, probably Ahmed.

Tiphanie entered the kitchen carrying an armful of plates and said, "I can deliver the tea for you, sister."

Serena smiled. "Father asked for me to bring it to him."

"Hmm," Tiphanie replied, hefting the plates onto a shelf. "I hope you still have your golden hairpin."

"Of course, sister," Serena replied, noting the coded reference to the stiletto blade sheathed on the inside of her left forearm. "Although I am certain it will not be required. Not with Father."

"Perhaps, but there are many potential dangers on the way to his office."

"And if any appear, they shall receive a most unpleasant surprise. See you later," Serena said, lifting the tray and heading for the doorway.

Tiphanie called after her, "I'll tell Lilliana to begin preparing the fish for dinner. The schedule says we have only the family and staff this evening."

"Good," Serena called over her shoulder. She climbed the stone stairs and turned right at the beautiful Persian vase that was large enough to hide a person. She walked the corridor to Father's office, her footfall silent on the patterned beige and red rug that stretched all the way to the main reception area. The still air carried a faint but pleasant scent of jasmine.

She tapped lightly and entered without waiting, as usual. Father glanced up from his screen and his face softened. Serena placed the silver tray on his desk.

He waved a hand towards the open door and said, "Close the door and sit in the chair, child."

Serena paused. Father had never done such a thing. Her senses reacted and she readied herself for whatever Father had planned. She crossed the room, closed the door, and returned to the ornate chair to Father's right. Before sitting, she ventured, "Shall I pour the tea?"

Without looking up from his screen, he said, "Yes."

She poured the tea into the two glasses mounted in elegant silver holders.

"And add a small spoon of honey to mine, please."

Serena's heart rocked easily in her chest. Father was the only man who, since she had been abducted from Rome, had not threatened her. The cause of her concern was his interest in her. She added honey to both glasses and stirred the tea. She laid the spoon silently on the tray and sat where indicated.

Finally, Father looked at her. The light from his screen accentuated the small pockmarks in the skin on his face. He clasped his hands together, offered a benign smile and asked, "How are you and my other European slaves?"

"We are well, thank you, Father," Serena replied in his language. "We appreciate that we owe our safety to your magnificence."

His eyebrows rose in surprise and he repeated, "'Magnificence'?"

"Sorry, I meant to say 'munificence', Father. Please forgive my poor knowledge of your language and my simple mistakes."

Father let out a throaty laugh, the kind of laugh Serena sometimes heard distantly when he played with his children.

"I not only forgive you, child. I thank you for making me laugh when there is such turmoil in our great Caliphate, and I complement you on having learned our language to such an advanced level."

"Oh, Father," Serena said plaintively, trying to recover from her mistake while also using it to her advantage, "I try but I am far from advanced."

Still smiling, Father said, "No matter. Let us drink our tea."

Serena took her glass and sipped. She watched the humour leave Father's face while he drank.

He placed the glass on the part of his desk covered in a dark green plastic and said, "I expect you are wondering why we are drinking tea together. This is not usual behaviour for master and slave, is it?"

Serena maintained her composure but her curiosity bristled. She replied, "If it pleases you, Father, then I am also happy—"

"No," Father broke in, suddenly serious. "Happiness is not the objective. Happiness does exist here, in this house, yes. But you see the anger on the streets, do you not?"

"Yes, Father," Serena answered in a demur tone, keeping her head lowered.

"And this is in the great city of Tehran, the capital of our Caliphate. The situation is far worse in the outer provinces."

Serena said nothing. She cared little and knew even less of the internal political situation of this brutal place. She only fought to survive, to protect her sisters, and to gain some revenge if God willed it.

Father went on, "But any happiness is fleeting here, child. Do you know why we live in this opulent palace?" he asked with a wave of his hand.

"No, Father," she lied.

"Because I helped the Third Caliph, and he rewarded me with this palace as a gift."

"Oh, I see."

"So I, and therefore everyone in my house, am permanently connected to the Third Caliph. If he were to fall, if he were replaced with a new leader, we would lose all of this. And probably much more."

The threat behind Father's words was plain. Serena sipped her tea.

"Things are such, child, that it is very difficult to know whom to trust. When things are in balance, peace comes easily. But when balance is upset, trust becomes impossible. Change happens at those times. And when it does, it is usually accompanied by great violence."

Serena's ears picked up. She wanted to question him but dare not. Her senses insisted that she should only listen.

"This Caliphate was forged from great violence, child. Decades ago, there were many countries and tribes in these lands. The First Caliph brought the core lands together. The Second Caliph brought peace and prosperity and learning, which led to a vast flourishing, but the Third Caliph has used every element of modern technology to wage war."

Father lifted his glass and sipped the tea, as though considering what more to tell Serena. He went on, "Without the technology, without the advanced computers and replicators, this Caliphate could not and would not exist. And now the time may be approaching when it shall fall."

Serena allowed a little gasp of feigned concern to escape her lips.

Father looked at her and nodded. "Yes," he said. "It is so serious. The Third Caliph is an ordinary man. His name is Saad. He has two younger brothers, self-styled Grand Viziers called Waqas and Affan. When they seized power from the Second Caliph, about seven years ago, they kept that leader's advisory body, called the Council of Elders. These are twelve leaders from the diverse regions of the Caliphate. Remember, child, the Caliphate has over two hundred and sixty million subjects that represent hundreds of tribes with thousands of customs and traditions."

Serena wondered if Father were speaking for her benefit, or rather to make sense of something to himself.

"But there are always conflicts. Intrigue. Subterfuge. The three brothers used to be very clever indeed, but many on the Council feel that they, and especially Saad, have made a mistake. And to correct the mistake exceeds even the abilities of all of our technology. The mistake is to threaten to invade India in the same manner he invaded Europe. But he seems to forget that India is not Europe. And today, his amazing weapons with which he began his crusades have lost their novelty."

Father turned his head back to his screen and went on, "Three weeks ago, a city in Sahara Province was completely destroyed. On the night it happened, two members of the Council of Elders were meeting in secret there. But no one is left who knows why they met. And what is worse, no one knows how the city was destroyed. Many say it was an earthquake. Others claim that Allah wanted to show his displeasure. Our computers have made the ludicrous suggestion that Europeans somehow managed to use powerful sound waves. But the truth is that no one knows for certain.

"Nevertheless, since then the Third Caliph and his Grand Viziers have grown more paranoid every day. They see betrayal everywhere. The other members of the Council of Elders manufacture false stories to turn suspicion away from them. At the same time, they raise their own private armies in their own territories. The respect and obedience the Third Caliph commanded even a year ago is being challenged with, I fear, dire consequences if he cannot remain in control."

Father let out a heavy sigh. "And this, child, is why we are having tea together."

Serena tilted her head and placed her hand above her eye in feigned sympathy and concern.

"If anything happens; if another member of the Council or some unknown and unsuspected usurpers wreak havoc here, in the capital city of the Caliphate, it will be difficult for me to protect you. You are already aware of the implant that can be used to kill you, yes?"

Serena made eye contact with Father for the first time since he started talking. "Yes, Father," she intoned.

"I have placed a block on anyone other than me giving the command. Ahmed cannot use this, nor any official or guard who takes a dislike to you or your sisters. You are safe. Only the Third Caliph himself can demand it of the computers, as he can of any slave it pleases him to kill. But if he is overthrown, which is now a clear possibility, my house will lose all prestige, and the fate of you and your sisters will be in the hands of Allah."

Serena had to stop herself from scoffing aloud. Her fate remained in God's hands—and it always would.

"Now," he said, "I have told you all I wanted you to know. I have some hope that these disturbances may settle down, somehow. But my hope is fading, child. The new decrees restricting movement are being disregard. Thus, I fear all of us will have to face difficult times. Thank you for the tea."

"Thank you, Father," she replied, standing.

Father gave her a weary smile. "Take these things and return to your duties, child."

Serena picked up the silver tray and swept out of Father's office, spinning around and deftly pulling the handle of the large door with a crooked little finger so it closed under its own momentum.

Chapter 35

08.11 Monday 3 September 2063

Captain Pip Clarke looked at the rows of residential houses that faced her and the company she led. They'd emerged through a barren forest where the autonomous troop transports had deposited them half an hour earlier. Now, they cleared the treeline to be presented with a selection of typically German middle-income streets lined with spacious family homes, most of which appeared deserted but undamaged. Smoke rose from a building five hundred metres away, which Pip's lens identified as having hosted enemy warriors.

She stifled a sigh and tried to get the taste of masonry dust out of her throat. The day's objective remained the same as it had for almost every day since Operation Repulse had begun: clear and secure the objective to allow second-wave units to move in. Today's objective was the town they faced.

Next to her, Mac sucked air in between his teeth and said, "Every one of those houses could be crawling with nasties."

She addressed her Squitch, "Confirm SkyMaster reports. Have the Scythes missed anything?"

"Confirmed. The urban area in front of you has been cleared."

Pip twitched an eye muscle to review the tactical situation in her lens. She opened comms to her troops and instructed, "Okay, all squad leaders. Same as. Send your Pathfinders ahead before you advance. Keep sharp and let's get this cleared so the replicators can come up to build our digs for tonight and deliver the chow."

Mac spoke, his Scottish accent thick with sarcasm, "Request permission to release the Pathfinder!"

Pip shook her head in amused dismay and said, "All squad leaders, permission granted to release your Pathfinders. And keep your heads down, everyone."

Mac took the silver metallic orb from his webbing and gave it a gentle lob towards the nearest property. It thudded into the dirt. Its flimsy legs jutted out and the little android began trotting up the slight incline between the houses. All along the line of advance, thirty or more Pathfinders did the same.

"Okay," Pip said, crouching, "might as well settle down and see what they can make happen."

The lumpen Barny Hines hurried over to MacManus and said, "Reckon there's some nice kit in those drums, don't you?"

Mac replied, "Dinnae be simple in the head, laddie. The ragheads will have had everything out of them that wasn't nailed down."

Hines' head tilted in reconsideration. "I ain't fussy," he replied with a shrug. "I bet they missed something worth having."

Pip leaned over and said, "Private Hines, if you must discuss breaking the law by stealing from the properties we liberate, could you at least do so out of my earshot?"

Hines began to stammer but Pip stilled him with a dismissive wave.

Then, the world exploded.

The ground fell away from Pip and came back to hit her hard on her right hip. The change in pressure sucked the air from her lungs. A high-pitched whine blanketed her hearing, making every noise sound distant.

The ingrained urge for self-preservation forced her to bring her legs up towards her chest to adopt the foetal position. Her training told her to get her arms over her head. Her Squitch was saying something but she couldn't make out what.

The ground around her shook and then was still. The high-pitched whine faded as her hearing returned. "Report," she croaked.

Her Squitch said, "You have suffered minor concussion caused by air-pressure changes."

"Okay," she breathed. She forced herself up onto one elbow and blinked. Her lens relayed data that a Spider in the fifth house along the street had detonated. A vast plume of grey smoke lifted slowly above the scene, dissipating as she watched. "Mac?"

"Aye," Sergeant MacManus answered.

She sat up, relief flooding her body that she was uninjured. She looked left and right at the line of troops. Most of them moved with similar caution. In her lens, data scrolled that named those injured by falling debris and told her they would withdraw to a safe distance for treatment with their battlefield GenoFluid packs. The advance had taken fourteen casualties with minor injuries.

She got to her feet and caught her breath as the disorientation gave her a moment's unsteadiness. However, her Squitch did not offer any warnings, so she knew she must be all right.

Mac pointed to a large piece of twisted metal in front of them and observed, "It's a good thing it blew when it did. Another second and it would've come down on top of us."

Barny Hines looked at the debris and offered, "Looks like part of an aircon system."

"Nothing worth having, then?" Pip asked.

Hines' face showed that he missed the irony. "Nah," he said on consideration. "And it's too heavy to carry, anyway."

Pip scanned the houses in front of them.

Mac asked her, "You think there are more?"

"My lens says the remaining Pathfinders are now nearly half a klick ahead, past the main shopping thoroughfare and approaching the local high school near the railway station. That's where the two squadrons of Abrahams are, so we should be clear up to there. Today, I think they want us nervous, to keep us on our toes. They could be holding bombs back for a new defensive line or counterattack."

"Aye," Mac agreed. "I reckon they're being canny with them. If they decide the game is up, then they might just try to level everything on their way out, and we'll be right in the shite."

Pip glanced again up and down the line. With a twitch of an eye to open comms, she said, "Okay, squad leaders, let's move out. Walking wounded to the rear. If any of your team members needs a hand, get them to relative safety then crack on back to the line. No slackers, if you please."

With her Pickup cradled in her arms, she advanced up the street, past the huge crater and surrounding lip of smoking rubble created by the Spider that detonated when its pulse hit the Pathfinder and decided it was a squaddie. In her mind's eye, she tried to stop scenes of imaginary young families that once lived here, the little children that ran and played in the gardens, the gentle laughter of grandparents and grandchildren gathered around—

"Caution," her Squitch announced. "A new contact has been detected in sector one-nine foxtrot."

"Christ, what now?" Mac said.

In Pip's view, a flashing orange sign denoted the 'new contact' beyond the tanks. She said, "Don't know." They reached a T-junction after which the incline in the road in front of them increased further. Pip paused and said, "Squad leaders, report." She listened as her corporals and sergeants reported in.

Across the broad road that denoted the end of the residential area, four autonomous tanks started up and trundled ahead of the line. They vanished into the grounds of the damaged high school.

Pip's Squitch said, "Danger. Seek cover immediately."

She heard Mac curse and all around her came the sound of shuffling boots. Pip raised her Pickup and backtracked, taking small, cautious steps lest some unseen hazard trip her. But her lens remained clear of direct threats.

"Update," she demanded.

"New contact of previously unknown design is in sector one-nine foxtrot. A Scythe has been diverted and is inbound; ETA twenty-two seconds."

Hisses and booms came through the air.

"Must be our tanks," Mac said.

Pip turned and said, "Let's back off." She hurried down the residential street they'd just cleared, pleased to see that her troops had taken up good defensive positions next to walls and in doorways.

An indicator flashed in her lens denoting an invisible dot in the sky sweeping in to deal with the problem. The Scythe came down and passed over the target. As it climbed, a volley of missiles leapt up to chase it, exploding in pops against the Scythe's shielding. The ACA pirouetted in the northeast and made another pass. More missiles, their tails burning as bright as a blowtorch, raced into the Scythe and exploded against it. The ACA pivoted over the target. There came a deep thump and a lazy plume of smoke drifted into view.

"Update," Pip repeated.

Her Squitch replied, "The battlespace is secure. However, this advance must pause until specialist units arrive."

Pip opened comms and said, "Okay, squad leaders. Not sure what's happened, but let's withdraw to the treeline." She closed the comms and asked, "What the hell was that?"

Her Squitch told her.

Mac, trailing Barny Hines, fell in alongside her as they returned past the ruined houses to the treeline. He asked, "Did you find out what happened?"

"Oh, yes," she replied.

"Can you nay tell us mere scroats?"

Pip smiled and replied, "The ragheads just hit us with a tank."

"A tank?" Mac echoed in disbelief. "Since when did they bother with tanks?"

"I know. It's a first. That's why we've got to pause the advance."

Mac shook his head and said, "They must be getting desperate for ways to hold us up."

Barny Hines lumbered alongside them and announced, "I've been thinking about those Pathfinder things."

Mac said, "Aye, have you now?"

"Yeah. You know how the Pathfinder tricks the sleeping Spider into thinking it's a soldier, so the Spider activates and blows it up?"

"Aye, so?"

"Well, when the Spider fully activates again, I s'pose it must see that the Pathfinder is not actually a soldier. So why doesn't it ignore it, go looking for some actual soldiers and blow them up instead?"

Mac looked at Pip and said, "Laddie makes a good point."

Pip replied, "I'm not sure. Maybe because it's lost touch with its Blackswan?" Pip looked at Hines for a moment and then added, "You know something, Private Hines? I think I prefer it when you're just rummaging around trying to steal anything you can get your hands on."

Hines' square face took on a look of hurt. He complained, "That's not fair, captain. It ain't stealing. It's the spoils of war, that's what it is. Honest."

Chapter 36

11.01 Monday 10 September 2063

Terry Tidbury strode to the entrance to the main War Room and grasped the hand of his visitor, shaking it firmly. He said, "Thank you for coming back from France, Sir Patrick."

General Sir Patrick Fox, commander of First Corps, nodded and replied, "No trouble at all, TT. Good to visit your lair and have a nose around."

Terry's adjutant, Simms, joined them and asked Sir Patrick, "Your usual tea, sir?"

"Thanks, yes."

Simms left.

Terry stuck out a hand and said, "We'll discuss the issues at the main console."

Sir Patrick's oval face tilted and turned at the screens around the exterior walls, nodding in approval.

Terry addressed the flaxen-haired operator at the AGE console, "Put First Corps' current deployments on the central display."

The two men approached the central holographic display as it came to life with a topographical, blue-hued map of central Germany. Small globes, cubes and pyramids indicated deployments of units and materiel, while shades of red denoted how far behind schedule Operation Repulse had fallen. Above the map were written the words, 'R-plus-forty-one'.

Sir Patrick waved a finger at the display and observed, "Looks quite bad when you show it like that."

Terry shrugged and replied, "This is today's locations. We anticipated there would be problems. The enemy was hardly likely just to roll over, was he?"

"I think his leaving those Spiders behind ready to snag an unsuspecting soldier was very bad form."

"It's caused more than one problem, but we'll come back to that in a moment."

Sir Patrick said, "The last few days, we've had numerous reports of the Pathfinder failing to stop the Spiders. We're being obliged to take higher casualties."

Terry said, "I've heard some complaints. That countermeasure is the best we can do in the circumstances. Given the range of the types of terrain we have to clear, it was always going to be almost impossible to account for every eventuality."

"Scant comfort for the soldiers tasked with recovering territory, TT," Sir Patrick replied.

Terry said, "Regaining enemy-held ground is unlikely to be an entirely risk-free endeavour in any action, general."

"What are the total casualties from those hidden Spider attacks?"

The figure, over two thousand dead and injured since the first deactivated Spider surprised the first NATO soldier, resolved near the top of the image.

"Hmm," Sir Patrick mused. "Given the cost in lives of this war to date, that in actual fact does not appear to be a high number. We could've done without those tanks, as well. Why on earth introduce a main battle tank at this stage?"

"The naming committee have given the enemy's tank the reporting name 'Moose'," Terry said. "And analyses show the enemy is manufacturing the things at former NATO facilities in occupied Europe."

"How efficient."

Simms reappeared carrying a tray on which sat two steaming mugs of tea.

Sir Patrick's face lit up. "Mugs? Excellent. On the continent, no matter where I go the tea always seems to be served in a cup and saucer, and there's never enough to drink."

"But the Moose's purpose," Terry said, taking a mug, "as with the deactivated Spiders, is to delay us as much as possible. And that's what I asked you here to discuss."

Sir Patrick nodded in consideration. He sipped his tea and said, "I'll be frank, TT. Some commanders are suffering from clear cases of overcaution. Indeed, I decided on the way here that if you didn't raise the subject, I certainly would."

Terry pointed at the eastern front, a jagged line running the length of central Germany. He said, "Then we need to make changes."

"Very well. Where are we furthest behind?"

"Oddly," Terry said, "it might be better to look at where we are furthest ahead."

The hologram zoomed to an area around Hannover. One globe denoting Polish First Army subdivided into more detailed formations.

Terry went on, "From all of the Attack Group East formations, the Poles are making the strongest headway. Pakla is like a rottweiler off the leash. He has a range of battlefield commanders who are incredibly able. But, most importantly, he seems to enjoy an endless supply of fearless troops who will not be deterred by any of the enemy's innovations. Repulse's timetable says he needs to reach Berlin by the end of October. I expect him to get there within a month from now."

Sir Patrick murmured his agreement and said, "Those Poles are fighting to free their country. Yet again."

"And it will be freed, again."

"I am quite sure, TT, that Pakla also shares our concerns regarding how soon the enemy will deploy new and better ACAs."

The image withdrew and shifted northwards. The front line straggled to the left.

"And Pakla's success is risking his flanks. There, on his left, we have a mix of British, German and Hungarian battalions moving more slowly."

"Yes," Sir Patrick agreed, "we should look at replacing some of the underperforming British commanders. But what about the others?"

Terry looked at the general and asked, "What do you mean?"

Sir Patrick's eyes narrowed. "Upsetting the European formations?"

"No. They are part of NATO and I am their commanding officer. There is no room here for nationalistic sensitivities. Now, if we look to the south, on the Poles' right flank, we have another mix: a majority of British, but also Commonwealth formations and units from the Baltics…"

Over the next thirty minutes, with Sir Patrick's advice Terry agreed the sacking of seven generals and the promotions of their replacements. Squonk would handle the initial logistics, to begin later in the day, with Terry speaking to each affected commander in person.

When Simms had delivered the next round of tea, Sir Patrick asked, "What about Attack Group South, TT?"

The hologram over the central display shifted upwards. Southern France and the Franco/Spanish border came into view.

Terry said, "The Americans are making a pretty good fist of it, all round. Although some elements of the Third and Fifth Armies are behind by up to two days."

The image enlarged to bring the southernmost section into closer view.

Terry went on, "Brooks and Garret are competent commanders, although AGS is far from exclusively made up of American forces."

"How are the US Marines performing? I assume they've ditched those death-trap exoskeletons that cost them so much on the English coast last year?"

"They have," Terry confirmed. "But, as with AGE, the hindrances the enemy has thrown in our way these last couple of weeks are costing too much time in the south as well." Terry folded his arms and let out a contemplative sigh. He added, "Although with the American generals, diplomacy remains the order of the day."

Sir Patrick nodded his comprehension. "I don't envy you having to deal with the politicians."

Terry shook his head and replied in dismissiveness, "Part of the job. I have no interest in our political leaders' personal relationships as long as I can keep them at arm's length when it comes to making the important decisions."

Sir Patrick picked up his fresh mug of tea and gave Terry a rueful smile. He said, "Difficult decisions remain the privilege of command, TT."

Terry let out a mirthless guffaw. "Choices are one thing; trying to anticipate the enemy's next move is quite another."

"He's erratic, to say the least."

"I don't like to speculate, Pat, but the newest intel shows that there's not a great deal of stability underpinning the enemy's empire. I keep hoping there'll be more internal destabilisation to stop him deciding on the Hitler Option."

"The 'Hitler Option'?" Sir Patrick echoed.

Terry looked at the general. "Yes, where he orders that ground be held at all costs. So far, we're getting not much more than nasty surprises; novelties we can cope with—assuming the field commanders can motivate their troops sufficiently—but we know from the number of dead warriors that a majority of them must be retreating. So, they could cause us even more trouble in the near future. We can't afford Repulse to be delayed further by any futile last stands, however extensive and well-coordinated."

"We still have a long way to go."

"And despite appearances, the whole operation is still very much in the balance."

"I appreciate your caution, but I don't see what could derail it now, TT."

"A great deal could 'derail' it, as you put it. Sooner or later, he has to hit us with better weapons, certainly improved ACAs."

"But we levelled his main ACA production plant—"

"He might have better construction replicators than we know."

"Pity about Hastings, don't you think?"

"A couple of his team made it out, and that in itself was a first. And the benefit of the success of Thunderclap to Repulse is incalculable."

"Absolutely," Sir Patrick agreed.

Terry paced around the central console. He said, "You know, Pat, I'm concerned that right now, we might actually be at our most vulnerable?"

"I have to disagree, TT. You are indeed the CO. It's your job to see all of the threats to Operation Repulse, both potential and actual, but I think you are seeing things at what we might call the 'negative end of the spectrum'." Sir Patrick lifted his mug of tea and concluded, "You remain at the head of the most technologically advanced army the world has ever seen. The prospect of Repulse being denied is infinitesimal."

Terry looked at the general and wondered how much of what the man said constituted his martial opinion and how much he truly believed. Terry decided that it really didn't matter. Time would tell. He smiled at Sir Patrick and said, "Shall we go downstairs and get some lunch?"

"Excellent idea, TT."

Chapter 37

23.01 Tuesday 18 September 2063

Serena Rizzi sat on the edge of her bed and whispered to Tiphanie and Liliana, "I have presents for each of you. Come here."

Tiphanie smiled but concern creased Liliana's forehead. They closed the window and unrolled the cotton cover that acted as a curtain. A lamp on the small bedside table threw a bright yellow light onto Serena's lap, on which she held a bundle wrapped in white material.

The bed squeaked when Tiphanie's voluptuous form sat on Serena's left, but made no sound when the waifish Liliana did the same on her right.

Serena contained her enthusiasm as she said, "I have something for you that I promised some weeks ago."

Tiphanie put her hand on Serena's shoulder and said, "Thank you, sister."

"You don't know what it is, yet," Serena answered.

"I have hope."

Liliana did not speak.

Serena unrolled the bundle on her lap to reveal two small, thin objects also wrapped individually in more of the same material. She said, "You know that for some time now, I have had my golden hairpin strapped to my forearm?" She lifted the sleeve of her *abaya* to show the others the sheath containing the stiletto blade. "Now," she said, "I have secured one for each of you." She handed each of them one of the two packages.

Tiphanie's face lit up. She unwrapped the sheath. She unclipped a small button fastener and pulled the stiletto out. The edge of the silver blade glinted in the lamplight. "It's lovely," she breathed. "Thank you, sister."

Serena pointed to the two securing straps and said, "See? You tie it to your forearm with those, and keep it safe with that clasp at the top. Then the weapon stays hidden by the sleeve of your *abaya*. If any man tries to violate you, you can make him regret it very much."

"Wonderful," Tiphanie cooed.

Liliana held hers unwrapped and said, "I do not want it."

"You should wear it, sister," Serena urged. "It might save your life."

"Might?" Liliana repeated in disbelief. She whispered in fear, "We are not allowed to carry such things. If Ahmed or any of the men in the house caught us with it, we would all be killed. Do you forget the implants they put in our bodies in Italy, sister? This," she said, holding the package up, "will cause us to be killed for certain."

Serena watched Liliana's lower lip tremble as her frightened eyes flicked from side to side. "Try to stay calm," Serena said, placing a hand on Liliana's thigh.

With tears welling in her eyes, Liliana repeated, "But they will kill us for having these. I do not think even Father would be able to stop them."

Serena struggled to think of a way to calm Liliana and encourage the younger girl to defend herself if she had to.

Tiphanie leaned close to Serena and said to Liliana, "Sister, they have already killed us. They killed you when they took you from Italy; they killed me when they took me from France. Please, see the truth. We have all been violated. And we probably shall be again. It is only a matter of time. We have simply been fortunate to have ended up here, in Father's house."

Liliana rubbed a tear from her cheek with the back of her hand and said, "I do not care. I shall not wear it. I am sorry, sister."

Serena said, "Of course. Do not be upset. I will keep it in case you change your mind."

"I will not," Liliana insisted with a shake of her head.

Tiphanie asked Serena, "Help me put it on."

Serena showed her how to balance the sheath on her thigh to be able to tie the straps more easily.

Tiphanie asked, "How were you able to get these?"

Serena replied, "They are quite easy to find at the Wednesday market."

"That market is huge," Tiphanie said.

"On the northern side, there are lots of stalls selling blades of all kinds, from little kitchen knives to scimitars."

"Oh."

"I have to be careful, of course. The so-called men there are often offended that a lone female is there. Then they are shocked that a Christian slave can speak their tongue so well." She finished securing the sheath on Tiphanie's forearm.

Tiphanie lifted her arm and moved it back and forth, murmuring in approval. She observed, "I must remember not to lift my arm too high in case the sleeve slides up my arm and someone sees it."

Serena went on, "I tell them my owner needs special knives for peeling figs and other—"

"Peeling figs?" Tiphanie queried with a chuckle.

"Yes," Serena replied. "I can keep most of them in a kind of unsure shock. But there are some…" she shivered. "You can see the hate in their eyes." She paused and then said, "You know Chundee, the knife-sharpener?"

Tiphanie nodded.

"I put those in with all of the kitchen knives, and when they come back, they are extremely sharp."

"It is a very good idea, sister," Tiphanie said.

Serena glanced back at Liliana and said, "I worry that we may find our lives getting worse soon."

"Why?" Tiphanie asked.

"Father spoke to me again this afternoon. I think he has come to trust me because I am a Christian and a slave. For whatever reason, he does not seem to consider me a threat." Serena watched the others stare at her. She went on, "I am sure he talks to me as a way to think out loud and consider his worries. Sometimes, he deactivates the translation so I do not have the Italian text in my vision. I think he may have forgotten that I can understand everything he says in his own language, even without the translation."

Tiphanie asked, "What did he say this time?"

"He said we should be ready in case we have to move again, suddenly. He said this palace might be taken from him and given to a more loyal supporter. Apparently, there are big rifts among the Council of Elders. There is fighting in the south among tribes and cities that used to be separate countries before the formation of the Caliphate. Also, there are accusations. Last month, an earthquake destroyed a whole city in the western desert—"

"But that is not possible," Tiphanie broke in. "There are no fault lines—"

"Exactly," Serena confirmed. "An earthquake happened where none has ever happened before, so there is much blame and many accusations. Worse, two members of the Council of Elders were killed there. Father thinks more trouble might be on the way here, to Tehran."

For a space, silence fell among the European women.

Liliana broke it with a sniff and said, "So, I think I should accept your gift, dear sister. Will you tie it on my arm for me, please?"

Serena looked at Liliana and her heart swelled with pride. "Yes, of course I will," she said.

Chapter 38

16.12 Wednesday 26 September 2063

The Englishman smiled at the receptionist, or 'front-of-house staff' as the embassy liked to call them.

The young lady, her hair swept back in a bun and a tight-fitting white blouse stretching over her lithe limbs, gave him a tight smile back. She said, "You really don't need to wait, sir. The pouch will be collected shortly."

He asked, "May I sit over there?" indicating a low, cream-coloured leather couch behind a coffee table.

"Of course," she replied with an indifferent shrug.

He left her and sat. He picked up one of the embassy's bland magazines and flicked through it. *Especially English* featured articles on the few things left about which England could still boast. These included a feature on his own cover story as a wholesaler of English piss-water that its producers laughingly called wine. He scanned the text and images, recognising some of the named brands he talked about at dreary functions.

Minutes passed. The receptionist took a call in Cantonese, then a second in English. Two lumbering giants exited the lift on the far side of the area, and the Englishman caught their American accents as they passed him and approached the large glass entrance doors.

When the doors opened and the Americans left, a courier in a brown uniform entered and hurried up to the receptionist. She handed him a grey satchel that was the diplomatic pouch and the courier left. The Englishman threw the magazine back onto the coffee table, stood, and followed the man out of the building and back to his autonomous vehicle.

With a twitch of his eye, the Englishman's lens would track the vehicle. Satisfied, he crossed the expansive stone courtyard and exited the grounds through the wrought-iron gate, nodding to the security guard sitting in a quaint little wooden booth. The sun beat down on the street in a cloying heat that only a vast city like Beijing could produce. He pushed up the sleeves of his fashionably thin sweatshirt and strode on towards the largest shopping mall in the district. Now that the diplomatic pouch was safely on its way, perhaps he would treat himself to something material before he enjoyed someone carnally.

In his lens, he looked at his list of contacts, trying to decide who he wanted tonight. He called Hu, the analyst who provided him with intel on China's deployments in Africa.

"Wha' you want?" barked into his ear.

"Want to meet up? I've got a new batch of the very best gear, sweetheart—"

"No," Hu shouted. "No, no, no. I doan' wanna see you. You hear me?"

"What? Hey, take it easy—"

"No. You go. Doan' call me ever. You hear? Ever."

The connection ended; the Englishman sighed. "Whatever," he said to himself. "You always came too quickly, anyway, you selfish bastard."

He reached one of the entrances to the huge mall. He twitched an eye muscle and zoomed and rotated the plan of shops that was digitally overlaid in his view. From the advertising highlights that ran down one channel on his left, he saw that Samsung had released its newest lens. This boasted a brand-new and hotly anticipated feature whereby the wearer could manipulate overlaid digital content by interacting with their hands. To the outside observer, the person would appear to be waving their hands in mid-air at nothing, but this innovation promised to be a game-changer in modern tech, and the Englishman considered it a just reward for what was in the pouch.

The Samsung boutique was on the fifth and highest level of the mall.

By twitching his eye, the Englishman ordered and paid for a latté, and then collected the cup of coffee from a window he strolled past a minute later. He got on an escalator and sipped the hot, bitter liquid. He called Fen, another of his habituals, who had been instrumental in gaining the dossier, a copy of which was now winging its way to London.

No answer.

He alighted the escalator, strolled past several shops, and got on the next escalator to take him higher. He switched to tracking the courier and smiled in satisfaction when he saw that the vehicle had reached the airport. He relaxed. In just a few hours, the pouch would reach its destination and his boss would have proof of what the crazy Third Caliph was planning next—and how China was pulling the strings.

Another three escalator rides later, he arrived on the highest floor of the mall. There were fewer people here. He walked towards the Samsung boutique, his mind made up to buy the new lens after scanning advance press reviews, and tried calling Fen again.

But the voice that answered did not belong to Fen. A woman spoke. "Hiya," she said.

The Englishman didn't reply. A digital question mark winked in the corner of his view, meaning that his interlocutor had requested visual as well as audio. He paused. He knew the voice but couldn't place it.

The female voice spoke again, "You wanna talk? I fink it good idea, yeah?"

The Englishman stopped walking. Dread congealed in the pit of his stomach. He willed it not to be so. He allowed visual contact. A woman resolved with a perfectly oval face, narrow eyes, and pursed, deep-red lips. She might have been the most beautiful Chinese woman he had ever seen. And he had seen her before.

"Good," she said. "You remember your manners, yeah?"

The Englishman suddenly did not know where to turn. He stood outside the Samsung boutique, with its array of internal and external body tech for today's modern citizen of the most advanced country on Earth.

The woman's head tilted in curiosity and she said in her broken English, "How you fink I not ever find you again?"

He stammered, "Where's... Fen?" although his detached common sense told him the answer.

"Fen already dead. We don't like traitors, yeah? And you? You fink your quantum encryption gonna keep you safe? You real English dumbass."

Recollections of the outrageous pain this woman had inflicted on him in June the previous year resurfaced. The memory made him shiver. He began to hyperventilate.

"I fink you better come in. We talk, yeah? Like the old days."

"Jesus," he panted, trying to get a grip. He'd been in tricky situations before. He just needed to keep calm and work out an escape. Without his bidding, a new image resolved in his view: a map to lead him down the escalators and into the underground vehicle park.

The woman said, "Okay. So, we do this easy. You go down, get in car. Car brings you to me. You tell me what you done. I put new bots in and you can live. If no, you die. Deal?"

Anger surged inside him. Anger at himself for getting caught. Anger at the Chinese secret service for giving a shit about him or what he was doing. He said, "From all the shit you've got going on, why are you even bothering with a dumbass like me?"

She smiled, looking dazzlingly gorgeous, and said, "You don't ask questions. You go to underground car. Now. Yes, or no?"

The Englishman determined his course of action. He spat, "Fuck off, you slit-eyed cunt." With his thumbnail, he hooked the lens out of his eye. All digital data immediately vanished from his view. He held it between his forefinger and thumb, and then twisted it over in a vain attempt to break it. For good measure, he threw it on the tiled floor and stamped on it with his foot, using the heal of his shoe to grind it. He lost all ability to be in touch, but she lost all ability to track him.

"Right," he said to no one in particular, "time to leg it back to the embassy. Fuck you, Beijing. I'm off to Blighty."

He turned towards the lift at the far end of the row of shops and ran. It rose to meet him. The glass doors opened and two men in leather jackets stepped out, sunglasses obscuring their faces, weapons drawn but pointing at the floor. He spun around and ran in the opposite direction. Another figure stood on the escalator coming up to that level. He ran past that and on to the down escalator. As he expected, a similar figure waited for him at the bottom of it.

The Englishman backed away, looking left and right. He had one last escape route. He turned towards the Samsung boutique. He could get out through the rear and escape via the cargo lift or emergency exit stairs. He rushed for the doors. They were locked. He shook the silver handle hard, even as his common sense told him that the building's super AI had locked the doors and would not open them until it was told to do so.

The Englishman turned back to face his tormentors. Beyond them was the barrier, made up of oblong cream panels topped with an elegant and continuous chrome handrail. On the other side of that rail was a five-storey drop to the fountains on the ground floor. His final choice became plain: more agony with that vile witch, continuing for hours or days or months and likely ending in his death at her pleasure—or a moment's agony now? The agents paced with caution towards him. Soon, even that last choice would be gone.

The Englishman decided. He pushed himself off the glass doors and ran as fast as he could, leaping up and over the handrail to plunge five storeys to the ground floor below.

Chapter 39

08.49 Monday 1 October 2063

David Perkins, the head of MI5, exited the lift on the fourth floor of Ten Downing Street and strode towards the prime minister's private flat. Although he disliked talking to anyone outside the intelligence community—usually because they seldom understood anything about his work—what had arrived in the latest diplomatic pouch from Beijing was little short of dynamite.

However, in its way, this also frustrated him. Now that the military operation to reclaim mainland Europe had been going on for two months, the subterfuge of his department's work had returned to more traditional ground. MI5 had retreated to where it belonged: in the shadows, securing information, defending England and the Home Countries, and engaging in the occasional act of violence.

The heavy panelled door swung open at his approach, the PM's effeminate aide holding it open.

"Good morning, Mr Perkins," Crispin Webb said.

Perkins simply nodded in response as he entered the flat. He strode along the corridor, hearing the door close behind him and Webb's soft footfall on the lush carpet.

"On the right, here," Webb said.

"I do recall," Perkins replied, unable to hide his irritation. Ever since the problem with the SPI protocols the previous year, he laboured under the added pressure of the PM disliking him, although he'd be the first to admit the feeling was mutual.

Perkins entered the spacious living area he had hitherto only seen on the screen in his Whitehall office. "Good morning," he said to the room.

"Thank you for coming, Mr Perkins," Dahra Napier said from the two-seater couch.

Perkins glanced at the young defence secretary, Liam Burton, and the foreign secretary, Charles Blackwood. Both men repeated the PM's welcome.

Webb offered, "Coffee? Tea? Something stronger?"

Perkins looked at him and replied, "No, thank you. I do not plan to take up too much of your time. Will the field marshal be joining us?"

"No," Burton said. "He's busy and has asked me to appraise him afterwards."

Perkins shrugged and said, "I could appraise him myself, but as he wishes." He withdrew the data-pod from his jacket pocket and said, "May I, PM?"

Napier nodded.

Perkins placed the data-pod in a port next to the screen over the fireplace. He said, "Computer? Display the English summary appended to this Chinese dossier."

"Confirmed."

Perkins went on, the urge to leave as soon as possible growing. "This is a dossier on present strategy—entitled Current and Future Threats—for the internal Chinese intelligence community, with recommendations to the politburo. According to the dossier, it is updated every month to reflect geopolitical changes and fluctuating exigencies. The politburo then debates its findings a few days later at its monthly meeting, and decides any necessary adjustments to Chinese foreign policy. This is the first time we have been able to obtain a copy of any of these dossiers."

Burton blew air through his teeth while Blackwood's eyebrows rose up his forehead. Napier sat and sipped what looked like coffee.

Perkins read the summary aloud, "One, a war between the New Persian Caliphate and India should be regarded as desirable. India is China's main competitor in shrinking global manufacturing markets, and a similar war as that seen in Europe would likely benefit many Chinese economic sectors. However, one potential drawback is that, unlike in Europe, a war between the Caliphate and India would probably involve the extensive use of nuclear and/or chemical and biological weapons, whose effects are likely to extend beyond the belligerents' own borders. Even so, an exchange of such weapons would also open opportunities for Chinese businesses, especially in the health care sector.

"Two: the cessation of all exports to the Caliphate as a result of it using banned chemical weapons in Europe does not appear to be having any effect whatsoever on its internal economy. The objective of demonstrating that the use of such weapons will not be accepted has not been achieved, hence the conclusions in point one above. In addition, the weapons' production facility abutting the city of Tazirbu is likely to resume producing weapons in the next few days. These will be next-generation autonomous combat aircraft that we expect will drag the European conflict into a quagmire with no immediate or short-term resolution in sight. Again, this may offer benefits to Chinese businesses that provide services in Africa through intermediaries into the Caliphate."

Perkins paused. The colour had drained from the PM's face. The other cabinet ministers also looked shocked. He concluded, "Three: thus far, the ongoing conflict in a relative backwater such as Europe does not impact China greatly. To date, compensation paid to legitimate business interests that have proved their European write-downs is less than one hundred trillion Yuan. As mentioned above, in the event a war between the Caliphate and India does break out, these losses will be offset by a factor of at least two hundred based on current projections of economic opportunities."

Charles Blackwood cast his eyes at the others and said, "My god, they really only think in terms of their enormous economy."

Burton asked, "Sir Terry will want to know the date of the dossier. How old is it?"

Perkins replied, "It's dated 21 August this year."

"Thank you," Burton said.

Perkins glanced around the room. "Does anyone have any questions?"

Napier spoke: "That's the summary. Have you read the whole dossier?"

"I have, PM."

"Is there anything else you think we should know about?"

The pointedness of her question, given their previous confrontations, was not lost on Perkins. He considered his response before replying, "The dossier goes into far more depth in justifying those summary conclusions. In particular, there are recommendations at the security and economic level—"

"For example?" Napier asked.

"For example, in the former case—security—enhancing ACA patrols in the mountainous regions close to China's border with India and accelerating the testing of an equivalent to NATO's SHF burners to defeat Caliphate jamming. This is in the event of a Caliphate victory over India. In the latter case—economically—this involves sending out advisory comms to select, government-owned multinationals suggesting they artificially inflate the costs of medical equipment by delaying deliveries of, for example, GenoFluid packs, until hostilities break out, at which point long-term supply contracts should be renegotiated in China's favour."

"I see," Napier said.

"If you have the time, PM, it is worth reading the entire document. If nothing else, it offers a remarkable insight into the mentality of the Chinese security apparatus, not to mention a damning account of the utmost cynicism at the highest level of their political order."

Blackwood brushed the sleeve of his jacket and asked, "And we got this from a reliable contact, yes? I mean, there's no hint this could be false and planted to distract or mislead us?"

Perkins replied, "None at all. The contact in question was the same one who first sent us evidence of the Caliphate's intention to invade Europe in January last year."

A silence hung in the air, and Perkins knew he did not need to add: *which evidence you all refused to believe until it was too late.*

"In that case," Napier said, "please pass on our gratitude for his or her hard work and resourcefulness."

"Thank you, PM," Perkins replied. "Will that be all?"

"Yes, thank you," Napier said.

"Er, if I may?" Liam Burton said, his eyes glancing from the PM to Perkins and back."

"Yes, defence secretary?" Perkins said.

"What is your personal opinion of this, Mr Perkins? What does your expertise tell you?"

Perkins understood the young man framed his question to flatter him, so he deflected by saying, "My 'expertise' doesn't tell me a great deal. But my contacts in the Indian government confirm that the country's armed forces are as ready as they can be. As he did with Europe, India expects the Third Caliph simply to invade when he chooses. The Indian intelligence services are convinced, rightly or wrongly, that the Third Caliph seeks world domination, and, like all dictators throughout history, he will not stop until he is stopped."

"Thank you," Burton said, sitting back in his chair.

"Well," Napier said, bristling, "that's hardly going to happen now, is it? Terry assures me that the operation to reclaim Europe is too far advanced to be prevented now."

Perkins looked at the woman, abruptly loathing her for her misplaced confidence in the field marshal. But he said, "I am not well-versed in military issues, PM. I would only note what the dossier says on the subject, and how a grinding, protracted kind of stalemate—or even new weapons to push us backwards—would benefit our enemies."

Chapter 40

18.00 Monday 1 October 2063

Terry Tidbury sipped the hot mug of tea, the small of his back resting against the desk in his private office. He waited as thumbnails of his generals flashed into life around the edges of the large wall screen.

Squonk spoke, "Sir Terry, all required attendees are present."

"Ladies and gentlemen," Terry began. "I will be brief and to the point. I had considered bringing our scheduled meeting forward but decided against doing so given that each of you has your own staff to manage and which you will shortly have to brief with some unwelcome news."

Terry drank from the mug again to allow his audience to acclimate to the fact that their lives—and those of the troops under their command—were about to become more difficult. He put the mug on the desk beside him and folded his arms. "We have received intelligence that the enemy might be about to bring its ACA production plant in Tazirbu back online. It was of course nothing less than remarkable that our forces were able to remove it from the battle at all, never mind for nearly two months.

"If our intel is good, and I have no reason to believe it isn't, then we must redouble our efforts to regain ground before he can produce and deliver to the battlespace more powerful autonomous combat aircraft. We know for a fact that a majority of his warrior group armies are retreating as we advance. But our advance has been to a notable degree dependent on the enemy being unable to deploy a greater number of machines.

"Now, we know he has—for reasons best known to himself—held a substantial part of his forces back in readiness for an assault on India. Latest intel also confirms that the Indian government is expecting an invasion in the nearest future. However, I believe we cannot rely on him continuing to make this mistake. If he chooses to postpone his attack on India, he will have ample reserves to deploy against us. And if the plant at Tazirbu does return to full production, Operation Repulse would face a material risk to its success."

Terry picked his tea up and drank, sensing again his lack of erudition when needing to emphasise the importance of a new development to his staff. He steeled himself to deliver more bad news. "When I was informed of this new intelligence earlier today, I immediately made inquiries regarding our own weapons' development programme. As you have already been briefed, our next-gen ACAs are on the way. But it will be weeks before all tests will be complete and they can go into production and deployment.

"Therefore, over the next two or three days, I will speak to each of you individually. But before I do, I want to ask you to consider a hypothetical scenario where we might suddenly be obliged to dig in, to protect our gains, against a resurgent enemy. I want each of you to analyse your section of the front and look for natural physical obstacles such as rivers, hills and mountains, as well as manmade ones like large conurbations. Obviously, do this in consultation with your own field commanders and the computers. But bear in mind that you should be as ambitious as possible. Any questions?"

"Yes," said Lieutenant-General Robert Kovar, commander of the Czech 41st Mechanised Battalion. "A large part of every day's advance involves getting survivors to the rear, managing PoWs, clearing bodies—many of which are usually in advanced states of decay—and making rudimentary assessments of the most urgent needs. If you are as sure as you sound regarding... this development, would it not be better to slow, rather than accelerate, the operation? Will one or two kilometres here or there really make a difference?"

Terry said, "Thank you, Lieutenant-General Kovar. Firstly, I am not as sure as I might sound. I still entertain hopes the enemy will continue with his mistake and we will be able to secure the mainland before the year's end. Secondly, I will not allow a sense to develop again that the advancement of Operation Repulse is some kind of optional tactic depending on the circumstances on any given day. You yourself were promoted three weeks ago to replace General Hrčka due to his failure to advance in line with the timetable."

Terry pushed himself off his desk and stepped closer to the screen. Sweat prickled the back of his bald head. "As I occasionally do with each of you during our individual discussions, I will use this opportunity to remind all of you that this is a live shooting war. We cannot be sure of our enemy's plans or his intentions. Today, we have the initiative. Today, we have the most effective weapons. Today, we have the momentum to drive us forwards. It is prudent to assume that our enemy probably does not appreciate these facts. So far, he has made piecemeal efforts that have transpired to be hinderances. And unfortunately, some of those efforts yielded him results. I order all of you to look at ways to accelerate the timetable on your sectors, and to make contingencies in the event the enemy makes a determined counterattack."

Terry paused before asking, "Any further questions?"

No one spoke.

"Very well. Before I conclude, I can inform you that our two new ACAs have been named the Scythe Alpha and the Scythe Omega. You will receive further details later today and a full presentation at the daily situation briefing the day after tomorrow. Thank you, ladies and gentlemen. I will speak to each of you individually in due course."

Chapter 41

15.15 Saturday 6 October 2063

Journalist Geoff Morrow looked at the destroyed refugee camp and wondered about the lives of the people who'd died there. Around him, the oaks and birches and limes and acacias still held on to the deep greens of their summer leaves. Geoff had found out that some of the last lakes in the country kept the water table high enough that these trees could survive, a rare area of green on a continent that became more desert-like every decade.

On the forest floor, however, none of the people who'd sought escape far from any towns or villages had survived.

Sergeant Savage was trudging through the low ferns up ahead, weapon at the ready. He called back over his shoulder, "They're all dead, Journo. They were dead a year ago, and they'll still be dead a year from now."

"Ha-fucking-ha," Geoff muttered under his breath. He called back, "Right. I'll take a few minutes here and catch you up."

"Don't make me have to come back and get you. Leipzig is only a couple of hours ahead and we're getting thirsty."

Geoff didn't answer. With the care a forensic investigator might take, he trod towards the remnants of light-blue commercial camping tents. All were singed around the edges, evidence that the camp had been burned, not visited by a Spider. Torn and rotten clothes and other debris littered the central space.

He sought physical remains until he realised that they would've been eaten by wild boars or deer or wolves or foxes. Damn. Just as he was about to leave and catch up with the soldiers, his eye alighted on an old-fashioned slate, its circular frame open. He trod over to it and twitched his eye muscle to tell his lens to try and make contact with it. He didn't hold out much hope. The owner had obviously been among the victims, so would hardly be able to approve the link—

Suddenly, his lens told him that the owner had disengaged the device's quantum encryption. Morbid curiosity surged inside him. The slate's condition had degraded as a result of exposure to the elements, but even though it was an older model, its battery still had twelve percent left. In addition, much data had been lost from the degradation. He selected the most recent media content, dated 3 July 2062, fifteen months earlier.

Geoff caught his breath at the video of a young father holding a baby. The man's rasping German voice sounded urgent, and Geoff's lens automatically provided a text translation near the man's head.

The man's round, earnest face beamed. "We have done it. We have come as far as possible from any built-up area." The footage panned around the complete tents and camping site this group of people had established. He went on, "We have provisions to last many weeks, as well as weapons to defend ourselves and our families. We know the army and the government will protect the country all they can. We only need to be resourceful, to hold out until we receive the all-clear and return to our homes. And we will!"

With that exultation, the footage ended. Geoff silently thanked the man for having the presence of mind to disable the quantum encryption so that his final words might be witnessed and referenced for posterity. The man must've taken such an action in the moments or even seconds before he and his family were killed. And given what had happened to Geoff's family in London during the infamous attack on 2 June the previous year, he appreciated the German's clarity of thought in those final moments.

Geoff looked at the faded and decayed remains of the camp. Yet again, he sent a notification to the NATO investigators in the follow-up waves, who would have the time and forensic aids to establish as many of the details as possible. Geoff wondered if the man in the footage had realised that his act of making the recording had probably attracted the Lapwing that had put an end to their secret resistance. Geoff asked himself why those people in 2062—which felt like a century ago now—had failed to work out how the enemy tracked, found, and killed them.

Geoff hurried away from the wrecked camp and through the fens to catch up with Sergeant Savage. His limbs became chilled with sweat when he ran. He had to leap over plants and shrubs and not trip on protruding tree stumps. He wondered if there mightn't be a handy path close by.

At length, he made out the khaki-clad back of Savage as the Royal Marine continued to trudge through the forest.

On hearing the noise, Savage turned around and asked, "Are they still dead?"

Geoff choked down a foul curse. Instead, he said, "Don't you give a shit about any of these poor bastards?"

"Nope."

"Why?"

"Because they're dead."

"But they died horrible, violent deaths."

Savage shrugged, "We've all got to die of something."

"Won't you care that someone will care about you when you die?"

"Nope."

"Why?"

"Because I'll be dead."

"Right."

"Would you like to shut the fuck up about now?"

"I need to file a report to London."

Savage flashed him a sardonic grin and said, "But you'll say nice things about the Royal Marines who are looking after you, won't you?"

Geoff tutted and replied, "If you insist."

"There's a good Journo."

Geoff fell back from Savage as they continued traipsing through the trees. He heard the sergeant mutter confirmations and instructions, including that they would form up at the edge of the forest six hundred metres ahead.

Geoff opened a comms link to his media outlet in London and spoke his report, not worrying about the quality of his language because Alan, or probably one of his underlings, would edit it to death anyway. "Day sixty-six of NATO's operation to restore freedom to the European mainland has revealed yet more tragic stories of those who were unable to escape. This morning, the company of Royal Marines with whom I'm embedded cleared the small village of Grandenborn in the countryside of central Germany. We witnessed familiar sights of burned houses and farms, and the church spire—over eight hundred years old—had been dashed to the ground. We saw little evidence of the owners and residents of the village. Perhaps some were fortunate enough to escape, but it is more likely that forensic investigators will identify human remains among the ruins, as has already been the case in so many towns and villages. It is still a fact that local populations of wild boar, deer, wolf and fox have grown substantially in the last year, and may also account for the lack of physical remains of the Caliphate's victims. Indeed, this afternoon while clearing forested area, we came across a destroyed makeshift camp…"

Geoff continued the report as, in front of him, the forest thinned. He attached the footage of the victim. He emerged out of the trees on the side of a hill that offered a view of Leipzig. It presented a dismal scene of widespread destruction; a flatness where no structure more than a few metres tall had survived and over which hung an anaemic white mist of sadness.

Savage called to him, "Looks like you've still got a few stiffs to record for posterity, doesn't it?"

Geoff didn't reply. He stared at the sergeant as the man muttered orders, observations and confirmations. Other Royal Marines sauntered around him, taking in the view and presumably discussing potential threats or tactics or whatever. Once again, intimidation shivered through Geoff when he watched the soldiers stand there in their equipment, holding their weapons.

He turned back to take in the view and muttered, "There's still so far to go."

A new voice spoke from behind him, "Chin up, mate, this war will be over soon, you'll see."

Geoff spun around to see another soldier walking behind him whom he hadn't heard. "You think so?" he said reflexively.

"Yeah," the young man insisted. "We've got them on the run good and proper now. This'll all be done and dusted before the year's out."

Chapter 42

21.12 Tuesday 9 October 2063

Mark Phillips walked along the restored footpath by the river Thames in central London. He wanted to call his sister, Maria, but had to get his breathing under control first. He tried the exercise his friend, Simon, had shown him. Mark focused on the dirty brown water flowing past in the darkness and inhaled the cool evening air. He exhaled after a few seconds and repeated the exercise. A minute later, he'd calmed down enough to make the call.

His sister spoke in his ears, "Hello, brother. How are you?"

Her simple question threatened to undo his work. "Only audio?" he said in complaint. "Why not video?"

"I'm tired, Mark."

"Oh, right. Okay. Well, er, sorry."

"It's all right. How are you?"

"I had to speak to Simon earlier."

"Ah. Did it help?"

"S'pose so."

"What happened?"

"Captain Shithead."

"But I thought you had all that worked out? You and him were getting along—"

"It's changed. I've been working on things apart from my job, you see? I've been following Squonk correlating all the data on the enemy and how he's behaving—honestly, being an airspace defence officer can be a bit dull sometimes—and looking at all the big numbers and then reversing the—"

"Mark," his sister broke in. "I love you, but please just tell me what happened."

"But I am," Mark protested, not sure of the point Maria was trying to make.

"The conclusion. Get to the conclusion."

"What? Oh, right. Ready for this?"

"Yes."

"I know for sure the enemy is going to hit us with new weapons soon, in the next few days."

"Okay."

"But that bastard Captain Shithead just laughs at me. He thinks I'm joking when I'm actually being serious. He says the super AI would know if that were the case and if the super AI says no, then it's not going to happen. I hate him. I really hate him."

"What about your other supervisor? What was her name, Chow?"

"Cho. Her name's Cho and she's off sick. They found a bunch of her relatives all dead somewhere in France."

"Dearest brother, how can you be sure you have found something that Squonk has not?"

Mark heard the whine in his voice, but he couldn't help it, "It's not easy to explain, but I have. I'm not just guessing, I'm really not. But Captain Shithead doesn't believe me."

"I believe you, brother."

"Thank you," Mark said, his panic and anger subsiding. There came a silence, so he said, "How are you?"

"I miss Martin. And Mum. And Dad."

"Oh, yes. So do I. Where are you now?"

"South. Very south. I can't say any more than that, you know?"

Mark had a feeling that he'd missed something. Recollections of Simon's advice raced through his mind, but he struggled to pinpoint where he'd gone wrong with his sister; he only knew that he had. "I'm sorry," he said suddenly.

She replied, "And I'm sorry your supervisor won't listen to you."

"I know," Mark shrieked, his panic rushing back. "It's not fair—I know they will—"

"Mark," she broke in again. "I believe you. But what difference can knowing make?"

"Some, surely? If the soldiers knew, they'd—"

"They'd do the same as what they're doing now: being vigilant, being careful."

"Oh. I s'pose—"

"I have to finish now. I'm on the nightshift and I'm already tired."

"Okay."

"I'll call you tomorrow and we'll talk more."

"Yes."

"And remember: everything will be the same anyway. Bye."

Chapter 43

06.13 Sunday 14 October 2063

Colour Sergeant Rory Moore stomped along the hilly dirt track. He eyed his fellow sergeant next to him and hissed, "It's getting ridiculous, grandad. The guys won't let me anywhere near the front line. I've been back in the regiment nearly two months and they're treating me like I've got the fu—"

"They're treating you like what you are," Jack Heaton broke in. "You're the regiment's mascot, its good-luck charm." He held his arms out and added, "So we're making sure you're okay, because if you are, then we are. Is that nay clear?"

Rory scanned the backs of the two rows of soldiers in front of them and then cast his eyes skywards. Thin clouds hid the early morning sun, but rays occasionally speared through into everyone's faces. Rory said, "This is bloody Doyle's work, isn't it? He was pissed off I wouldn't agree to be his poodle, so he's told—"

"He wanted you to be his adjutant to keep you out of harm's way."

"I don't want to be out of harm's fucking way, grandad. The war's still on. Doesn't matter to me what anyone else thinks my role in it should be, I want to be where the shit is going down."

"Aye, do you now?"

"Well, I think so."

Heaton shook his head and replied, "Listen to yourself. How many guys have we lost to those blasted Spiders? You remember why we got transferred out of Germany and down here, to help the Yanks?"

"Yeah, yeah. I had an important date lined up in Germany. And now it's postponed, again."

"Because they lost so many troops because they had the balls to keep advancing despite the risk."

"I get it, grandad."

"And while the Yanks were getting on with the job down here, we had generals getting sacked and lower ranks getting court-martialled for slacking off. That little trick the enemy pulled with the dormant Spiders showed up a lot of units, laddie."

"Maybe. But this is a volunteer army now, not a professional one like we joined. Well, it was professional when I joined. When you joined, the British Army was still fighting the Nazis, weren't you?"

"Aye, and when your mother gave birth, the midwife gave you such a slap, your—"

"Caution," Rory's Squitch announced. "The advance will commence in sixty seconds. You are in the second line. Standby to receive new orders."

"Okay," Heaton said. "All squads, move into formation."

Ahead of them, the two lines of troops divided, the left turning to the south; the right turning to the west.

The company captain spoke, "Attention, all troops. Scythes are inbound to clear the ground ahead. Given that it's a bit hilly, it might take longer than usual to get a green light to advance. Each company's Falarete team needs to keep a sharp lookout, just in case. Also, watch out for caves and other hidden depressions, and don't get caught out. Extra grog for all ranks if we reach Bilbao by sundown. Good luck, everyone."

"'Grog'?" Rory echoed. "Who even uses that word anymore?"

"Can you see the ACAs yet with your young eyes?" Heaton asked.

"Negative, grandad. Not even with magnification."

Rory's Squitch announced, "Danger: the enemy is deploying an autonomous combat aircraft not previously encountered."

Rory stopped. Ahead of him, the company's squads stopped fanning out along the low ridge. Heads shook and shoulders shrugged.

Heaton turned to Rory and muttered, "I'm glad you said you wanted to be where the shit's going down. Looks like you're in the right place."

From behind them, wing after wing of Scythes raced overhead to meet the enemy. The sun broke through the cloud and Rory shielded his eyes to watch the NATO aircraft lead the advance. His spirit rose at the sight of friendly ACAs sweeping into battle to defend and protect the advancing NATO troops. The hisses of displaced air faded as the ACAs sped on.

The captain spoke again, "We're getting reports that the inbound enemy machines have a different sig to anything else. Check your kit, people. If things get hot, you'll need a full mag."

Rory said to Heaton, "The last time I was in Spain, I went through a whole ton of shit. I really think this country doesn't like me. You think maybe we should take cover?"

Heaton said, "I don't know. There's plenty of cover around if it gets that bad."

"Besides which," Rory said with a nod to the east, "there are two battalions of 6th US Marines over there. Much tastier than us English engineers."

"Aye," Heaton agreed.

"Right, here we go," Rory said. He twitched his eye muscle to zoom to the far horizon. Small digital arrows flashed to indicate the Scythes. They engaged the enemy machines. Suddenly, the sky was filled with ACAs climbing, diving, pitching and pirouetting. Rory held his breath. He could hardly follow the action, and additionally the laser shots were invisible—a fact he'd come to loathe about this war, when death and destruction were so often delivered without indication or warning.

Finally, he spied puffs of black and grey smoke over the more distant hills. Any relief quickly evaporated when his lens told him these damaged and destroyed machines falling from the sky all belonged to NATO.

"Shit," he said.

Heaton took a step back and asked, "How much time d'you think we've got before those bastards come for us?"

"I dunno," Rory replied. "But I've been here before, grandad, and it is not a good day out."

"You're nay just saying that?"

More NATO Scythes fell out of the sky, trailing sparks and smoke. The new enemy ACAs held an undulating, shapeshifting formation Rory had never seen before. "Christ," he breathed, "the Scythes can't get near them."

Heaton grunted his confirmation. "Our super AI has only got one choice."

Rory's Squitch spoke, "Danger: NATO assets in the battlespace will be destroyed in sixty seconds. Prepare to retreat or seek cover."

Heaton said, "I don't think we should object to that advice, Sergeant Moore."

Rory sensed Heaton backing away along the dirt track. Rory's memory threw up images of fighting off a Spider singlehandedly and how close the engagement had been. His breathing accelerated. More Scythes twisted and dived and dropped out of the sky, vanishing behind the further hilly ridges. Puffs and trails of smoke marked their demise like a drunk with a smudged, grey marker pen.

Rory said, "We need reinforcements. Where are the reinforcements?"

His Squitch answered, "Reinforcements will arrive in the battlespace in ten minutes."

Rory breathed, "Christ. When they wipe out the Scythes, we won't last ten seconds."

"Danger: NATO air assets in the battlespace have been destroyed. Seek cover immediately."

Rory caught his breath when the troops furthest from him abruptly dissolved in flames. A bright orange flash encompassed each soldier for a second before they collapsed. In panic, Rory looked to the sky to see the enemy ACAs, each marked with a red arrow, streak across the sky.

"Let's go," Heaton yelled, leaping from the track.

Rory followed, vaguely aware of all the able NATO soldiers also scrambling off the high ground and heading into depressions. He left the path and descended into the low, brown scrub. Recollections surged up from his memory, but at least this time he could take comfort that the enemy would not be able to jam transmissions in the battlespace as it had at the beginning of its invasion.

Ahead of him, he made out Heaton's helmet-clad head bobbing up and down. The older man moved at a speed that belied his years. Rory followed him down into an anonymous valley, jumping over small shrubs, his boot occasionally sliding on the sandy dirt between them.

Heaton vanished to the left so Rory steered after him. They ran on, around a high slab of rock, skidding and stumbling ever deeper.

Heaton stopped and gasped, "We must've come down at least thirty metres. That should do for now."

"If we're really lucky," Rory said, in between gulping in lungfuls of air, "our stupid Squitches will start telling us to 'wait until friendly forces have retaken the battlespace'."

Heaton grimaced and said, "If that's happening all along the line, we're going to be decimated."

Rory demanded, "Update?"

His Squitch replied, "Seek cover immediately and wait for friendly forces to retake the battlespace."

"Fuck," Rory spat. "That's exactly what the thing told me last year when we were all fucked."

Heaton said, "Take it easy, laddie. It's not the same at all. We've got reinforcements on the way. Besides, we're only here to protect the Marines' flank."

"Well, they're toast today, that's for sure."

"Aye."

"You know what happens next, don't you?"

"What?"

"They'll come back and start picking us off, one by one. They don't fucking quit. Once they've barbequed the Yanks, they'll swoop about looking for units, even individuals, and they'll cook all of us, too."

Heaton put out a hand and repeated, "Listen, it's not the same as last year. We've got the reinforcements. Up there are mobile Falarete teams for exactly this eventuality. The picture is not totally black, laddie."

Rory said, "Squitch, do Falaretes work against this new enemy ACA?"

"Affirmative."

"It says Falaretes work against it."

Heaton nodded, "See? It's not the same."

"Current status along the rest of the line?" Rory asked, although he knew what the answer would be.

"Your rank does not authorise you to access that information."

"Fuck you very much," Rory answered.

"We just need to wait it out, that's all," Heaton said.

"You think so?" Rory asked in a rhetorical tone.

"Aye."

"You take your chances, grandad, and I'll take mine," Rory said, removing the small circular control for his Squitch from his trouser pocket.

Heaton smiled in realisation and did the same. The two veterans deactivated their Squitches, put on their BHC sleeves, and thus concealed, waited for friendly forces to retake the battlespace.

Chapter 44

10.03 Sunday 14 October 2063

D ismay suffused Terry Tidbury's tired limbs. The flaxen-haired operator glanced back at him. On the large screen above the Attack Group South station, the news worsened relentlessly. He divided his attention between that screen and the station next to it, whose screen displayed a map of the German border with Poland and the deployments of Attack Group East.

Thousands of NATO soldiers were dead on this Sunday morning, none of whom he'd expected would die today, not like this. The counterattack had been bound to come, sooner or later. Operation Thunderclap had succeeded and helped Operation Repulse to begin and establish an almost unassailable lead. And the enemy teetered on the precipice of a headlong confrontation with India that had tied down such a proportion of his forces that Repulse was also aided.

But, however late to the party, the enemy had now most assuredly arrived. To Terry, the morning's events constituted a contradiction: they were both expected and a surprise; both anticipated and unprepared for. He felt a modicum of relief at his foresight in discussing this eventuality with each of his generals in the preceding week. At least they should've made preparations.

"Sir Terry," the flaxen-haired operator said. "Squonk has run into a block trying to activate reserves of Scythes at one of the main stores in southern England."

"You have my authorisation. Fix it," Terry barked.

"The person in command is refusing to cooperate."

"Audio, now."

A new voice sounded in the War Rooms; old and suspicious. "Who is this, really?" the man asked.

Terry heaved in a breath and replied, "I am Field Marshal Sir Terry Tidbury, Supreme Allied Commander, Europe. To whom am I speaking?"

"Er, I'm just a stores master. I, er, no one else is here, and—"

"Please lift the block on the reserves of Scythe autonomous combat aircraft in your stores and hand control of them over to the super artificial intelligence."

"Oh, Lordy. Yes, sir. I've done that. Sorry Sir T—"

"Thank you." He glared at the operator and ordered, "End, now."

The operator nodded in confirmation. Terry shook his head. "Squonk? Update. Attack Group South first."

The super AI replied, "Reserve wings of ACAs are in the battlespace; however, the enemy's attack is supported with extensive deployments of warriors. In less than ten minutes, the only tactical option available will be to withdraw all forward units in northern Spain to behind the Pyrenees."

Terry nodded in comprehension. He could not let his emotions overrule his common sense. "Very well. Commence the withdrawal of all forward units."

"Confirmed."

"And what about Attack Group East?"

"Greater numbers of reserves are being deployed due to the lack of natural land or other features that can be used as defensive positions. Subordinate commanders are aware of the gravity of the situation and are reacting accordingly. Nevertheless, the enemy has also supported its attack along sections of this front with warriors. The enemy's autonomous combat aircraft will eliminate NATO positions before the warriors advance. In less than thirty minutes, the only tactical option available—"

"Very well," Terry hissed. "Commence withdrawing forward units."

"Confirmed."

Terry took a step back from the screens, an appalling and utterly alien sense of enfeeblement enveloping him. For seventy-two days since 1 August, Operation Repulse had succeeded with no more than the enemy making half-hearted attempts to ensure the retaking of European territory cost more NATO lives than it should have. But now? It seemed as though—

"Sir?" the flaxen-haired operator spoke, breaking into Terry's thoughts.

"What is it?"

"General Pakla, Polish First Army, is asking to speak with you."

Terry gave a mirthless chuckle and said, "He's 'asking' to speak to me, is he? Very well, audio only."

Pakla's forthright, accented English filled the War Room, "Field marshal? Request permission to hold my forces in position."

"Request denied."

"But we are almost on the border of Poland. Please, Sir Terry, I would not ask you if I was not certain of my troops' ability."

"General, the ability of your troops is the last thing I would question. But the choice is not ours. The enemy has deployed superior weapons and we must react accordingly. Your current deployments offer insufficient cover. Please begin the phased withdrawal we discussed earlier this week, especially in the event of something like this happening."

There came a moment's silence before Pakla conceded, "Very well. Can we speed up the deploying of our own better weapons?"

"I cannot be certain, general. If we can't get the Alpha and Omega deployed within the next week, there is a real risk that Repulse could be reversed. Good luck over there."

The connection ended and the operator said, "Sir, I've got General Abrio of the Italian 2nd Dragoons, who has a similar request given that his forces are close to Italy, and Lieutenant-General Robert Kovar of the Czech 41st Mechanised Battalion, who is about to cross the Czech border—"

Terry raised a hand to stop her. He said, "Squonk? Red-level comms to all commanders at battalion level and above, now."

"Confirmed... Comms open."

"Attention, all ranks. This is SACEUR. Follow the super AI's recommendations for tactical withdrawals. Our reserves of Scythes are not unlimited and we do not have the firepower to withstand this counterattack. This is a new and unknown threat that the X–7s and X–9s cannot stop. Retreat is the only tactical and strategic option at this time. That is all."

Terry took a step back and watched his world take a battering. To defend England against insurmountable odds, as he had to last year when no one entertained a hope of the country surviving for more than a few weeks, was one thing. But to suffer such a painful setback when Operation Repulse had been proceeding almost according to its original plan, was a new and deeply unwelcome feeling.

The future of the entire operation now depended on the rapid production and deployment of the new Scythe Alphas and Omegas.

Chapter 45

10.58 Sunday 14 October 2063

Pip yelled at her squad, "Go, move it, get in there—now!"

Eight young recruits sprinted the short distance from shelter in the damaged sports centre across the pockmarked football field and into the waiting autonomous air transport.

Sergeant MacManus appeared next to her. "All clear. Is there enough room for us to get on that thing as well?" he asked, nodding towards the AAT.

"Sure," she replied. "Where's Hines?"

"Behind me."

She reached the ungainly craft and boarded it. Inside, the squad were stowing their weapons and strapping themselves in. The smell of stale sweat permeated the interior.

MacManus clambered in followed by the ungainly Barny Hines. The door slid closed.

Pip's Squitch said, "Secure yourself. The journey will involve mild turbulence."

As soon as she had done so, the aircraft whined and lifted off the ground. It accelerated and gained height.

Pip observed the furious expression on Hines's face. She opened comms only to him and said, "You did great getting us all out back there. Thanks."

Hines just grunted his acknowledgement.

The autonomous air transport flew straight and low. Through the small windows opposite her, the fields of south Germany flashed by.

Pip called up the strategic overview in her lens. She leaned to Mac and spoke over the noise of rushing air, "It's all going according to plan. We're pulling back all along the line."

"It's a wee shock, is this."

Her Squitch announced, "Caution, the enemy is attempting to outflank this part of the line's withdrawal."

"What?" Pip said. "Explain."

In her lens, a map of the withdrawal resolved that showed the little flotilla of AATs as they fled headlong in front of the enemy's new ACAs. However, on either side of the NATO aircraft, more of the enemy's faster machines had advanced and now had the potential to engage their NATO targets.

"Mac?"

"Yeah?"

"We might actually be in the shi—"

The AAT suddenly fell out of the sky.

Mac cursed.

The aircraft came up level and the pressure on Pip's torso almost prevented her breathing. She leaned towards Mac and gasped, "Reinforcement Scythes have arrived."

The AAT descended and slowed. Pip glimpsed damaged buildings through the windows opposite.

Her Squitch said, "Prepare to disembark and seek cover."

She asked, "Are the reinforcement Scythes sufficient to defeat the enemy's new ACA?"

"The battlespace is too dynamic to sustain a response."

"Shit." She opened comms to the occupants and scanned their young, determined faces as she spoke. "No dramas, people. We've got reinforcements above us. We touch down, grab our kit, leave and get to cover. Piece of cake, right?"

She collected their nods and half-smiles and a sense of reassurance came to her. As she looked at each soldier, their name, rank, specialisation and date of birth resolved digitally in the air next to them. Most were only two or three years younger than Pip, but to her, they had the faces of children.

Except for Hines. His mouth and heavy jowls were set in a rictus of anger. She decided his bravery more than compensated for his compulsive light-fingeredness.

The AAT bumped down onto the ground and the door slid open. Pip's Squitch instructed her to disembark. She followed the troops out, the last to leave. She hit the ground and took in the buildings around her. They consisted of sheer metal sheets at least ten metres high. To the south loomed large silos presumably for hemp processing. Half a dozen AATs had set down in the wide concrete area between the buildings and troops were trotting out of them. The air smelled fresher and a warm breeze blew across her face, helping her to focus.

Her Squitch advised, "Seek cover immediately."

"Cap?" MacManus called. "We've got a storied building with two underground levels just over there."

"Good. Tell the corporals to get their squads down there, then."

"Aye."

Pip turned to the western sky and strained to see the aerial battle taking place there. She said, "Update."

Her Squitch said, "The reinforcement wings of Scythes have engaged the enemy."

"Are more reinforcements on the way in to this sector?"

"Affirmative."

"Does this enemy counterattack extend along the entire front?"

"Affirmative."

She magnified the view in her lens and saw patterns of erratic smoke in the sky, although the machines themselves were too far away to make out.

Her Squitch repeated, "Seek cover immediately."

Pip turned around in a complete circle. Troops were still alighting the autonomous air transports and jogging towards the relative safety of the buildings.

"Cap?" MacManus yelled from the long, low building with the underground levels. "My Squitch says this contact can still go *tae rat jobby*."

Pip strode towards him.

Her Squitch announced, "Danger: an enemy ACA has targeted this landing zone. Seek cover immediately."

Pip broke into a sprint. Mac's face creased in concern. He stood at the top of a concrete ramp down into the building, wide enough for a vehicle, along which most of the troops had descended.

Mac waved his arm, urging her to speed up.

She accelerated, the weight of her kit forcing her limbs to work harder. A dangerous red hued her view. The enemy ACA was nearly on her. She lengthened her stride, desperately trying to reach Mac. He leapt forwards, caught her arms, pivoted, and threw her down the ramp. She landed heavily. The impact of laser shots vibrated though the concrete. She rolled into a foetal position, the sounds of hissing and the popping of the concrete surface terrifying her.

The heat receded through the surface on which she lay. She opened her eyes. The entrance to the ramp was blackened and chunks of concrete had been blasted off in reaction to the laser shots.

"Mac?" she asked, pulling herself to her feet. She heaved her body up the ramp, the air becoming hotter, as though she were entering a vast oven. She reached the top and there, on the left, were the shapeless remains of Sergeant MacManus, burning furiously but otherwise still. Across the landing zone, more bodies burned and an injured squaddie cried in pain, dragging himself towards the nearest building.

Pip's spirit broke. "No," she said. "That's it. Enough."

Her Squitch advised, "Danger: the enemy ACA has re-targeted this landing zone. Seek cover immediately."

"No," she repeated, accepting everything and nothing; understanding everything and nothing. Tears ran out from her eyes. She reflexively dropped the magazine from her Pickup, took a new one from her webbing, and slotted it into her weapon. She held the Pickup out in her right hand and unclasped the webbing from her tunic, so it fell to the steaming ground. Sweat poured from her face, neck, arms, and lubricated the movement of the material of her uniform against her skin. She paced further away from the building, into the open area where NATO machines and soldiers burned and hissed and crackled in an overbearing weight of heat.

Her Squitch repeated, "Seek cover immediately. Any attempt to engage the enemy ACA with your Pick—."

"For the last time, no. It's enough. It's time. I've earned this."

Captain Pip Clarke raised her Pickup and aimed into the sky. When her lens indicated from where the enemy ACA approached, she turned to face it.

When it came into range, she opened fire.

Chapter 46

19.07 Monday 15 October 2063

Liliana shivered and her terrified eyes implored Serena. "Please, sister, no. I cannot do that. I am sorry."
Serena felt a twinge of disappointment but little surprise. "Very well," she said. "Stay here in the kitchen and help with preparing the food."
Liliana sniffed and nodded. "Yes. I am sorry."
"Don't be. But you must try to be ready. If the rumour is true and I have only one chance, I will take it. And that will mean the worst for all of us. Now, wipe your face and come along."
Liliana did as Serena said. Together, they left the laundry room and entered the chaotic kitchen. The house's own cooks hurriedly diced and chopped fresh vegetables, herbs and spices. Tiphanie stood at the huge sink cleaning and organising the tableware and cutlery.
"You, slave," Ahmed cried the minute Serena emerged with Liliana.
Serena left Liliana with Tiphanie and approached Ahmed, the man looking older every time she saw him.

"Father wishes to see you. Follow me," he snapped, turning and leaving the kitchen.

Out in the wide corridor, guards milled about. Serena sensed much concern emanate from them and wondered what could be happening. The riots had worsened the previous evening, but finding out facts was incredibly difficult, even though she spoke their language fluently. Only so much information could be gleaned from listening outside closed doors or hoping to overhear some snippet in the bustling market.

Ahmed strode on, his black *kandora* swishing over the exquisite rugs, and passed the opulent vases. He spoke to her without troubling to look over his shoulder, "We are about to face a very difficult dinner here this evening, slave. Father is going to ask you for your help. Not 'order' you; not 'tell' you; but 'ask' you. Do you realise what a privilege that is?"

Serena kept her head down, not least to hide the shock on her face. The frustration of not having certainty about what had happened to cause this level of stress in everyone in the house both excited her and threatened to overwhelm her.

Ahmed said, "But whatever he 'asks' of you, you must not refuse or deny him. Is that clear."

"Yes."

"Good. Here we are." Ahmed's bony hand emerged from his sleeve and he rasped on the door with his knuckles. He pushed the door open and indicated for her to enter. She did so and turned back to see Ahmed close it behind her.

"Child, come and sit here, please," Father said from behind his desk.

She did so, noting the tiredness on his face and wondering if the silver in his jet-black hair had spread in the last few days.

He pinched the bridge of his nose and said, "We have a special guest who will bless our house this evening. He and his entourage will spend the night here before leaving in the morning. This special guest is His Highness the Third Caliph."

Serena gasped and put a hand over her mouth.

Father nodded. "Yes, this was my reaction also when his staff told Ahmed that he would honour our humble home."

Serena tensed her muscles to stop the trembling that had begun in her legs. The rumour was true. The Third Caliph, the man responsible for destroying her family, her country, and her life, would be here, in Father's house.

She put on her most demure voice and said, "May I ask why he blesses our house, Father?"

Father's shoulders sagged. He replied, "There are severe pressures on him, child. Rumours of an assassination. Attempts at a coup d'état. He needs to stay with an ally he can trust."

"I see."

"Given this, while he is here, no individual is allowed to come to within two metres of his person. However, when we have dinner in the grand hall, someone will have to serve him. Currently, he is distrustful of his staff—"

"But Father, forgive me for interrupting you, I am only a slave. I cannot possibly serve food to such an exulted per—"

"I am asking you to," Father broke in. "It is because you are a trusted slave who has been with my house for a year and a half, who has learned our language, that you will be allowed to approach the Third Caliph and serve him food, on behalf of my house. The same house that His Highness has blessed so greatly."

"Oh," Serena said, numbness spreading down from her shoulders. She straightened her spine and added, "Then I shall not let you down, Father."

Father smiled and said, "Child, do not be nervous. It is just one meal, one dish even. And if His Highness escapes his present troubles, he will be sure to bless our house even more in the future. Can you manage for the next hour or so?"

Serena looked into Father's kind face, his dark, pockmarked skin shining in the warmth of his office. "Yes, Father," she whispered.

"Good. Cook Reza has planned a sufficient range of dishes for our exulted guest—"

"Forgive me, Father," Serena broke in, her objective crystallising in her mind's eye. "Will his brothers be here also?"

"No, child. They are in other provinces ensuring support for His Highness. There will be few people around the table. In truth, these are stressful, unstable times. This is not a normal visit in normal circumstances. But remember, in the morning he and his entourage will leave and everything will be as it was. Now, go and prepare yourself."

Serena stood and gathered the folds of her *abaya*, muttering, "Yes, Father. Thank you, Father," and hurried from the room. Outside, Ahmed had gone. She moved as quickly as she could. She passed more guards and realised that none of them bore any weapons that she could see.

Sounds of bustling chaos greeted her when she entered the kitchen, but she heard nothing. The aromas of a dozen spices assailed her nose, but she smelled not a single one. Men and women worked together to prepare the dishes. The huge table in the middle of the room was laden with vegetables and fish and cuts of lamb. She strode to Tiphanie and tugged the woman's arm. Tiphanie followed her into the laundry room.

When she closed the door behind them, she whispered, "I have to serve the Third Caliph his meal this evening."

Tiphanie's face dropped in shock. Realisation dawned and she asked simply, "Will you?"

"If I can, yes."

"But why you?"

"Because the Third Caliph trusts none of his subjects."

A sly look crossed Tiphanie's face. She said, "But he thinks a subservient European slave would not dare—?"

"Precisely," Serena broke in. "They regard women as less than human, and slaves from Europe as beyond contempt. They would not dream a mere slave would even dare to do anything."

"My God," Tiphanie replied. Her eyes welled with tears. She nodded and kissed Serena softly on the lips. "God be with you, sister," she whispered.

"God will be with both of us," Serena said.

She followed Tiphanie back into the kitchen. There stood the personal maid of Father's wife. She held a folded *abaya* and told Serena that it was clean and to put it on.

Serena took it and thanked the woman. She retired again to the laundry room to change, for a final few moments in private. She dressed in the new *abaya* and ensured the stiletto in its sheath was high up her forearm and well hidden. Then, she prayed for guidance from the one true God.

When Serena re-emerged into the kitchen, the young cooks were carrying plates of sauces and finely cut cold vegetables out to the grand hall. At the doorway stood a tall, thickset man with a mean face similar to Ahmed's. He looked as though he wanted to kill Serena. But Serena didn't mind.

She waited at the back of the kitchen, a reassured calmness settling over her. Memories replayed themselves: helping people in her hospital in Rome; her little brother Max—certainly long-since dead—and the night she watched a flying bomb destroy the block of flats in which her mother lived. Then, the abduction, the feeling of violation when the first warrior raped her, the first of many. Oh yes, so many mem—

"You, slave. Come along. We do not keep His Highness waiting."

Pulled from her reverie, Serena blinked and advanced to the table. On a silver platter sat a cake of *Tahchin*, a mixture of rice, chicken, eggs and saffron. She lifted the platter. The young cooks and her two sisters made way for her to leave, but the thickset stranger remained in the doorway.

He growled at Serena, "I am His Highness's food taster." He withdrew a small spoon from the folds of his robe and scooped a chunk from the centre of the *Tahchin*. He put it in his mouth and stared unblinkingly at Serena while he masticated the sample.

She held his evil glare for as long as she thought appropriate without raising suspicion, and then cast her eyes down in supposed fear and respect.

He asked, "Are you armed?"

Serena feigned her reaction and replied, "For a slave such as I to carry any weapon would mean instant death."

The piercing black eyes considered her answer before saying, "So, hurry up. His Highness has had a difficult day and is hungry. Do not let the meal arrive at the table cold."

She made to pass him, but he put a hand up and added, "You must only put the platter down in front of His Highness. Do not pause. Do not look at him. Serve him and leave." He moved aside.

Serena left the kitchen and carried the platter along the broad corridor as though her feet barely touched the floor. The vast, ornate double doors stood open to receive her. She glanced at the guards, who appeared nervous.

She entered the great hall. The Third Caliph sat at the head of the large oval table with his back to her. Several more men sat on either side, muttering in conversation. Father sat at the opposite end of the table and paid Serena no attention whatsoever, his head lowered as he listened to a smaller man next to him.

Part of her spirit reeled in the sudden understanding that not one of them suspected that she planned to do anything other than serve the food. She thanked the one true God as she had been thanking Him since finding out the man responsible for all of her pain and anguish would be within reach. It had been a long journey, but God had guided her to this hall at this moment in time. Her breathing lightened and her spirit rose in acceptance that the moment had arrived for her to give her life for a far higher purpose.

Serena took the last few steps to the table. As instructed, she placed the platter in front of the Third Caliph. She moved her arms away and bowed low. As she did so, she drove her right hand up her left sleeve and unclipped the button holding the stiletto in its sheath.

Serena raised herself. In a single fluid motion, she withdrew the weapon from her sleeve and plunged the blade deep into the side of the Third Caliph's neck.

THE END

Coming from Chris James in 2024
The Repulse Chronicles conclude with:

The Repulse Chronicles Book Seven

Aftermath

For the latest news and releases, follow Chris James on Amazon

In the US, at:
https://www.amazon.com/Chris-James/e/B005ATW34C/

In the UK, at:
https://www.amazon.co.uk/Chris-James/e/B005ATW34C/

You can also follow his blog, at:
https://chrisjamesauthor.wordpress.com/

Printed in Great Britain
by Amazon